"DON'T PUSH ME."

Renford's gaze went bleak. "For your wife's sake, I'm trying to be nice to you, Crandall," he said quietly. "Don't push me."

A wicked light danced in Crandall's eyes. He spurred his horse around to face the sheriff. "Damn, can't abide a nosey sheriff," he murmured, "especially when he's a snotty kid!"

Crandall spurred his horse straight at Renford, then pulled him up to rear back on his hind legs, and came down. Renford had to throw himself to one side, barely escaping from the flailing, iron-shod hoofs. He rolled over once and sprang to his feet to see Crandall, tugging at his gun.

He thought for a fleeting instant of the .45 at his own hip, but he didn't pull it. He wanted to avoid that as long as possible. He hadn't had to use it except to bluff, and he didn't want to.

He saw Crandall's gun was stuck in its sheath and lost no time taking advantage of the opportunity. He lunged forward and caught the gun just as the rancher finally succeeded in yanking it free of the stiff holster. With a twist he pulled it away from Crandall and hauled him out of the saddle.

Crandall pulled himself upright. He was blind with rage and whiskey, but he was not drunk—at least not drunk enough to impair him physically. His long sinewy arms shot around Renford and his driving feet carried them both backward into the tie rail. . . .

LONE HAND

T. V. OLSEN

LEISURE BOOKS   NEW YORK CITY

A LEISURE BOOK®

March 2001

Published by

Dorchester Publishing Co., Inc.
276 Fifth Avenue
New York, NY 10001

ISBN 0-8439-4845-0

The name "Leisure Books" and the stylized "L" with design are trademarks of Dorchester Publishing Co., Inc.

Printed in the United States of America.

Visit us on the web at www.dorchesterpub.com.

Editor's Note

At the time of his death, T. V. Olsen left behind six unpublished Western novels and nine unpublished Western short stories. One of the nine short stories, "Jacob's Journal," subsequently appeared in *Louis L'Amour Western Magazine* and is included here. The second of these stories also appears in this collection under the title "Center-Fire" and the third as "Five Minutes." It was due primarily to Bill Pronzini, who had proposed preparing a new collection of T. V. Olsen's previously published Western magazine fiction, that the author revised, edited, and had newly typed all of his previously uncollected stories for possible inclusion. It is these enhanced versions of the stories, benefiting from the author's greater maturity and depth of understanding, that form the basis for the text of this book. The only exceptions are "Jacob's Journal," which exists in the author's typescript, and "Center-Fire" and "Five Minutes," which exist only in holographic manuscript versions.

TABLE OF CONTENTS

Except for a single summer he spent in a cabin on Buffalo Lake in Woodruff, Wisconsin, T. V. Olsen lived the first thirty-three years of his life at his parents' home on the east side of Rhinelander. Olsen attended Rhinelander public schools. In junior high school it was his intention to become a comic strip artist, but he found the more he drew, the more he became interested in the storylines rather than the illustrations. He took a night school vocational class in creative writing while still in high school, and a Western novel he had begun in that class was in rough draft when he was graduated in June, 1950. He worked for a year at menial jobs, the only question in his mind at the time being which one he hated more violently before he enrolled at Central State College in Stevens Point which later became part of the University of Wisconsin system. He continued writing while in college and in August, 1953 turned again to the novel he had in rough draft. When he completed it in the spring of 1954, it ran 75,000 words. That summer he received a notice from the August Lenniger Literary Agency which invited submissions of book-length manuscripts that would be read and analyzed for a fee of $35. He sent in the manuscript with his fee. Six months later he heard from John Burr, who had once been editor of Street & Smith's *Western Story*. Burr sent a lengthy critique and suggestions for revising the book and cutting it down to 60,000 words. It was published in 1956 as HAVEN OF THE HUNTED and is still in print. It was not easy, apparently, to follow this first novel at once with another. So, for a number of years, while developing plots and working on various novels, Olsen wrote short stories, including the one that follows.

Having crested the slope above the Lansing place, Tim Younger paused to blow his sorrel and enjoy the cool morning. A hint of the mild New Mexico winter was in the cold breeze, blowing down from the Sierra Madres. Tim hunkered further into his frayed mackinaw, but without even a silent complaint. He liked the briskness of winter in the higher country.

Then he mechanically felt the weight of the sack of money in his pocket. A grimness straightened his mouth, and some of the pleasure went from the morning. The secret behind that money was one for which a man had already died.

The early sunlight streamed across the pine and cedar timbering this side of the slope and picked out the deer trail through the trees. Tim Younger guided the sorrel down the trail toward the Lansing cabin, set in a little clearing, partly encroached upon by young pine.

He reined into the yard, seeing Sue Lansing leave the cabin and head for the adobe chicken hut with a pan of feed. Tim dismounted stiffly. Sue's warm smile and greeting barely pierced the taciturn barrier that he threw up against the world.

"'Morning," he acknowledged gruffly. "Let me."

He took the pan from her and scattered feed to the chickens, aware of Sue at his side. The crown of her honey-tinted hair just reached the bridge of his nose, and it decreased a little his perpetual sense of his own inferior height.

They walked back to the cabin and inside. He removed his hat and set the pan on the table, looking about the room while Sue lifted the stove lid and stirred up the embers. The small two-roomed cabin was commodious enough for Sue, who lived alone now. Everything was scrupulously clean, and a fairly successful effort had been made to lessen the crudity of the place by the use of a brightly patterned oilcloth on the table, red curtains, and cans of house plants in the windows.

After refusing a cup of coffee twice, Tim reluctantly agreed to a cupful. Sue got two cups and walked to the stove.

"Getting cold, isn't it?" she said.

"Yeah. I had to break the ice this morning."

She nodded cheerfully. "I have to break it every time you visit."

Tim only looked more morose. He watched her pale thin hands as she poured the coffee. Her brother's death had spoiled much of the good that the high country had done for her waning health. *She's too young and pretty to go this way,* Tim thought vaguely. He wondered why she stayed, a lone woman in a lonely cabin.

She returned the coffee pot to the stove and came back to the table, seating herself and motioning him to a chair opposite her. He pulled the canvas sack from his mackinaw pocket and set it on the oilcloth in front of her. She shook her head, smiling.

"How much this time, Tim?"

"Not much."

"How much?"

"Well, the usual half." He ran his fingers through his dark hair and ducked his head toward the table to avoid the warmth of her eyes. "I had the gold assayed in town and turned into money for us. I banked my share already. I'll bank this for you on my next trip to town. It's not safe for you, having this much money in the cabin."

"But Tim . . . half?"

"It's coming to you," he said patiently. "The gold's only half mine. It was Tom's, too. With him gone, his share is yours."

"And you work like a dog to dig it out."

"Someone has to," Tim said, uneasy at this talk.

12

"But you didn't have to bring the money here. It's extra trouble for you, and you could have banked my share with your own."

"I wanted you to see it first, so you'd know you were getting it."

"But Tim," she said in surprise, "I trust you."

He looked at her squarely. "*Don't* trust me," he said flatly. "Not me, not anyone. When your back is turned, your friends become throat-cutters."

"Like you are?" Sue asked, her golden-flecked eyes laughing at him.

"Maybe," he said morosely. "How can you say?"

"You sound very worldly, and very wise," she said musingly, "and so bitter that it's . . . well, . . . a little silly. I'd trust you with my life. So there."

Tim muttered something and drained his cup, then stood up, buttoning his mackinaw over his chest. "Thanks for the coffee."

A disappointment that he judged must be anger touched her mouth, then flickered into a smile. "You don't want to talk . . . as usual."

Tim shrugged. "Do you want more gloom?"

She laughed, but any further reply was arrested by the sound of a horseman reining up in the yard.

Sue opened the door and said: "Hello, Sam," to the rider's greeting.

That would be Sam Travis, Tim thought without enthusiasm.

Sue stepped back as the rancher loomed imposingly in the doorway, smiling. He advanced into the room with a nod at Younger, then set a bulky sack of food on the table. The movement brought him beside Tim, who looked dwarfed next to Travis's great bull-shouldered frame. Sam's cold, supercilious eyes regarded Tim amusedly, and then as though by the very dynamic will and dominance of his nature he could thrust the smaller man back. Sue, at Sam's back, did not catch this interplay. Only Tim felt a stir of wrath.

He showed none of this. Instead he said quietly: "I'll be going, ma'am. See you, Sam."

Sam nodded, smiling enigmatically. Tim could feel Sue's eyes on him as she followed him to the door and watched him mount the sorrel. She said good bye with a note of trouble in her voice that made him wonder, but he only nodded a response before he rode out of the yard.

Tim guided the sorrel up the slope with the memory of Sue's voice a warmth in his mind. Then he increased the horse's pace roughly. *She's just grateful,* he thought, *and you're just a damned fool.* Besides, there was Sam Travis.

Tim felt a guilty awareness that it was becoming increasingly hard for him to see beyond the bulwark of his own suspicious cynicism. That was the effect, he supposed, of these months of guarded wariness. If anyone should learn that he'd found the ancient mine whose secret had been lost since the days of Spanish rule — the same half-legendary mine for which hundreds of men had scoured these mountains in vain — all his precautions, his careful covering of his trail, would be for nothing.

Only a year before Tim had been one of many purposeless chuckline drifters along the Mexican border country. One day he'd come upon an adobe shack where an aged Mexican lay dying of cholera. Tim had cared for the man, easing his last moments as best he could. In gratitude, an hour before he died, the Mexican had directed Tim to a metal box buried under the dirt floor of his hovel.

In the box was an age-yellowed map, and the old man told him its story. It showed how to find a lost mine in New Mexico Territory, the northernmost of all the old Spanish gold workings. At one time, when the Comanches began raiding heavily in the district, the Spaniards had sealed off the mine with a man-made avalanche, then cleared out of the mountains, leaving in their haste several jackloads of gold bars, raw nuggets, and dust enclosed in the mine.

The Spaniards never had the chance to return for their gold. The War with Mexico came, and in its wake the ceding of the Southwest to the United States. The mines and caches of New Mexico had become lost in maps and letters filed in dusty archives.

Tim, broke and discouraged, decided he could lose nothing. He had the map translated by a good *padre* and came up north to try his luck. In the town of Sentinel he'd met Tom Lansing, an Eastern mining engineer who had brought his ailing sister out West in an effort to restore her health. Tim had liked Lansing immediately and decided to make him a proposition.

"I need mining know-how and money for a grubstake," Tim had said. "You need fresh business opportunities out here. How about it?"

Lansing had told his sister only that he was going gold hunting with Younger. Leaving her at the cabin he'd built for her, he went up in the mountains with Tim.

Riding now up the trail, rocking loosely in the saddle and sunk in thought, Tim recalled their precautions to keep the search and its object a secret — precautions that went for nothing. After they'd located the mine, following a week's planning and searching, Tim had gone to Dry Gap to register their claim. Returning to camp two days later, he had found the engineer lying beside the dead camp fire, shot through the back of the head.

Tim, a born woodsman, found nothing that would help him track down the killer. After telling Sue and the sheriff, he'd set to digging out the rubble blocking the mine entrance, his rifle near at hand. He was ridden by a constant sense of being watched, yet saw and heard nothing.

Ever since, he'd been intermittently bringing in some small amounts of gold to be assayed. It was best to channel it off in a slow trickle — as though he'd only prospected it and found a good vein — until he'd accumulated enough money to hire men and equipment for operating the mine on a full scale.

It was slow going, because he scrupulously set aside exactly half of each amount in Sue's name. Meanwhile, because trust came hard to Tim, he'd kept her in ignorance of the real extent of the find. She might unthinkingly let the secret out, to Travis or another. Tim pacified the small guilt he felt by thinking of the day when he could tell Sue she was independently wealthy.

He also had a wistful hope that he might forget his past bitterness and present harsh temper enough to find a better footing with her, to stop fighting the friendship she offered.

Sunk in thought, Tim found he'd reached the crest of the slope. He glanced back down, seeing the cabin through the trees, and the door opened. Sam Travis came out, mounted his horse, and started up the trail, the violence of his movements telling of his angry mood. *He hadn't stayed long*, Tim thought, a little surprised and oddly pleased. Travis was an important man but, with his overbearing ways, not the right one for Sue.

Tim rode on leisurely, building a cigarette. There was the sound of hard-beating hoofs tattooing the trail behind him. That must be Travis, pushing his horse hard. Tim didn't turn as the rider reined alongside him.

"I want a word with you, Younger," Travis said.

Tim glanced at Sam now, seeing something ugly in the man's face, and a heightening wariness touched him.

Sam said: "Did Tom ever tell you to take care of Sue if anything happened to him?"

16

"Not that I know of," Tim said dryly, "and he can't now, can he?"

"Then keep away from her, Younger. She doesn't want you around."

"That right? I'll have to hear her say that, Travis."

Sam's big hands twisted on his pommel, the veins standing out. He said softly, a wild, almost maniacal note in his voice: "Ride out of here, Younger . . . right now. If you ever come here again, I'll beat you to ribbons."

Tim stopped his horse and quartered around. "Have you gone crazy?"

"I've asked her to marry me half a dozen times. She always stalls. I didn't know why, but now I do. You've been playing for her on the sly ever since Tom died."

A dangerous glint touched Tim's light eyes. "Be careful, Sam," he said softly. "Be very careful."

Sam swore viciously, and the hot and uncontrollable rage in his eyes gave his play away before he made it. He began to lift in his saddle to throw himself at Tim. But Tim simply sidled his horse away from Sam's. Travis, unable to check his lunge, pitched from his horse. His hands, reaching to seize Tim, only brushed Tim's saddle leather. Sam fell clear to the hard ground, the wind leaving him in a driving grunt.

Sam rolled over, his hands tearing savagely at his mackinaw, ripping it open. *He has a gun under it*, Tim thought, and wasted no time in what he knew would be useless talk. He swung a leg over his saddle, poised in the stirrup, and fell out of it onto Sam, landing with knees on the big man's belly. When Tim rolled away and came to his feet, he was holding Sam's gun, trained on its owner.

Sam, at first doubled with pain, got slowly to his feet, shaking off this bruising punishment with the constitution of a bull. His wild eyes sought Tim.

17

"I could break your neck any time," he gasped.

Tim smiled. He backed away till he reached his horse, then shoved Sam's .45 into his saddlebag. It was safely out of Sam's reach there. No one except Tim could get near that sorrel.

Tim invited gently: "You can start now."

Surprise showed on Sam's heavy face. He came on, slowed by wariness at first, then rushed in. Tim was upslope from Sam. He used this gradient to help counter Sam's additional size and weight, balling his body into a driving lunge that stopped Sam's rush and carried both backward downhill. They rolled over and over, down a bank of crumbling brown shale, and smashed up suddenly against the bole of a scrub pine. Tim was caught between the tree and Sam's pinioning weight. Sam caught Tim's head in both his big hands and drove it savagely against the base of the tree.

Panicked pain drove Tim's knee up into Travis's groin. Sam groaned and rolled away. Tim shook off his hurt and dizziness, a frantic urgency driving him to his feet, trying to concentrate on Sam, lurching after him again. But, before he reached him, the terrible punishment Sam had already taken at last caught up with him, and he fell to his knees with a groan, doubled up, white-faced, and swayed back and forth.

Tim walked unsteadily up to his horse. He held onto the pommel for a moment, supporting himself that way and breathing slowly. Then he hauled himself into the saddle and headed down the trail.

Behind him came Sam's harsh voice. "I'm going to get you, Younger. Depend on that."

Tim spent the rest of the day hunting. Having had no luck, he headed back for his camp late that afternoon. It was set in a wind-sheltered grove of pine on the base of a mountain.

Tim turned the sorrel into the deep grass behind the camp, built up his fire for supper, and headed for the sack of bacon hanging from a tree back in the grove. He stopped suddenly.

Was that a sound? He listened, feeling a rippling of the skin at the back of his neck. There was only the faint soughing of the wind in the pines, a lonely, familiar sound, good to his ears. Still, Tim relaxed only a little. He lifted the sack from the tree limb, and stopped. This time he could see it . . . the dark, nearly formless shape of a man moving through the trees far off to his left.

His eyes straining in the dimming light to make out the shape, Tim was unaware of the other intruder, moving like a shadow, who came silently and swiftly up at his back. He was unaware until something exploded on the back of his head.

The crackle of the flames was the first sound to break through the fringes of Tim's consciousness. His head ached poundingly with the effort of turning it to view the men crouching beside the fire a couple yards distant. There were two of them. One was a small, wiry Indian, an Apache from the look and build of him, in cast-off white man's trousers and calico shirt, frying bacon over the fire. That was the one who'd gotten him from behind, Tim guessed. The other man was Sam Travis.

Seeing Tim conscious, Travis walked over and hunkered down beside Younger. Tim pulled tentatively against the thongs that bound his hands and feet but found them to be rawhide and quite secure.

Sam's laugh was subdued and malicious. "You see, I told you I'd get you."

Tim shifted, cold and cramped. "What is this, Sam?"

"Why, it's like this. I was curious about the gold you've been digging out of the hills. I asked Sue about it. It sounded like you had a good thing. I checked with the assayer in town, and he confirmed it. So I had Silva, here, keep an eye on your camp. He scouted out your mine and found some gold bars and dust

19

inside . . . old Spanish stuff. That explains your surly hermit act. You wanted to keep folks away from your diggings. You're a potentially rich man, Tim, I'd judge."

Tim felt the futility of a dismal, helpless rage. Then a thought flashed at him, and he said: "Sam, you murdered Tom for the gold, didn't you?"

"No, Silva did that job." Sam jerked his head toward the Indian. "Not for the gold. I didn't know about the gold, then. A good Indian, Silva, he does things for me. Lansing shouldn't have gotten in my way with Sue. That was a mistake."

Cold understanding settled over Tim. He had the picture now. No wonder he'd found no trace of Tom's killer. No wonder he'd felt he'd been watched yet saw no one. An Indian had done both jobs.

And Tim recalled Tom Lansing's bitter opposition to Sam's courting of his sister. With Tom gone, an obstacle was removed for Sam. Two months of stark loneliness should make any woman turn to the nearest outlet. Only Sue hadn't turned.

"What're you thinking, Tim?"

"That you're seven kinds of a fool, Sam," Tim said coldly. "The mine is registered in my name and Tom's at the claim office in Dry Gap. You'll never get away with it."

"You think I can't? Figure it out. You have a lot of mined stuff up in that mine already, Silva tells me . . . enough to make me rich. I can take it out of this country and sell it where no one will trouble to trace it back here. I can do that before anyone knows you're missing. It'll be a long time before anyone finds your body at the bottom of a remote cañon where you fell by . . . accident. Oh, yes, think it over, Tim. I want to keep you alive a while so you can think a lot about it."

"You're a sorry kind of man, to rob the girl you're supposed to be courting."

"Not at all. She'll have her share." A cold gleam was in

Sam's eyes. "I wondered what she saw in a runt like you. Hell, it was the gold she had her eyes on, not you. Only now it'll be me because *I'll* have the gold."

In the wash of a cold shock, Tim realized the full extent of Sam Travis's overriding ruthlessness. It had blinded and twisted the man into an unfounded jealousy of Tim and let him order Tom Lansing's murder without the quiver of an eyelash.

"Get that grub ready," Travis told the Indian, and then stood, towering over Tim.

Sam's face went stormy with a sudden violence. He kicked Tim viciously in the side, then kicked him again. Tim rolled over, holding his breath against the wracking pain.

"Grub," said the Indian laconically. Travis went to sit by the fire, where he and the Indian ate in silence.

Afterward, Silva nodded toward Tim. "Feed him?"

Travis shrugged. "Cut him loose. Give him a plate."

The thongs removed, Tim rubbed his stiffened wrists to start the restricted circulation, his mind working. If there were a way out of this, it had to come soon. He walked to the fire, squatted, accepted a plate of beans and bacon from the Indian, and ate.

The night was coming down over the grove. Travis crouched by the fire, opposite Tim, a rifle on his lap. The firelight was on Travis's face. Tim breathed painfully because of his aching ribs and considered Sam with a passionless hatred. The Indian had no gun, only a knife at his belt.

Borne clearly on the wind, the soft nicker of Tim's sorrel came out of the night, downslope beyond the grove. The Indian and Sam were instantly alert.

"Our horses are hobbled the other way . . . up the slope . . . aren't they?" Sam asked Silva.

The Indian nodded.

"Must've been your horse, then, Younger," Sam said.

"I left my horse up there, too," Tim lied. *Maybe it would*

21

help, he was thinking, *if you could get one of them out of the camp.*

Sam hesitated a long moment, then glanced at Silva. "I'm going up to take a look. There must be someone out there. You got a rifle around camp, Younger?"

"No," Tim said truthfully. He had a rifle up at the mine but always left it there, opining that if a man didn't carry trouble, it wouldn't follow him.

Sam hesitated again.

"I got my knife," said Silva. "I see after him, Travis. You look. Get rifle."

Sam nodded. "Silva knows how to use his knife, Younger. Don't try anything. Anyway, I won't go far." He stood up and walked out of the circle of firelight.

Sam would be back in a minute and furious at his lie, Tim knew in sudden driving urgency. *Suppose*, Tim thought, *he could deal with the Indian. That still left Sam with his rifle.*

Tim thought: *if I had a gun . . . ?* Then, unbidden, it came to him. He had a gun — Sam's — in his saddlebag, where he'd shoved it before their fight that morning. Sam, his mind too full of his own overmastering passions, had forgotten that.

Tim looked idly over his shoulder. His saddle, with the saddlebags, lay where he'd dropped it at the foot of a pine. He gauged the distance to it — four yards, maybe less. But, if he moved, the Indian would be on him with that knife. A white man's reflexes usually came out second-best against an Indian's.

Tim calculated his chances narrowly, then half stood, bending forward to rub his hands briskly over the fire.

"What you do?" Silva asked sharply.

"My hands are cold," Tim said. "Do you want me to quit breathing, too?"

"You got big mouth, feller," Silva said.

Tim gathered himself. *Now*, he thought, and shot a hand down, picked up a flaming brand from the fire, and flung it in

Silva's face, all in one motion.

The Indian screamed an Apache curse and pitched on his back, clawing at his face. Tim did not see more because he was running, crouching low. He reached his saddlebag and tore it open, as Silva rose to his feet.

Tim's hand plunged into the bag and came out with Sam's gun as Silva lunged at him, an oily glint of firelight pooling along the blade of his raised knife. Tim shot him when he had covered only half the distance. The Indian fell on his face, his outflinging fist plunging the knife into the ground six inches from Tim's toe.

Tim retreated, backing into the grove beyond the firelight. He waited for Travis to rush into camp on the wake of the shot. Travis didn't come, though, and a dark silence grew over the camp. The crumpled form of the Indian lay unmoving.

Tim waited. Tension ran along his nerves. *I've got to draw Sam back into camp*, Tim thought. *He'll be out there, watching. I've got to give him a sight of me.*

With a coldness in his belly Tim forced himself, step by wary step, back into the camp light. He waited, his back crawling with sweat. There, off to his right, moving in the trees, was something.

He flung himself down, rolling desperately away as Sam's rifle crashed out. The kick-up of the bullet flung decayed pine-needle loam in his face.

Tim, on his feet then, dove for the shelter of a pine. Another bullet gnawed away bark and green wood an inch from his shoulder. Tim groaned, lay flat and still behind the tree, and watched as Sam, with an exultant grunt, left the shelter of his own pine. Tim, his head cautiously raised, saw Sam's hulking shape move forward.

In the darkness, Tim, holding his breath, braced the barrel across his forearm, lined Sam's shoulder along the sights, and squeezed off his shot.

The heavy .45 slug flung Travis around in a half circle, and he went down.

Tim got to his feet and came up to the man. He struck a match, and its light showed Sam Travis huddled against the base of the pine tree which had sheltered him, holding his shoulder, sobbing words painfully, without coherence, in a voice Tim no longer recognized.

The next morning Tim sat in Sue Lansing's kitchen and did not refuse coffee the first time she offered it.

"It all must have been building up in Sam a long time," Tim finished quietly. "I'm sorry I had to tell you this."

Sue stood by the stove. She said softly: "I'm very sorry for Sam. Even after Tom, I'm very sorry."

"And nothing more?"

"Tim, Tim, you're very blind . . . still."

"No, not any more, Sue. My trouble was that I wanted too much money . . . too fast. I saw the greed in Sam last night, too, and it wasn't pretty. Crazy as his talk was, Sam made me think. I don't want the gold. I don't want anything if I can't have you. Only I'd thought Sam and you . . . ?"

Sue shook her head very slowly. "Sam never had a chance, not even before Tom brought you to supper that first time. Tim, why do you think I've stayed on here by myself?"

Tim stood up, taking her by the arms, seeing the gentleness and goodness of this girl through the black tissue of distrust and cynicism that he had drawn like a veil over his every thought.

"There's not much to start with, Sue. I've got to make myself over. You'll have to help me."

"There'll be time for it, Tim," she said gently. "All our lives."

24

By the time T. V. Olsen began diligently writing Western short stories — between the appearance of his first Western novel in 1956 and his second, THE MAN FROM NOWHERE, in 1959 — the American magazine market for fiction had retreated considerably from its halcyon days. One of the longest survivors among Western fiction magazines was *Ranch Romances*, launched in 1925 and edited by Fanny Ellsworth until her retirement in November, 1953. She was succeeded by Helen Davidge (later Helen Tono following her marriage). It was to this magazine and Helen Tono that T. V. Olsen sold the majority of the short stories he wrote during this period, beginning with his first published short story, "Backtrail," appearing in the 1st April Number: 3/23/56. It was adapted as a teleplay in 1957 and broadcast on "Dick Powell's Zane Grey Theatre" on the CBS network. "Vengeance Station" was first published in *Ranch Romances* (2nd October Number: 10/18/57).

At first, when the kid topped the crest of the sun-scorched ridge and saw the stage road below, twisting across the desert like a sun-basking snake, he thought it was a mirage. When it remained stable in his vision, except for the heat shimmer, he knew he'd made it. The knowledge brought little relief.

Bowie Adams, twenty years old, looked back over the barren sweep he had covered, along the path of deeply ploughed imprints made by his own dragging feet. The Averyson boys were not in sight now. But they were there, all the same, hanging like vultures to his trail, keeping at a distance because they figured they could afford to take their time.

After shooting Bowie's horse from under him and his canteen full of holes, the twins, Henny and Tobe Averyson, had been satisfied to hang back a mile or two and follow Bowie's wavering track from horseback. They'd figured the desert would finish the job of killing him for them, and the idea appealed to their sadistic natures.

But they were newcomers to this country, and Bowie Adams was not. At least his familiarity was sufficient to permit him, after taking his bearings by the blazing sun, to hold to a rough northerly direction till he reached the stage road. If the Averysons had known of the road, they'd have picked him off long ago.

Bowie had been traveling steadily on foot since that morning with the heat just as steadily sapping his endurance. He'd long since abandoned his saddle. He had stripped it from his dead horse and carried it on his shoulder for an hour, till he realized that its dead weight might mean the difference between his making the stage route or not. Bowie had left the saddle on the desert. In another hour his rifle had followed.

Now, with the slowly lengthening shadows of late afternoon extending gaunt fingers across the land, Bowie stood for a moment atop the ridge facing the road, savoring his brief victory. It would be brief indeed, because the showdown with the Averysons must come later, if not now.

Bowie had kept the .44 which he had taken, with its holster and belt, from the dead body of his kid brother, Jimmy. At thought of Jimmy, rage built in Bowie's eyes which were hard and pale and older than their years warranted. He caressed the smoothly worn butt of the .44.

For another minute young Bowie Adams stood on the ridge, squinting over his back trail. There was no sign of the Averysons yet. He descended the ridge to the road, a tall, gangling boy who looked as lean as rawhide, and as tough. He wore dust-laden Levi's and a threadbare shirt. His pale eyes were red-rimmed with sun glare under a low-pulled, grease-stained Stetson.

He hoped the evening stage, due along here at any time, would reach him before the Averysons did. The force of his hatred, the desire for revenge, were so overpowering that he could taste them. Yet, his exhaustion warned him that he was in no condition to take on one, let alone two men. He needed grub, a few hours' sleep, and a good horse and rifle.

He was in luck. In another quarter hour the stage swayed up the road, its yellow wheels flashing back the sunset. The driver hauled to a stop, cussing the team till the stage body settled on its thoroughbraces.

To show that his intentions were peaceful, Bowie had unbuckled his gun belt and laid it at his feet. The gesture impressed the driver, for this uninhabited stretch of stageline was infested with road agents as well as occasional bands of marauding Apaches.

The driver, a narrow, long-jawed man with the shrewdly perceptive look of a long-time frontiersman, gave Bowie an appraising glance and spat on the ground. "Lost your horse, son?" he asked.

Bowie merely nodded, knowing his thirst-contracted throat muscles would not form words.

"Get in," the driver said. Then he added: "Hold on."

He uncorked a canteen and handed it down. Bowie drank gratefully, strapped on his gun, and climbed through the narrow doorway. His eyes didn't at once accustom themselves to the interior gloom for the dust curtains were pulled.

He did make out the form of a single passenger on the opposite seat. Then he slammed the door and sank into his seat with a deep sigh of relief for the darkness. Even the bucking and swaying of the stage, as the driver kicked off the brake and flicked the team into motion again, was soothing to his drained body. He was asleep almost as soon as his back hit the horse-hair-padded cushion.

Later, with the edge worn off his exhaustion, the jouncing of the stage jerked Bowie to wakefulness again. The coolness of twilight had settled over the land, and the other passenger had pulled up the dust curtains.

He was grinning brashly at Bowie, a plump young man about six years Bowie's senior, with sandy hair rimming his almost bald head. A hard derby hat rested on one knee, and the black sample case at his side told that he was a drummer.

He was talkative, a born salesman. "My name's Roy Wheaten . . . ," he began, and left the briefest pause into which Bowie inserted his own name.

"Going far, friend?" Wheaten asked. This time, without waiting for a reply, he went on: "Whiskey, that's my line. I sell the stuff anywhere and everywhere. I enjoy the work. I hate these damn' stage jaunts in between, though. Be in Strang City tomorrow, anyhow. That's a relief."

His eyes brightened with another thought. "We stop at Ocotillo Station in another hour. We'll have a change of horses and supper, too. It's the one bright spot in the trip." He grinned and winked.

"How's that?" Bowie asked politely but without interest.

He was thinking of the Averysons. Even an hour's stop would give them a chance to catch up, and they'd ride hell-for-breakfast when they found that his trail ended at the stage road. Still, their horses, already exhausted from a desert trek, might break under the pace and force a stop. If he could just make Strang City before they caught up, he had money enough to get a horse and a rifle. Then he'd force the showdown on *his* terms.

"The station keeper, old man MacGreevey, has a daughter named Amy." Wheaten winked again. His pudgy hands made suggestive outlines. "Gets under a man's skin, that one. I haven't gotten anywhere with her so far. I keep trying, on every trip through. She's beautiful, Adams, just beautiful. I can't understand why she stays buried out here. I can't figure what she wants."

"Maybe to be left alone."

Wheaten peered at him in surprise, then chuckled. "Hell, you don't know women, kid. They all want something. They all hook some poor sucker to cough up the goods." He folded his hands across his belly and looked ruminatingly at the ceiling. "As soon as I find out what that little gal wants. . . . Yes, sir. Old Roy never met a girl that wasn't after something. For a girl like that, a man would climb to the moon if she gave the word." He chuckled again. "It won't be that hard to get her, though."

Bowie Adams shrugged. He was too disinterested even to be disgusted by the drummer's sly talk and oily manner. His thoughts were filled with the consuming hatred of the two men who had shot his kid brother in the back and left Bowie himself to die under a desert sun. He was living only for the moment when he could catch the two across the sights of a rifle or a shotgun.

In an hour, as Wheaten had predicted, they rolled into Ocotillo Station. It was a low adobe building, squatting on the limitless desert floor, with brush corrals built against the sides and rear.

Bowie got down stiffly, batting at his dusty pants with his hat. A bald tub of a man with a smile wreathing his round, cheery face wheezed out of the doorway.

"Howdy, Smoky. How many dead passengers this time?"

The driver swung lankily to the ground. He was tired and ill-humored. "Howdy, Mac. Two live ones, present and unaccountable."

MacGreevey roared. A girl leaned with folded arms in the doorway behind him, smiling a little. *Wheaten had underrated her*, Bowie couldn't help thinking.

She was as different from her short fat father as night from day. About seventeen, she was small and slender, with high-piled hair that became a honey golden nimbus against the lamplight. Her eyes, a fine level gray, were the most serene Bowie had ever seen. They met his own coolly.

Now Wheaten puffed his way to the ground, shouting boisterously: "Howdy, honey! It's your drummer boy, back from the wars."

The smile left her lips, and she turned quickly back into the building. MacGreevey hesitated, then snickered tolerantly as he greeted Wheaten. Bowie Adams's own reaction was simple and uncomplicated — he felt like smashing the drummer's leering face. Tight-lipped and wordless, he filed into the building with the others. The dining room was cool, resisting the lingering heat of day.

The men sat at the table while Amy MacGreevey silently

31

served the food. Wheaten's eyes followed her graceful movements. Once he tried to grab her wrist as she passed, but she sidestepped, without looking at him, and walked back to the kitchen. The drummer laughed and pounded his knee, then winked at Bowie.

"She's a good cook, too."

Bowie ate in ravenous silence. After the meal the driver and MacGreevey went outside to check the fresh team the hosteler was hitching up and to see that the axles were properly greased. Wheaten attempted a conversation now and then, but Bowie, busy with his own thoughts, drank his coffee without answering. He didn't notice the drummer get up and go into the kitchen.

Abruptly his reverie was broken by the faint sound of a muffled scream. Bowie thought it came from the kitchen. He noticed then that Wheaten was gone. He glanced through the doorway where MacGreevey and the driver were chatting by the team, evidently oblivious to what he had heard. Bowie got up, skirted the table, and entered the kitchen. His glance swept it. It was empty.

He hesitated. Then his eye fell on the back door. In two strides he reached it and flung it open. Roy Wheaten had backed the girl against the building. One arm was around her waist, while the other hand was clamped roughly over her mouth.

His eyes rolled toward Bowie, and his jaw dropped in surprise. With a frightened squeak he released the girl. Bowie stepped in and hit him. Wheaten gasped in protest as he tried to protect his face.

Bowie hit him in the soft belly with all the force of work-toughened young muscles behind the blow. The breath left the drummer in a long *whuf-f-f*. As he lowered his hands to his belly, Bowie slammed him on the point of the jaw, and dropped him in an inert heap.

Breathing only a little harder, Bowie swung to the girl. She still shrank against the building, her eyes wide, one hand at her throat.

"Are you all right?"

"Yes."

Her voice was steady. She pushed back a wisp of hair from her eyes.

Bowie looked at Wheaten, his eyes hard. "You'd better get back inside, then."

Amy drew a deep breath. "I think I'll stay out here for a while." She added: "I feel a little dizzy."

Bowie glanced sharply at her, wondering if she'd read his intention — to knock more of the starch out of Wheaten when he came to. Her next words confirmed it.

"There's a lot of hate in you, mister."

He said coldly, to cover his embarrassment: "If there is, what of it?"

"Nothing." She pushed away from the building. "It's your business. But don't hit Roy again . . . not on my account. He's not worth it. It won't change the way he is."

Even the resilience of youth hadn't kept Bowie's nerves from being scraped raw by what he'd been through. In his guilty knowledge of himself he knew that she was right. The long-contained spleen of his hatred for the Averysons had burst the tidewall of its fury on Wheaten. The urge to kill must have shown in his face when he hit the drummer, and that urge was not yet spent. It roughened his voice to deliberate rudeness.

"You must kind of like it . . . the way he is . . . if you can defend him after what he did."

Hurt showed in Amy's widened eyes, then they flashed with anger. "I can't stop you from thinking what you will," she said, as though the words left a bitter taste in her mouth. "Maybe I shouldn't even care, knowing what I do of men. Since I turned fourteen, every other male passenger that stopped here has

33

pawed me with his eyes. I know what's in their minds. What happened with Roy was the first time . . . and I didn't invite it, no matter what you think. I thought you might be a man who could think differently about a girl. I guess I was wrong."

She turned and almost ran into the kitchen, slamming the door behind her.

On the ground Wheaten groaned and stirred. He got slowly to his feet, retrieving his hat which had fallen off. He took out his handkerchief and wiped a trickle of blood from the corner of his mouth. His sallow eyes were baleful in the light from a window.

He whispered, "I'll get you for that, kid."

Bowie took a step toward him. The drummer gave a bleat of fear and vanished around the building. Bowie stood for a moment in bitter indecision, then walked away from the station to the farthest end of the corral. He hammered a fist against a post and stared bleakly into the ocean of darkness that was the desert night.

Amy MacGreevey's words had revealed to him how far he was gone in his corrosive hatred. It had begun to include the rest of humanity. It had made him use a rough tongue to a decent girl.

He heard soft footsteps coming up behind him and wheeled, his nerves taut, a hand dropping to Jimmy's .44. Amy gasped. He relaxed and faced her, feeling foolish.

"You *are* on edge," she said softly. "I thought there was something eating you. I came back to tell you I was sorry for what I said."

He made no reply. He knew he should be apologizing to her, but he couldn't bring it out.

She said timidly, as though she felt his resistance: "I told you I know men. I made it sound all bad. But seeing so many different ones come through, year after year, you get to know the good from the bad. I guess I know when a man needs help."

He felt a warm pleasure that she thought of him as a man. He tried to tell himself it was foolish — women always tried to soften a man, and he couldn't afford softness now.

He said, his voice still rough: "You have trouble enough of your own. Don't take on mine."

"You took on mine when you trimmed Roy to size." Amy smiled hesitantly. "Call it a favor returned."

Bowie tried to hold her off with brief curt answers to her questions, but it didn't work. He badly needed to talk to someone, to get out the thing cankering in him. He found himself telling her the story.

The Adams family, he said, had run cattle up in the Tonto Basin country since right after the Civil War. His father, Liam Adams, a Confederate cavalry officer, had brought his wife out to Arizona in 1866 and built up his own ranch single-handed. Thanks to the many natural barriers, he hadn't had to hire hands to patrol the driftlines.

As his herd grew, so did his five sons. The Adamses were well on their way to becoming a family of prosperous cattlemen when the Averysons rode into the Tonto Basin. The Averysons sprang from a breed of feuding folk common to the deep South hill country, and they brought their way of life with them.

A shiftless lot by nature, the Averysons had been content to let the Adamses raise the beef, while they skulked nearby, running off small bunches of Adams cattle. These they butchered back in the cañons or sold to random cattle buyers who didn't ask questions. Liam Adams was a patient man, but once needled to action he hit hard and deliberately.

While the Averyson men were out rustling Adams beef, Liam and his five sons had ridden over to the mean cluster of Averyson shanties, gotten the women and children out, burned down the buildings, and ordered the whole shabby clan out of the basin.

Retaliation had been swift. The Averysons had surrounded the Adams ranch house at night and riddled it with bullets, killing Liam Adams and three of his sons. Then they had melted back into the hills.

Only Bowie and Jimmy Adams remained to continue the battle, and they were both level-headed enough to know they couldn't maintain a two-man guerrilla warfare against the whole clan. Their mother had died years before, so there was nothing to hold them here.

They'd loaded a wagon with a few salvaged necessities and started out of the basin. One of the older Averysons and his twin sons attacked the wagon, emboldened by the success of the previous raid. But Bowie and his kid brother were both crack shots. When the overconfident Averysons rode in too close, the old man was shot dead, and both twins rode back to their clan, leaking from a half-dozen wounds.

Bowie and Jimmy went down to West Texas, bought a small spread with their father's savings, and settled down to what they hoped would be peaceful ranching. But they hadn't reckoned on the feuding tradition of the Averysons, how far they'd go to get an eye for an eye. When the twins, Henny and Tobe, were well enough to ride, they'd ferreted out the trail down to Texas.

It was the custom of Bowie and Jimmy to split their work and separate all day long for their individual chores. This was necessary, as theirs would have been an over-size burden for four men, and they couldn't afford as yet to hire riders. It was work till dark, topple exhausted into your blankets, then stumble up again with the dawn.

Three days ago each Adams had ridden out as usual on his rounds. Jimmy was to mend fence toward the east, while Bowie ranged miles to his south. Jimmy had not returned that evening. Next morning, sick with worry, Bowie had followed the boy's twenty-four-hour-old trail to the bottom of an arroyo on the east range.

Jimmy had been shot twice in the back at close range by a rifle — or rifles. Bowie had judged that there were two ambushers, from the abundant tracks which covered the loose-soiled bottom and banks of the arroyo.

The tracks made easy following — as the Averysons had intended they should. They'd stuck at first to sandy country and finally headed into the desert. Bowie hung relentlessly on through that day and most of the night.

He'd hardly hit the trail the next morning when a shot from a sand ridge had killed his horse on its feet. More bullets riddled the canteen on the cantle as Bowie sprawled half-stunned behind the carcass. Then the Averysons rode out into plain view, shook their rifles at him with taunting laughs, and galloped off.

The only thing to do was to strike north for the stage road that he knew roughly bisected the desert. Time and again he'd caught sight of the Averysons hanging tenaciously to his trail. It was a sure thing that the stage had carried him only briefly beyond their reach.

Amy listened wide-eyed. When Bowie had finished, she stared into the black gulf of night. Her voice was a whisper. "Then they might be out there now . . . anywhere . . . waiting."

"They might, if they caught up," Bowie agreed. "They'd sneak around and size up the guns before rushing in. That's their way."

Her hand, small and warm, touched his where it rested on the post. "I'll tell Dad and Smoky. They'll. . . . "

"They'll what? Go fooling around in the dark and get shot for their trouble? If Henny and Tobe are out there, they'd only have to wait to put a bullet into anyone who comes after them. This is my problem, Miss MacGreevey . . . no one else's."

The starshine caught the lean planes of Bowie's young face, and what she saw there put a quick catch in the girl's breath.

"You *want* to face them," she said unbelievingly. "You're so full of hate, you'd carry it through, even if they walked in and wanted to call it quits. All you can think of is. . . . "

"Jimmy," Bowie said harshly, but grief broke into his voice. "My kid brother. Those Averysons are full of nothing but hate and killing. All right. Then a man can face them only in like fashion."

"But Bowie, the world isn't all like that. You can't believe it is."

"I've seen nothing to show it in a contrary light till now. My father and brothers were good men. What did it get 'em?"

"That kind of thinking can lead to a lot worse. But I guess I shouldn't say more. It wouldn't be any use, would it?"

"No, ma'am," he said stonily. "Not a bit."

Amy shook her head in a quick, frustrated way, then turned and headed for the house. Bowie took a step after her, but stopped in his tracks. Both of them had been caught up in the intensity of his story, that was all.

What did a girl know about what it did to a man to see his father and brothers killed before his eyes? Still, her words oppressed him, and for a moment he thought he hated Amy MacGreevey as much as the Averysons. A man's duty was clear, and a girl had no right to foul it up and get him confused when he needed all his faculties.

Saddled with these wry thoughts, it suddenly occurred to Bowie that, if the Averysons were prowling around the station, he might make a plain target against a lighted window. He pushed away from the post and tramped back to the building. The stage should be rolling any minute now anyway, and he told himself it would be a relief to get away from that girl and her fool talk.

He walked through the empty kitchen and into the dining room. Amy, her father, his hosteler, and the driver sat stiffly at the long table. The scared tenseness in their postures warned him — too late.

A pistol barrel rammed into the small of Bowie's back. Henny Averyson's raucous chuckle crackled in his ears. Henny had been flattened against the wall by the doorway, and he had simply stepped quietly behind Bowie.

"A dumb play. You walked square into it, Bowie. And you Adamses always lorded it over us as being so all-fired smart!" Henny yanked Bowie's gun from its holster and nudged his spine. "Step over to the table and sit down. Put your hands out flat and keep 'em in sight." He lifted his voice. "All right, Tobe."

Tobe Averyson slouched through an outside door that opened on the front yard. They had stationed themselves to catch Bowie between them, no matter which way he entered. Bowie's lean hands curled into fists on the table. They had him for fair this time.

He wondered where Wheaten was. The drummer must have walked a distance from the station to sulk by himself, and the Averysons had missed him.

The twins kept their guns trained on the room at large, but both watched Bowie steadily with all their hatred glinting in their eyes. Neither had changed since Bowie had last seen them close up, back in the Tonto Basin country.

Both were as narrow as laths, with too-pale skin that had boiled ruddily in Texas sun and wind. Their tawny uncut hair fantailed over their collars. Their lips were compressed to lines that matched their narrowed eyes, reflecting the lifetime vigilance of a feuding people.

Henny laughed often, and he was the talkative one. Tobe's closest approach to humor or to conversation was a thin grin and a few pithy words.

He gave both now as he eyed Bowie. "Do you think he'll die fast as Jimmy, Hen . . . with a bullet in his spine?"

"Don't reckon, Tobe. Bowie's a tough one. He's pure rawhide, clear through." Henny grinned. "Even a day under that sun couldn't dry him out. He did it on foot, and it almost killed our horses. Bowie won't die fast at all, Tobe."

There was a tight dryness in Bowie's throat. They were not making idle chatter. He would die slowly. And they'd sweat him a while with this sort of talk, because it was all part of the game as they played it.

Someone was coming on foot across the yard. Tobe swung his gun to cover the doorway. Roy Wheaten walked into the room, his face surly, looking at no one. He had pulled off his hard derby and was running a handkerchief around the inside band.

Tobe said sharply: "Come in, mister."

Wheaten looked up in surprise, his round ruddy face blank. His jaw dropped at sight of two lean, hard-eyed men with guns pointed at him. There was no saying what fantasy seized his brain at the sight. He simply turned with a terrified sound and lunged for the shelter of the stagecoach.

Tobe's gun roared and bucked. Through the door Bowie saw the drummer jerk as he reached the stage. He grabbed at the paneling and tried to claw his way up. Tobe fired again. Wheaten turned under the impact, facing them as he slid down to lay, unmoving, in the dirt. Bowie's gaze shuttled to the others. He had seen too much sudden death in his young life. Wheaten's end could hardly touch him. But the shock on the faces of the girl and the three men showed plainly that they hadn't grasped the full scope of their danger till now. It was

40

unlikely that Henny and Tobe would leave anyone to carry tales.

Henny's voice cut the stillness. He motioned with his gun. "All right, you, girl . . . on your feet."

Amy stood slowly. There was only the faintest tremor in the spread fingers with which she lightly supported herself against the table. Her chin was up, her gaze level.

MacGreevey's huge bulk made his chair creak as he shifted. "Now, hold on!"

"Shut up," Henny said leisurely. He grinned. "We're taking her with us. Stand back, girl, away from the others."

Sweat sprinkled MacGreevey's forehead. Bowie Adams had tagged him as spineless, obsequious — but the knowledge that his daughter was in danger galvanized the fat man to action. With a bellow of rage he piled out of his chair and drove at Henny.

The Southerner pulled back a step in astonishment, then pulled the trigger. MacGreevey's massive form spun with the slug's impact, and he plunged to the floor like a dying rhino.

Amy screamed and came at Henny, her fingers clawed. They raked down his face. Henny shouted with the pain. Tobe slouched forward, his gun lifted to slam against Amy's head. Bowie braved himself for a moment until Tobe was close to the table.

Then he came to his feet, slipping his hands under its rim. He lifted the table and heaved it over on Tobe, carrying him to the floor and pinning him by the hips, while dirty dishes cascaded over him.

Bowie bent to snatch up Tobe's fallen gun just as Henny flung Amy away with a sweep of his arm. She fell against the wall. Henny's gun barrel swung in a tight arc toward Bowie.

With no time to check his sights Bowie squeezed off a snap shot. Henny brought his hands up to his chest, his shoulders

41

hunching together as though he were suddenly very cold. He dropped to his knees, then fell in a crumpled sprawl.

Cursing, Tobe had kicked the table away, and now he rushed Bowie bare handed. There was a shot, a deep, heavy roar that was almost deafening between the cramped walls. Tobe grabbed at his shoulder with a yowl as his charge carried him into Bowie Adams. Bowie shouldered him away, and Tobe sat down hard on the clay floor and stayed there, groaning.

Amy had snatched a Winchester from its wall pegs. Sobbing, she levered it again and swung it to a level for another shot at Tobe.

"No, Amy!" Bowie lunged, wrapped a hand around the muzzle, and jerked it down as she fired. The slug hammered into the floor. He took the gun from her suddenly limp and unresisting grasp.

There was a dazed look in her young face. "You hate them," she said in a dull voice. "Why did you stop me?"

The driver had knelt by MacGreevey. Now he glanced up at Amy. "Your dad's all right, girl. The shot just creased the old buffalo's skull. He'll be right as rain in a few minutes. Give me a hand, boy."

Bowie and the driver carried MacGreevey to his room and eased him down on the sagging bed. The driver returned to the dining room to see to the wounded Tobe. Bowie and Amy stood by her father's bed. Color had left the girl's face as reaction clamped its panicky hold on her. With a muffled moan she came into Bowie's arms.

He held her gingerly, feeling very awkward about it, and talked soothingly, his lips against her bright hair. "You were right all along. Revenge and hatred are plain wrong. I didn't know how wrong till I saw them in your face. Anything that could make a girl like you want to kill a man is no good . . . no good to anyone, Amy."

She drew back from him, lifting a tear-stained face. "But I understand now what you went through, Bowie. I thought they'd killed Dad, and all I could think of was hitting back, any way I could." She shuddered. "Thank heaven you stopped me in time. If I'd killed a man who was already wounded and helpless. . . . "

"You'd have carried the memory all your life," Bowie said soberly. "It took that to make me see it."

The driver appeared at the door. "Stage'll be rolling in five minutes. We're behind schedule now. I'm taking that Tobe feller in to the U. S. Marshal in Strang City. The other one's dead. You coming, son?"

Bowie looked thoughtfully at Amy, then her father. "Not this trip, Smoky. They'll need an extra man around here for a while."

Amy's smile was radiant. Bowie answered with a grin. It came stiffly to his lips, because he hadn't smiled in a long time. But he managed it.

In an article he titled "What Do Americans Want in Westerns?" in *The Roundup* (2/62), T. V. Olsen entered the controversy then at issue among members of the Western Writers of America between the traditional Western and the off-trail Western. In describing what he felt the proper direction for the Western story, he also summed up the significance of his own tremendous contribution to what would become increasingly the direction of his own fiction: " . . . a commercial Western fictioneer of today would do well to regard each book as a new creative challenge in development of plot and situation and highly varied characterization, with mature and intelligent concepts of theme and treatment — but strive simultaneously to recapitulate more truly the traditional elements that have made the Western beloved of Americans: the historical feel of the place and the people and the times, the sense of freedom of a wild and wide-open land, sex presented more honestly but still not sensationally, tough-minded men who did what they damned well had to and never mind about Mr. Jones, a swift, close-knit pace carried by lots of fast-moving action, and the decisive triumph of good over evil by a protagonist who can make mistakes and commit an occasional wrong because he is understandably human." What in effect Olsen was accomplishing at the time in his own Western fiction was to remove the Western story from the idealized models that harked back to Greek drama and the epic poems of Homer and Vergil and to populate his stories with realistic human beings who, notwithstanding, are caught in the same web of moral questions as found in Classical precursors — is this right? is this wrong? how ought one live? what is most important in life? So-called mainstream fiction had long abandoned any pretense it had ever made at addressing such questions, but T. V. Olsen was asking them in a stronger voice than ever before, following the trail Les Savage, Jr., had blazed in which the focus increasingly is turned toward psychological motivations directly related to the historical events, circumstances, and personalities of the period and place where the story is set.

The Man They Didn't Want

Will Evans rode his gaunt nag into the Kansas cowtown of Sun City in the early morning. Evans was a weather-darkened man of thirty with bleached hair, and eyes that were squinted and sun-wrinkled at the outer corners as though from a long habit of watchfulness. He pulled up at the blacksmith's shop because Bleak Denton had come to the doorway and was grinning widely.

"So you came back, son."

"I said I would," Evans replied with just a touch of tentative defiance.

But there was only cheerful welcome in Bleak Denton's long face. Bleak was nearly sixty, his gray hair almost gone, but time could not erase the unbending power developed by a lifetime of blacksmithing.

"Light down, boy. Where've you been?"

"Sonora and points south." Evans swung from his saddle and cuffed back his hat, as gray and colorless as his worn clothes. "I was chasing a bank robber. It was my last hitch as a bounty hunter."

"You'll really settle here, eh?"

"That's my idea." Evans glanced down the street. "It won't help your business to be seen talking to me, Bleak."

"The hell with all of them," Bleak said calmly. He stoked his pipe.

Evans smiled humorlessly. With Bleak Denton he was welcome; he knew it would not be so elsewhere. Evans had been a professional bounty hunter since he was twenty-five, a man on his own with no official status as a lawman who had been commissioned to track down any man wanted for

47

a crime and collect a large reward.

Two months earlier Evans had come farther north than ever before in search of Race Peel, a killer and train robber. He had finally cornered Peel in Sun City and wounded him in a saloon gun fight. During his brief sojourn in Sun City Evans had made one friend — Bleak Denton. It had been Denton who had counseled him that bounty hunting was a young man's game.

"And you're growing out of it," he had added. "It's time to settle down, son. My advice is . . . make it here."

He had shown Evans the rich grasslands that had been granted to the railroad by the federal government and that the railroad disposed of to the first comers at fantastically low rates. Land had no economic value to the railroad if it were not settled and developed.

The quarter section that Bleak pointed out did not need the blacksmith's glowing commendations to fire Evans with enthusiasm. He would locate his farm there, he decided. He made a one-tenth down payment to Hardell, the railroad agent, and had almost enough money left — saved from five profitable years of bounty hunting — to pay for the rest. One more bounty should do it.

That job had taken him far south in pursuit of a train robber. It was finished now, and Evans had enough money sewed in the lining of his jacket to finish paying for the land and enough left over to build and equip the farm. Will Evans had returned to Sun City, this time to stay.

One obstacle, the highest of all, still remained to be hurdled. Sun City was settling down from the wildness of its beginning as a wide-open trail town. As a result of the influx of sober farmers replacing the roistering cowhands of the old days, Sun City had already begun to develop a small-town clannishness that bordered on prudishness. Across all the face of the South-west no man was more hated than the professional bounty hunter, the nonprofessional lawman who cared nothing for the law, who hunted down a wanted man as impersonally as he might hunt an animal — for a bounty. With small-town gossip running from resident to resident like a brush fire, it was not long before all these upright farming folks knew that one of these hated manhunters intended now to make his home among them.

Even before Evans had left Sun City that first time with his prisoner, an ugly black resentment had been readily stiffening the ranks against him. One hot-tempered young farmer named Willis Richie had even shouted after him as he rode out: "Don't come back, Evans. We don't need your kind."

But he had come back.

It was as though Denton had read his thought. "You'll have to win 'em over, son. But that's only half your trouble, and maybe not the worst half."

Evans nodded. He had heard of cattle baron John Rhodes and how he had sworn to drive every last one of the sodbusters off the land that his cattle had grazed as open range for nearly thirty years.

"I had an idea trouble might be starting," Evans said.

"It's in full bloom right now," Bleak said grimly. "It's grown to clashes in town and on the range between farmers and Rhodes's Double Bit hands. You probably didn't know that most of these settlers are kinfolk . . . they all came West together from a big Tennessee clan. You know how these Southern hill-country folks hang together. That's why Rhodes has held off from starting a full-scale war.

"Mostly, big cattlemen drive off settlers by picking 'em off one by one. But Rhodes knows, if he jumps one of these families, he'll have to take on the whole clan at once. He hasn't been willing to risk that . . . not yet.

"Only a few weeks ago, though, he hired a new foreman . . . a bully boy named Grant Rudabaugh who used to be a trouble-shooter for the railroad. He's fixing to import a lot of professional gunmen who'll burn down every farm on the range."

"I know Rudabaugh," Evans said slowly.

He and Grant Rudabaugh were in like professions, and their trails had crossed more than once, never pleasantly. Rudabaugh was shrewd, ruthless, utterly without scruple. Rhodes had picked the right man for the job.

"So you came back!"

The acid voice broke like a wash of ice water over Evans's thoughts. He turned slowly, his reins trailing through his fingers, to find Willis Richie standing behind him. The stocky farmer's meaty fists hung loosely, and his thick legs held a belligerently wide-spread stance.

"Enjoy your stay, Evans. It won't be a long one."

"Why?" Evans asked. "Has the railroad upped the price from two dollars an acre?"

Richie's sun-ruddied face flushed darkly. "I told you once that we don't want your kind. We have trouble enough with old man Rhodes and his cow nurses without man-killers coming in to make more."

Evans took two steps forward and hit Richie in the face. The solid smack of the blow could be heard for a block. Richie hit the dust on his back, rolled over, and came to his feet, holding his bleeding mouth. His eyes were wild with hatred, but he held himself in.

"I won't fight you, Evans. You can't make me. You've picked up enough dirty tricks in your bar-room brawls to kill me and claim self-defense."

Evans's hands were fisted at his sides. He said in a trembling voice: "Listen to me, Richie. I never went after a man who hadn't been convicted, and I never killed a man while I was bringing him in . . . which, I grant, some bounty hunters do. You were there when I wounded Peel. I could have killed him as easily and saved a lot of bother."

"The hell with you!" Richie said wildly, beyond reason now. "I have a wife and four kids. They've had a hard time of it. This was to be our new start. How can I raise good kids with a killer like you living on the next section? My youngsters deserve a decent chance."

A hard core of anger formed behind Bleak Denton's merry blue eyes. "And, I suppose, Will Evans doesn't?" he said softly.

Willis Richie ignored that. "Stay and you'll regret it, Evans. That I promise you."

He turned on his heel and walked away.

Will Evans stared at the ground. "Maybe I should push on to where I'm not known. It'll be hard for a man to fight the land and men at the same time." He thought a moment, then came to a decision. "But, whatever happens, I aim to make my home here."

As a consequence of Evans's constant labor — and Bleak Denton's help, when he could spare it, plus his advice, which he could spare anytime — the nucleus of a small farm soon began to take shape on the virgin quarter section.

One hot morning Evans sat on the crude wash bench, feeling better than he'd felt in days, as he worked at fashioning pails for carrying water. He had cut the tops from some big, square coal-oil cans and was rigging them with wire bails. He left off work briefly to allow a contented eye wander over his house and barn.

Newly completed, the barn was the typically crude farm building of that country, built of cottonwood poles and with a sod roof. But the house, in proud contrast to the usual soddy, was a two-room building, constructed wholly of sturdy, only slightly used lumber that Bleak Denton had scrimped together through some minor miracle and freighted here on a borrowed wagon.

Evans felt it was built to last a lifetime, and he could annex onto the house over the years. It symbolized the permanence in his new beginning. He felt good about it. Let the past stay buried, with no regrets.

His busy hands stilled as his eyes circled the short-grass plain rolling to the distant Rockies. Small eddies of dust billowed with the wind, kicked up by the passage of a lone rider, approaching from the direction of Rhodes's sprawling Double Bit. *They've got the Indian sign on me already*, he thought, and went back to work. He didn't even glance up when the rider finally reined up in the yard.

"Mister Evans?"

He looked up swiftly, then stood, pulling off his hat. He saw a piquant-faced girl of about twenty who sat her saddle with an easy grace. She was tall, slim, and rebelliously bare-headed. The wind toiled with and stirred a few silken wisps of honey-tinted hair.

"I'm Susan Rhodes," she said.

"You're John Rhodes's daughter?" Evans hazarded.

"Yes."

"Does he know you're here?"

"Coming was my idea. I'm not answerable to Father or to anyone for what I do."

He looked at her, proud in the saddle, thinking her pettish and a little spoiled. "Well, Susan, you've had your look at the black sheep. What else do you want?"

Her gray-green eyes were candid. "I want to warn you. Father means to drive every nester from the range, and he intends to start with you."

"Why me? Others have been here longer."

"Because he knows the others would stand together against him, but not a man of them would lift a finger to help you. You'll be targeted first . . . as an example to the others."

Evans considered that briefly, and then nodded. "Thank you for the warning . . . and good bye."

"It was a long ride for a few words," she said. "Do you mind if I step down a minute?"

Evans stared hard at her. "You don't just buy plain trouble, do you? You like it in spades."

Susan Rhodes slapped her quirt angrily against a leg of her Levi's. "I told you, I'm not answerable to anyone."

"I can see that. But I'm not stirring up a hornet's nest with John Rhodes by letting his daughter make my place a dropping-off station. You just turn that nag around and point for home."

Susan threw back her head as though she'd been struck. "You're afraid of Father, aren't you? . . . just like all these slavish settlers? I've long wanted to see just one person stand up to him and that head-on arrogance of his. I'd heard of you as a tough man, Mister Evans, used to facing up to trouble. I thought for a while you might be that person. I see I was wrong."

"Trouble is what I'm trying to leave behind. Skedaddle!"

She rode away, her back straight and angry. Evans looked after her for a moment, then shrugged, and resumed his work.

He cleaned up at noon and went in to eat. When he heard riders approaching, he moved swiftly to the door, because it sounded like a body of men. There were three of them, sitting their horses in his yard. As though by prior agreement, they had fanned out about the doorway, seemingly to circumvent any move he might make toward the rifle he'd leaned against the corner of the house.

Grant Rudabaugh was in the center, a blocky, middle-aged man with a harsh and bigoted face and the coldest eyes Evans had ever seen. For money, it was said, Rudabaugh would frame his mother for murder. Now Rudabaugh laughed softly, spuriously.

"Well, they told me, but I didn't believe it . . . ! Will Evans, a hoe-and-plow man! Having fun, Will?"

"Why not?"

Rudabaugh regarded him almost benevolently. "Why not?" he echoed. "Maybe we'll show you why not. Meet Wake Carruthers and Turk Krell."

Carruthers was a small man whose eyes looked out, hot and vicious, from his pinched and predatory face. Krell was a greatshouldered brute with a face like a wax-molded image left in the sun till it began to melt. Evans had only to glance at them to know what kind of men they were. His eyes moved to the rifle he had leaned against the house.

"Go on after it," Rudabaugh said. "I hear you bounty hunters are some shucks with a rifle. Let's see."

"You'd like to rawhide me into going after it, wouldn't you, Rudy? Then you'd shoot me when I reached it. That would make it easy. I'd be out of your way, and you'd have it cinched as self-defense."

Rudabaugh kept grinning. "You read a hell of a lot into things. All I know is, Rhodes wants you moved off . . . and, mister, that's what we're going to do. Turk!"

Turk Krell piled laboriously off his horse and tossed his reins to Wake Carruthers, then turned his massive ugly face to Rudabaugh. "I'll cut him down to size," he rumbled. "You name it, Rudy."

"About knee high, Turk," said Rudabaugh. "Don't be too rough . . . just show him we mean business."

Krell moved like a shaggy bear across the dry-packed mud of the yard. He was outclassed from the beginning, Evans knew. Krell was only a couple of inches taller, but he outweighed Evans by nearly a hundred pounds.

Evans blocked Krell's first free-arm swing, catching it on his forearm, but even so the crushing weight of the blow almost knocked him off his feet. He tried to move out from the cabin wall where he had backed, realizing too late that he would stand a better chance against the lumbering giant in the open.

Krell smothered him with his weight, beating him about the head and shoulders until he fell to his knees, sick with pain, trying to grab Krell about the legs and heave him off balance. Krell slammed him in the face and broke his hold, flattening Evans on his back.

"That's enough, Turk!"

Rudabaugh's voice was like a clangoring echo in Evans's ears. He climbed back to his knees with an effort of will, bleeding from nose and mouth. The image of Krell, towering over him, blurred his eyes, then cleared and sharpened.

"That's just part of what you're buying into, if you stay," Rudabaugh said harshly. "Drift. There's nothing for you here."

A blaze of anger and pain erupted in Evans. With a sudden gathering resurgence of power he launched himself from his knees, driving head and shoulder into Krell's bulging stomach. With a soughing wind-driven grunt of hurt, Krell fell back into his horse. The frightened animal shied away, and the big man was thrown to the ground.

Evans spun and ran for the rifle. He wheeled with it in his hands, throwing the sights up and centering on Rudabaugh's chest. Rudabaugh was caught startled and off guard, with his gun half drawn from its holster.

"Finish your draw," Evans said softly, "then drop the gun. Do the same, Carruthers, then Krell . . . one at a time."

When the three guns were thrown to the ground, Evans motioned Rudabaugh and Carruthers off their horses. "It's a long ride back to Double Bit," he said conversationally, "and a longer walk."

"You can't do this!" Carruthers bleated.

"Can't I?" Evans waggled his rifle at them. "Pull off your boots, boys."

"This is a mistake, Evans," Rudabaugh said harshly.

"It's your mistake. You're not big enough to carry out Rhodes's orders, Rudy."

Holding the rifle on them with one hand, Evans slapped the horses into a bolting run toward their home ranch. The three men followed, stiff with hatred and humiliation, leaving boots and guns in Evans's yard. The cold, hollow eye of Evans's rifle followed their retreating backs.

Evans finished his day's work as always, prepared and ate his meager supper, tidied his two rooms, and settled back for the evening with a book. He was ready this time when he heard a rider pull up in the yard. He picked up his rifle from the table, turned down the lamp, and moved quietly to the open doorway.

"Who is it?" he called softly.

"Me. Susan Rhodes."

He stepped into the dusk-shrouded yard, seeing the girl dismounting from a hard-driven horse. "I thought I told you. . . ."

She faced him with a white-faced dignity. "Mister Evans, I'm here to warn you."

"Again?"

"Again. Rudabaugh is almost crazy because of what you did. He and those other two gunmen staggered in at supper time, half crippled. In spite of that, they're coming back tonight to burn you out."

"Come inside."

He followed her in, and she wheeled to face him, her hands clenching and unclenching at her sides.

"I tried to talk Father out of it. He just laughed. He says they have a free hand and his blessing."

56

He pointed to a chair, and she sat, running a tired hand through her pale hair. Backed by warm lamplight, it formed a nimbus of tangled light about her face.

"Will you trust me?" she asked quietly.

"Yes, I think so."

"Then, listen. Let me stay here. They won't dare burn the house or shoot at it with me in it."

"I can handle them."

"I know you can," she said impatiently. "But, if we do it my way, we might avoid bloodshed."

He dropped the butt of his rifle to the floor and watched her wonderingly. He had been wrong, gauging her as the spoiled daughter of a wealthy rancher, interested perhaps in a small flirtation on the side. This was an unselfish woman who would put up her own life as surety that there might be no bloodshed between men who could be of no personal concern to her.

It occurred to him that this might be a transient whimsy, such as a spoiled girl would indulge herself in for a passing thrill. But her look was direct and serious, he saw, showing she was fully aware of the magnitude of making a choice that would pit her against her own father.

As if reading his thought, Susan said: "If you wonder how I can turn against Father, it's because you've never seen him break a man. I have. He isn't purely mean, like Rudabuagh, but he's arrogant and hard . . . too hard." She shook her head. "I don't know," she said wearily. "He wasn't always like this. After my mother died, he stopped caring what the world thought. He directed every feeling he had into his ambition, no matter who was hurt by it. Perhaps when he hears about this . . . how his own daughter stood against his hired killers . . . it may cool his well-fed arrogance down a notch."

Evans pulled up a chair and sat facing her, leaning his elbows on his knees.

"You know, there's a lot more at stake here than just my case. It involves hundreds of other settlers . . . those here now, and those yet to come. You had a hard choice to make, turning against your father, but you may be helping many by it."

Her eyes showed amazement. "I had heard all bounty hunters are hard, cold men. Yet, you want only good for people who have treated you like a leper."

A smile changed his dark face. "It's a world mostly full of pretty good people. The main trouble for most of them is they want to make their own standards apply to everyone else."

He stood and walked restlessly to the door, where he stared into the black gulf of night, listening. He was turning away when he heard the horses coming. He moved swiftly to douse the lamp. The saffron glow sank and died into darkness. He went to the window and strained his eyes, peering into the outer gloom, picking out the spectral forms of three mounted men.

Then he was aware of Susan's moving to his side. She put a hand on his arm, and there was an audible catch in her breathing as she saw the men. There was a wry irony in this for Evans — having Rhodes's daughter help him against Rhodes's hired gunmen.

The riders cautiously dismounted.

"Hello, the house!" It was Rudabaugh's voice. "Sing out, Evans! We know you're here."

"All right, Rudabaugh," he called, "I hear you. I can pick off all of you from here. Mount up and clear out!"

Rudabaugh's laugh was frosted with hatred. "I came here to burn your place to the ground, Evans. I'm going to. But not you with it. I want to see you take a long walk first, without your boots. Walk out with your hands up . . . or be roasted alive."

As he spoke, the three men were already moving out of view

toward the shelter of the barn.

"Wait a minute, Rudabaugh. Susan Rhodes is in here with me, and she won't leave. Think about that before you start throwing bullets or fire."

There was dead silence for a long moment. They could hear the three men talking in low hurried voices. Then Rudabaugh's wicked, high shout came.

"Here's your answer, Evans!"

A shot crashed through the window, and the whole pane collapsed in a tinkling shower of glass. Both Evans and Susan had moved away, so the slug went wide.

Evans's first reaction was stunned disbelief. He knew Rudabaugh, and the two with him were no better. But utter disregard for a woman's life was virtually unknown among Western men.

"I should have known," Susan said bitterly. "The fact of my being a girl would be more a goad than a deterrent to Rudabaugh. He hates me . . . he hates all women. I heard Carruthers say once that some woman made Rudabaugh the way he is."

Evans interrupted harshly. "You're getting out, Susan . . . right now! I'll call to Rudabaugh and tell him to hold his fire a minute."

His words were torn apart by a volley of slugs, crashing through the window, the doorway, and the walls, which were covered so far only by sheathing. Evans went down on the floor, drawing Susan beside him.

"You see?" Susan asked. "He'd as soon kill me, too, then burn the place around our ears. I think he welcomes the chance to kill a woman, even though he'll be forced to ride clear of the country afterward."

They heard running footsteps outside, and in the window there was a burst of flame which fell to the floor. A man had run in close and thrown in a piece of burning kindling, soaked in coal oil.

"Grab that!" Evans snapped at the girl and lunged to the window.

He saw a spectral form, flitting back toward the barn. He lifted his rifle and shot, once, twice, a third and fourth time. Every shot missed. Then the man was safely behind cover.

Evans turned to Susan, hearing the hiss of the dying torch as she dropped it in one of his improvised water buckets.

"This is no good," he said. "I can't see to hit them, and they can come in close and hit us any time. Wait! The window in the other room opens on the back, and they won't be watching there. Outside the cabin I'll at least stand an even break."

"An even break," Susan cried, "with three against one? Oh, if I only had a gun!"

"You're going to ride for help. Come on!"

Evans climbed through the high, narrow window of the back room, then helped Susan through.

"Your horse is around at the front," he said. "We'll get mine."

He got his horse out of the brush corral at the rear, and bridled it. Susan swung on bareback.

"The closest place" — Evans hesitated, his jaw clenching — "is Willis Richie's. And he probably won't help me. But you haven't time to try elsewhere. Try to get Richie . . . and bless you, Susan."

She looked down, and he could not see her expression in the night, but her hand reached swiftly, impulsively and touched his face. Then she turned his horse and was gone into the darkness.

Evans circled to the front, sliding along the wall. As he turned the corner, he saw another flare of oily torchlight in the yard, illumining the massive form of Turk Krell. Turk threw the torch. It arced high and hit the roof in a shower of sparks. The flickering glare threw uncertain light far over the yard as Krell turned to lumber back to the shelter of the barn.

Evans stepped into view. "Krell," he called.

The huge man wheeled clumsily, pulling at his gun. As it leveled up, Evans fired once, and then again, from the hip, holding his rifle low. Krell's great frame jerked spasmodically. He then slid down and pitched on his face.

Rudabaugh and Carruthers had sighted Evans, and both opened up from the barn, driving him to cover behind the well. The roof of the house had caught fire now.

Rage burst in Evans's mind in a crescendo of red fury, and he forgot caution, forgot that he might hold them pinned down here till Susan came with help, forgot everything except that these men must pay for destroying his home.

He skirted the well and ran head-on for the barn. The very rashness of the unexpected maneuver caught Rudabaugh and Carruthers off guard. They both fired wildly, and then turned to retreat deeper into the shadows of the barn.

Evans dug his heels in hard, stopping a half-dozen yards from the cowering men. In the flickering light thrown by the fire he could see fear darken Rudabaugh's face as he swung up his pistol to match the upswing of Evans's rifle. There were two shots as one, and then Rudabaugh fell over backward.

Carruthers had gone down on one knee and now began fanning his gun empty. A bullet whipped through Evans's shirt; another creased his scalp like the thrust of a running iron. Evans had seen more than one gunman lose his life by spraying slugs in this manner — fanning was rarely accurate beyond a couple of yards. In that second Evans took careful aim and sent off his own shot.

He felt the futile click. The loading tube of his repeating

Spencer breech-loader held seven cartridges, and all were expended.

Carruthers stood, his narrow face pinched and grinning. He had fanned four shots to no effect. He cocked his pistol and lifted it at arm's length to send off the fifth shot with care.

A gun roared in the yard. Carruthers groaned and fell back to his knees, holding a shattered arm. Willis Richie, on horseback, lowered his rifle and started across the yard.

"You all right, Evans?" he called.

Evans's legs weakened with relief, and he had to sit on the ground. Richie and Susan Rhodes swung from their horses.

"She couldn't have gotten to your place and back," Evans said. "How did you get here so soon?"

"She met me when I was almost here," Richie replied. "I'd heard shooting from your place, and it struck me that you were making a one-man stand for all of us."

Sunrise had only begun to streak the eastern sky when Richie and Evans returned from town with Bleak Denton, driving a wagon filled with lumber. By tacit agreement they felt it was necessary to throw up a new house immediately, in defiance of John Rhodes.

They were lifting lumber out of the wagon when a light rig drove up, containing Susan Rhodes and a tall, aristocratic-appearing man with iron-gray hair. It was John Rhodes. The men stopped work and watched like three stiff-backed tomcats as Rhodes climbed down from the high seat and gave his daughter a hand.

Rhodes cleared his throat uncomfortably. "Is it too late for an old man to say he was a fool? When Susan told me . . . when I saw Rudabaugh and the others for what they were, how they would have murdered my own daughter to get at you for spite, Evans . . . I saw very suddenly how near I came to making myself like them. Mister Evans, Mister Richie, I'm eating crow . . . but I think you're big enough to let this apology be a start."

Willis Richie rubbed a tired hand over his unshaven jaw. "Well, Mister Rhodes, you might have spared yourself that speech. *We* never wanted trouble in the first place."

"I know," the rancher said hastily. "But I owe Evans at least something. Five of my hands will be over later in the day to lend a hand on the new house."

Evans hesitated, his glance lifting to Susan. Her smile was warm and full.

"I'd take it kindly of you, Mister Rhodes," Evans said then. "A man needs a home."

All of T. V. Olsen's short stories, as his Western novels, deal in part with relationships between men and women, love, courtship, and in the later novels marriage and occasionally divorce. Olsen himself was married for the first time on April 17, 1970 to Jacqueline Brooks Michalek, a marriage that ended in divorce a little more than a year later. During this time Olsen had been researching and writing his first major historical novel, THERE WAS A SEASON (1971). It concerns young Jefferson Davis during the years 1828-1833 when he was an Army lieutenant on the Wisconsin frontier and Davis's bittersweet love affair with Sarah Knox Taylor, daughter of Zachary Taylor, later hero of the Mexican War and President of the United States. While researching this period, Olsen read Beverly Butler's FEATHER IN THE WIND (1965), set in Wisconsin in 1832, and came to know her. Totally blind since the age of fourteen (a result of glaucoma), Beverly had gone on to earn a Master's degree from Marquette University and had established herself as a noteworthy author of young adult fiction. The two were married on September 25, 1976. From this union both would prosper, personally and professionally.

Stampede!

The trail herd had pushed well north of the Nueces when the two riders caught up with it. The herders were making night camp.

"Saul Holly?" a 'puncher said in answer to a question from the pair. "That's him over there by the wagons with the two women."

The younger rider laughed and cuffed back his hat. He was a sandy-haired, cocky boy of eighteen who seethed with a core of highly nervous energy. "Two women on a cattle drive? Russ, boy, we stumbled on the right diggings!"

His companion, a big, smoky-eyed man in the mid-twenties, regarded the kid without anger, as though this were an old story. "We came looking for work, Cort, not trouble." His voice was quiet. "Let's keep it in mind, huh?"

The kid shrugged impatiently, and they rode over to the wagons where Saul Holly heard them out. Old Holly was not a big man. He stood five feet seven with a stocky, oak-strong body, his seamed face weather-darkened to a mahogany grain, his thin, unkempt, white hair like a misty nimbus about his bare head. His worn range clothes were more disreputable than his men's. Sixty-one now, he had pioneered in the great post-Civil War cattle drives to Abilene, Ellsworth, Wichita, and now to Dodge, the last great mecca for the Texas trail drivers. Saul Holly had become a living legend on the Chisholm, and Russ knew it and stated his request with respect and brevity.

Holly nodded, eyeing the two newcomers with humorous, tolerant eyes, as though he liked what he saw. "Riding the chuckline, eh? Sure, I can use you boys. I'm undermanned this drive."

"Thank you kindly, sir," Russ said.

"And who might you be, young fella?"

"Russ Kindred, sir, of Texas. This here is Cort Davies, likewise."

Holly gave each a horny handclasp and gestured to the two women. "My wife Andrea, gentlemen, and my daughter, Joan." His voice took on a strong note of pride.

Russ Kindred had heard that old Holly took his womenfolk along on trail drives but had supposed this to be just another of the legendary tales that had grown up around the little giant. Looking at his wife, Russ's puzzlement mounted. Andrea Holly was all of thirty-five years younger than her husband, and she was one of those rare women who was really beautiful. Even her men's clothes, as rough as any trail hand's, could not hide her grace. Dying sunlight brought out highlights in the rich gold-red hair, framing the faintly oriental sculpture of her slim face, held in the dutiful placidity of a faithful wife. But the sultry languor of her dark eyes and the pouting coral of her full underlip seemed to hold an invitation. Russ was suddenly angry at himself. It was not usually his way to pass judgment in short order.

Young Cort Davies was staring hard at her, and Kindred had to jolt him out of it with a hard elbow in the ribs. *The old story again with Cort*, he thought wearily — *an attractive girl.*

"Joan," the old man was saying to his daughter, "take these fellows over to the cook and tell him to fix them up. We ate already, boys," he added in explanation.

The daughter nodded and led the way to the chuck wagon. She was about nineteen, as tall as her father, and her long stride was businesslike and masculine. Except for the wealth of tangled, tawny hair, tied carelessly at the back of her neck with a piece of limp ribbon, her trail hand's clothes gave her much the appearance of a tall boy.

The bald, wiry little man in a greasy apron straightened from pouring water into the dish-piled wreck pan. "Hi there, sis. Something?"

"Saul just hired these two, Joe. Feed them, will you?" Her voice was level and clipped, like a man's — yet with a low-voiced modulation that Russ found oddly pleasing. She had turned her back to rejoin her father when the irrepressible Cort swept off his hat and made her a bow of mocking gallantry.

"Ma'am, fo'give us ignorant hogs, but it ain't often we see one lovely lady in a cow camp, let alone two! Ma'am, I'm befuddled. Your mammy must have married when she was five years old."

"Not that it's any of your business," Joan Holly said coldly, "but my father's first wife . . . my mother . . . died when I was born. Saul married Andrea seven years ago. Now . . . any more questions . . . stupid or otherwise?"

Cort lifted his hands in mock dismay. "Don't shoot, ma'am! I surrender!"

Joan set her fisted hands on her hips. "Listen, you owl-eyed knucklehead," she said levelly, "keep your place and you'll get along. Otherwise. . . ." She snapped her fingers, and walked away.

"Well," Russ said dryly, "you been taken down?"

"Plenty, partner," grinned Cort Davies.

"You don't want to run afoul of that gal," cackled old Joe, the cook. "She'll skin the hide off you faster'n I could put a fly off a buffler's horn with a bullwhip. Say, you boys hungry or not?"

A week of sun-seared prairie rolled behind the northward-trekking drovers, with Russ and Cort swallowing the dust of the drag. Finally they paused on the south bank of the Brazos, a broad gulf of yellow-churning waters. A bad crossing at any time for Texas drovers, and the water was high this season. But old Saul Holly had crossed at flood tide on other occasions. Sitting his shad-colored pony on the muddy shore, Holly presented a figure of tremendous vitality and knowing confidence that held everyone calm and ready to follow his lead.

"Push 'em hard the whole way," Holly roared, "and I'll see you at camp on the other side."

There were a few scattered shouts of approval as Holly slapped his horse's rump with his coiled lariat, plunging the beast into the roiling waters. The lead steer, caught up by this example, followed. The first animals and riders splashed into the whirling backwater, dropped into the swift current of the deep central channel, and began doggedly swimming. Tee Jones and Ace Leadbetter dropped back from point positions, turning back bunch quitters. The herd put the south bank behind and forged for the far shore. They floundered up the smooth sand bar of the north bank and surged to high ground.

The wagons followed, old Joe driving the chuck wagon, cursing and pushing the team hard. Behind him, Joan Holly drove a second wagon piled high with the warbags of the crew. Russ Kindred had hung close to her on his horse with no real expectation of trouble, for he'd long since found Joan to be as capable as any man at every trail job from steer-cutting to cooking. Cort would be up ahead, Russ supposed, near Andrea Holly. Russ shook his head gloomily. No good could come of that.

Joan's wagon had just pulled into a shallow current. Suddenly Russ saw the rear wheel on the off-side beginning to lower — then the whole stern of the wagon canted abruptly into a steep drop-off that the front wheels had missed.

Russ reined his dun in close, shaking out the coils of his rope. He twirled out a huge loop, got it over the hub of the rear wheel on his side — the one still on steady ground — and then over the whole tail of the wagon box. Joan was shouting at the harnessed animals, putting them into the full effort of righting the wagon that was beginning to tilt awkwardly as the lip of the drop-off crumbled and dropped the rear wheel deeper. With the added impetus of the swirling current, the wagon would be thrown over on its side in a moment.

Russ spurred his dun through the shallow water to take up the slack in his lariat. It dragged taut, and the dun's full straining weight was thrown into the effort of keeping the wagon on an even keel. The off-wheel stopped sliding. Joan threw a swift, startled glance over her shoulder. She hadn't noticed that Russ had spotted her danger seconds before she had.

"Lift 'em out of this!" he shouted at her, and she complied with shouts and handy rein work. The sagging off-side of the wagon heaved up and pulled clear of peril. Kindred dismounted and stood in knee-deep water to undo his rope and loop it over the wagon tongue, where he could add a stabilizing pull in case of further trouble on the crossing.

"Thanks, cowboy!" Joan said, and, to his surprise, she added the white flash of her smile — the first he'd seen. He nodded and motioned her on. The crossing was finished in comparative safety.

Joan swung down as Russ dismounted. She took off her hat, cuffed the dust from it. Her face had resumed its usual stony expression, making it — not plain — but angularly regular, like a handsome boy's. *She'd been pretty with that brief smile*, Kindred thought. Even now, she was an impressive girl to look at, with her faintly dust-powdered, tawny brows and the fine, level gray eyes of her father. And Kindred had discovered he liked her boyish frankness. It gave him an ease with her that his usual reserve toward women denied him.

"Thank you," she said stiffly. "You maybe saved my life."

"Nothing," Russ said. He couldn't help adding: "You

wouldn't smile again, I suppose."

She stiffened angrily before she saw that his blunt, young face held only good humor. She lowered her gaze. "I'm not fine to look at. Not like Andrea. Not much point to smiling."

"Why, ma'am, I never call a lady a liar, but. . . ."

Joan flushed. "Don't spread me taffy that way, mister. I'm not used to it. I'm just Saul Holly's tomboy brat. He had three daughters. I'm the one he couldn't marry off. So, if I wanted to play a man, he figured to get some use out of it. That's why I'm here."

She turned away, half shy, half angry, at having revealed so much of herself.

Holly rode up. "Son, that's a sharp pair of eyes. You knew what would happen before it happened, and you was ready. Say, I ain't seen you a whole lot. Where's Dirk been placin' you?"

"On drag."

"I'm tellin' him to try you somewhere else. We'll have you on point before this drive's over."

"On point," Russ Kindred said dazedly. "Yes, sir. Thank you."

Holly turned jovially to his daughter. "Still alive and kicking, eh, Blondy? Your sisters would be fainting sick by this time!" He cuffed her lightly on the head as he might a boy.

Joan drew away with an irritable toss of her disarranged hair. "Don't do that, Dad," she said sharply.

"What do you mean?" Holly asked. "You always liked it."

"I'm not a child, Saul!" She swung lithely back to the wagon seat and flicked the wheelers into motion.

Holly stared after the wagon. "Saul! Saul, she calls me! Now what in Tophet's ailin' that girl?"

They made camp not far from the north bank. With coming night, a chilled ground mist gathered and thickened, turning to

72

a pink pearl about the ruddy glow of the fire. There was a clink of tinware and no talk as the tired crew wolfed supper, squatting comfortably slack about the fire. With two women in camp, there was a natural restraint on an easy flow of man-talk. Russ had noticed, however, that with Andrea Holly the men were apt to be shy and stumbling, but with Joan they joshed like a comrade. And Russ thought that the blunt forthrightness of her, that he found appealing, would probably frighten most men.

Holly took a stubby pipe from his mouth and spoke to the trail boss, breaking the silence. "Think there's likely to be trouble along the way with one of those border gangs?"

Dirk, a sun-blackened string of a man, shrugged taciturnly. "Hard to say. I hear talk back in Dallas that Tunstall and his gang were riding up this way."

Holly nodded inexpressibly, his big face lined and stolid. "Assign the night watch, Dirk."

Andrea Holly sat near her husband, giving Cort Davies a glance of arch warmth, and the kid was getting all calf-eyed under it. It was the sort of thing, Russ Kindred reflected, that was not supposed to go on, or, if it did and you saw it, you were supposed to pretend you didn't.

Russ Kindred lost his appetite. Cort had no control where women were concerned. He could forgive the kid because they were partners and because presumably Cort would outgrow it, but forgiveness wouldn't take the boy off the hook if it came to trouble. As for Andrea Holly, married to an old man, he could not say how much blame she deserved. Russ simply did not like the woman, and he couldn't say why.

The crew began to split for the night watch. Andrea Holly left the fire and walked casually to the rear of the wagon. Because he was watching for it, Russ was the only one to see the glance she gave Cort over her shoulder before she disap-

73

peared around the tailgate. Cort finished his supper without haste, picked his teeth for a while, and exchanged insults with another 'puncher. Then he got up, stretched, and walked to the tailgate of the wagon with his cup and plate, dumping them into the wreck pan. Russ looked away to answer a remark from the 'puncher next to him. When he looked again, Cort was gone.

Russ stood, hesitating. He thought: *Maybe I'm wrong, but I've got to know.* He walked around the wagon and sent a swift glance into the darkness, seeing Cort gliding like a slim wraith into the fog that abruptly swallowed him. Russ's gaze went the circle of the fire, saw no one watching, and promptly followed Cort.

The black trunks of a meager stand of blackjack timber grew out of the misty obscurity. Russ stopped dead in his tracks as the voices of Andrea and Cort reached his ears. He could see them dimly, standing apart in the grove.

"You'd do anything for me, Cort?" Andrea asked musically.

"Ma'am, you name it!"

"Cort, I do need help. I need it very much." Her low voice was warm and seductive. "Saul has treated me badly."

"Ma'am, you say the word. . . ."

"Your night watch will be finished at midnight. Meet me here, then, and I'll explain. You're sweet, Cort, for understanding." She patted his cheek. "Now hurry on to your watch before you're missed."

Russ shrank tightly against the ground in a shallow, wind-worn hollow as Cort, returning, tramped past him not two yards distant. Kindred waited till Andrea had followed a moment later, then walked slowly back to camp with the step of an old man.

What can I do? he wondered, groping his way through the thick fog which was no deeper than the gray confusion in his mind. Andrea knew what she was doing. Whatever she had in mind, she meant to drag the kid down with her. *What can I do?* Russ asked himself again, and there was no answer. Cort was smitten with Andrea Holly as a boy can be with an older woman. And if Russ presumed to tell him the right of the matter, the boy would not believe him, would only hate him.

It's your hot potato, Cort, he thought, but that wasn't right, either. A man did not stand by and watch his best friend destroy himself without lifting a finger. He must make a token effort, at least.

At camp, Russ went out to the remuda to find Cort, cutting a horse from the string, readying for his night watch.

"Now you'll chase cattle for a while, eh?" Russ asked in a low voice.

Cort's voice was sharp in the gray silence of the fog that all but hid them. "Don't try to be funny, Russ!"

"I don't feel funny," Russ said slowly. "I don't feel funny at all."

"Get off my back, damn it! I've seen you and the whole camp watching in your smug way. I know what I'm doing! She's fine and sweet, and that damned old Holly treats her like a dog!"

Russ said flatly: "You been took, kid." He saw the blow coming but not in time to duck it. Cort's hard-knuckled fist hammered his jaw, and the ground seemed to lurch and lift and slam him in the back. He dragged himself gingerly up as Cort swung to the saddle and pushed off to the bed grounds. Russ looked after him until horse and rider were lost in darkness and fog. Russ only stood, a blackness in his mind, tasting bitter wrath at Andrea Holly.

"Oh, Russ." It was Joan's voice at his back, full of compassion and pity. He turned, squinting at the pale oval of her slim face.

75

"He hit me." There was pain in his voice but not from the hurt of the blow. "He wouldn't listen. He just hit me."

"I know. I saw it. I followed you. I thought you might . . . might need someone."

"How can a woman do what she's doing?"

"Andrea?" There was a bitter edge to Joan's voice. "She's been doing it the seven years of her marriage to Dad, after he took her out of some dance hall in Dallas. She's sneaky and cruel, and she takes it all out on me when Dad isn't around because she knows I would never tell him. Saul's too big, too easy-hearted to think bad of anyone. Sometimes she baits him cruelly, and he is too simple and blunt a man to know what she's doing. Some day he will know, and, when he does, it will kill him. And sometimes I could kill her!"

Russ was shocked by the terrible, bitter intensity of her. "Not you! Not a woman."

"Why not? Only another woman could see her clearly. Even though she takes constant pains to remind me that I'm a very poor sort of woman, dressing and acting like a man!"

"You never knew any women but Andrea?"

"How could I, growing up on Dad's ranch with my two older sisters married long before and the nearest neighbor fifty miles away?"

"Maybe that's it. Growing up, seeing what kind of woman Andrea was, you never wanted to become one yourself." She shook her head in confusion. "I don't know. It's all so mixed up. Why am I telling you these things?"

"Things build up in a person. Maybe you had to tell someone."

"I don't know how to begin to be a woman!" she said, looking up at him, and her dimly seen face seemed softened and appealing.

"Why . . . Joan," Russ said wonderingly. He took her arms

and drew her in, kissing her gently. At first her body stiffened in startled rebellion, then her lips became pliant and soft with acceptance. When they drew apart, her eyes were shining, womanly and wanting.

Russ said soberly: "I'm fond of you, Joan. Remember it . . . in case anything happens."

Her voice was quick with alarm. "What could happen? Russ, is something wrong? Something you haven't told me?"

He hesitated. He had not told her of Cort's midnight rendezvous with Andrea, and he decided not to. If there was a risk to be taken, he would rather take it alone. He had to know for certain what Andrea was up to. It was the only way to save Cort.

For hours, Kindred lay rolled in his blanket, feigning sleep. He knew it was midnight when the first watch of nighthawks came straggling in and the sleep-logged second watch made ready to ride out. Kindred got a horse and rode with them, falling casually behind in the fog. He cut off then at right angles and headed for the blackjack grove, silently hoping he wouldn't be missed. When he saw the dark shape of a lank-boughed oak lifting out of the neutral grayness, he dismounted, ground-hitched his horse, and went ahead on foot, moving like a shadow into the grove. He saw Cort standing in a little clearing by his horse, the man and animal one nebulous shape to his straining eyes.

Kindred went down on hands and knees and flattened himself beneath the shadowy, low-growing branches of young oak brush. Here, a man might stand a yard away and not see him for the heavy mists. The sounds of muffled hoofs and snapping twigs reached him, the sounds of a whole body of riders, heading into the grove.

Cort straightened with alarm. He had expected only Andrea. The strange riders dismounted with a heavy creaking of leather and rattling of bridle chains.

"Hey, who's the kid?" one of them asked, just as surprised to see Cort as Cort to see them all.

"He's with me!" It was Andrea Holly's voice. She came on horseback into the clearing and moved swiftly to the side of one of the riders. "David, this is Cort. He'll help us."

"Ah, I see!" David said dryly. "Though, when you told me you'd get one of your husband's crew to help, I didn't think you'd pick on a boy."

David! Kindred thought quickly. And the man had the clipped accent of an educated Englishman. This was David Tunstall, the black-sheep scion of a British family who led a gang of border thieves, raiding road herds in the wild country north of the Brazos. Kindred had heard much of the man. But why was Andrea Holly meeting Tunstall as though by pre-arrangement?

"Missus Holly," Cort said in half-frightened voice, "what is this? Who are these fellows?"

"Now, Cort," Andrea said soothingly, "you gave me your promise, remember? Won't you hear me out?"

The boy only relaxed slightly under the vibrant warmth of her voice.

"Saul is a brute," she went on. "I'm leaving him . . . now . . . tonight. And, because I believe I've earned it, I am going to collect for all the misery he has caused me. I am going to take his herd from him and sell it in Dodge. Mister Tunstall and his men will help."

"Tunstall!" Cort gasped.

"Cort . . . please, listen. I didn't want to do it this way, but it's the only way. I'm married to an old man. He owes me for seven years of my life, tolerating his crotchety whims. But he would give me nothing, and I couldn't take it without help. This drive gave me the chance, so I contacted Tunstall. We'll share in the profits, all of us. Oh, please, Cort . . . we need your help. It isn't as though Saul couldn't spare this herd. He's tremendously wealthy, and there'll be other years for him, other herds. But this is my one chance!"

Cort's voice was low and miserable and unpersuaded. Now, Russ knew, he was only a badly frightened boy. "What did you want me to do, ma'am?"

"It's easy, lad," Tunstall drawled. "If we're to take Holly's bloody herd, it should be now . . . at midnight . . . when cattle are most restless. Your job, as one of Holly's crew, someone they will trust, will be to draw off the attention of the night watch by some ruse, giving us a chance to get in close and stampede the herd off the bed grounds."

Cort was silent and motionless for a long moment, and Russ's heart sank. Cort's very hesitation was acquiescence, he thought. And then abruptly Cort wheeled and lunged through the standing men for the edge of the clearing, making a sudden break that took the jayhawkers by surprise.

"Catch him!" Tunstall shouted.

Two men dragged Cort down, just as he began to plunge through the brush into a mantle of fog that would have covered his escape. Tunstall undid the lariat from his saddle and tossed it to a third man.

"Tie him," he said curtly. "Gag him."

For a moment there was no sound but Cort's wildly thrashing struggle, then he lay helplessly bound on the dank ground.

"Well, my dear," Tunstall said coldly to Andrea Holly, "he's no more a thief than you are a faithful wife. There's your answer, though even a chap his age should have seen that you're a tramp who'll play every end against the middle to get what you want."

"What do you care?" she asked just as coldly.

"I don't," Tunstall said conversationally, "and I'm in no hurry. The nighthawks are still our biggest problem. Without this boy to help us, we'll have to take our chances on picking them off."

Andrea shrugged. "Well, once it's done, it should be no problem to get the herd moving and stampede it over the camp."

"No. No, that'll be easy enough." Tunstall scratched his chin. "Of course, when the herd goes over the camp, your husband and some of his party may be. . . ."

"Are you getting soft in the head?" Andrea Holly interrupted with a low fierceness. "If we get away with Saul's herd and don't disorganize and cripple him first, what's to prevent him from following us? He outnumbers us two to one. I'm going all the way with this, David."

"All right, men!" Tunstall called. "You know your positions. Let's push it, lads."

Mounted again and ready, the riders filed from the grove, Andrea Holly with them, leaving Cort Davies bound, hand and foot, in the clearing. Russ Kindred came stiffly to his feet before their lessening shapes were swallowed in the fog. They'd be headed now for the bed grounds of the herd, a half mile from the camp.

They'd need time to circle behind it, if they were going to run the herd over the camp, and they'd need time to dispose of the nighthawks, unless they could take them by surprise. That should give Cort and himself time to warn Holly, convince him of his danger, and get a counter-threat organized against the raiders.

Cort stirred and grunted, seeing Kindred as the older man bent to cut him loose. "You're lucky, kid," Russ told him. "You're getting a second chance."

Holly accepted their warning with startling readiness when Russ and Cort swiftly roused him. Pausing only to snap a few brief questions, he belted on a gun and swung stiffly out of the wagon where he slept to wake the sleeping crew. In seconds all were mounted and ready, having gathered up their gear and stowed it into the two wagons that Joe, the cook, and Joan Holly were to drive beyond the present camp site out of the way of a possible stampede.

At Holly's forward sweep of arm the mounted men thundered out of camp, straight for the bed grounds to hit the raiders, if possible, before they hit the herd. Riding at the forefront with Saul Holly, feeling a sudden, perverse exultation in the wide-open pace of his horse, Russ Kindred glanced sidelong at the old man, renewing his admiration. In this world of night and fog and dimly moving shadows, Holly rode with a boldly wild impetus that set the pace for his men and carried them in his wake. It was also Holly who first picked out the betraying sounds in the gray bank of silence ahead. He hauled in his horse, bringing the others to a halt with an upraised arm.

"They got the herd started," he said. "Pull far to the side so you won't get caught in front of it. Half of you" — with lightning composure he rattled off names to avoid confusion — "go with Dirk, hit the raiders from the rear. The rest of you come with me. When the herd comes through, we'll hit it from the flank and try to turn it into a mill."

They started up their horses, and then the thundering herd and shouting riders were sweeping on them, drowning all other sound. Russ picked out an outburst of shooting as Dirk and his men hit the jayhawkers, and he was aware of no conscious thought save being swept by the irresistible tide of stampede, riding at the flank to lend his whoops and horsemanship to the milling. For a long time, it seemed to Russ, the herd ran straight without a break, until it was as though he'd never known anything but the choke of dust, the whoops of men, the roar of guns, the rumbling cadence of surging hoofs.

Then, almost imperceptibly, as the daring riders at the front relentlessly crowded the lead steers, the animals turned gradually in a circle, and blindly the others followed that lead. The fog was lifting at last, as suddenly as it had settled much earlier, giving way to a white flood of full moonlight that highlighted the frightened cattle in sharp clarity. The problem of the riders who'd begun the mill was to keep clear of its center, for that would be the inevitable direction of the lead steers that they were turning.

Russ hauled up his heaving horse, the sobbing breath searing his lungs. He saw now in the full light, despite the dust and the night shadows, a rider coming up fast from the opposite flank, one of the raiders, trying to divert the efforts to turn the herd. It was too late. The lead steers were turning back on the rest of the herd, closing a great circle, driving into the others in a head-on collision of climbing, goring, frenzied animals.

"You fool," Russ gasped, for the raider was caught in the shrinking space within that circle! The raider's hat whipped away suddenly. A white face, seen by Russ Kindred in the moonlight, was fixed in a terrible scream. He saw it in the brief seconds before the circle closed, and Andrea Holly was swallowed and vanished in the mass of heaving backs.

It was dawn on the prairie. Holly's surprise counter-attack had broken and scattered Tunstall's gang. Some had been shot down, the leader among them. A few escaped. Cort, Russ, and old Saul hunkered exhausted by a wagon while Joan served them coffee. They watched the saddle-weary men drift, one by one, into camp and immediately head for the coffee pot.

Presently Holly glanced shrewdly around at Cort. "You got somethin' to say, young fellow?"

"Yes, sir," Cort said meekly. "I just don't know how to say it. Reckon you know most of the story already, anyway."

"Put it this way, son," Holly said gently, "I knew Andrea."

"Dad!" Joan said softly, "you knew?"

"Almost from the day we were married, honey. Hell, in the back of my mind, I knew it was wrong then. I knew she was near young enough to be my granddaughter and likely marrying me for money. But there's no fool like an old fool. I didn't see what she was till afterward, and even then I hoped she might change. But she was no good, and she couldn't. Now, I just pity her."

Cort stood suddenly and walked quickly away.

Russ said: "Cort!"

"Let him go, son," Holly said sharply. "He'll have to fight it out by himself. It's the way a boy becomes a man."

Joan laid a hand on his arm. "Let him go, Russ. . . . There are women like Andrea . . . but not many. Cort will learn that in his own time."

Russ looked down at her, seeing in full daylight the fine strong lines of her slender face. "You know," he said, "you're one in a million yourself."

Old Saul Holly chuckled and drained his coffee cup. "I always said you had sharp eyes, son."

Joe R. Lansdale in the second edition of TWENTIETH CENTURY WESTERN WRITERS (1991) concluded that "with the right press Olsen could command the position currently enjoyed by the late Louis L'Amour as America's most popular and foremost author of traditional Western novels." It was Lansdale who asked T. V. Olsen to write a Western story that included an element of the supernatural. "Jacob's Journal" was the result. In the event Lansdale never had occasion to use it, which is why it was available for first publication in *Louis L'Amour Western Magazine* (11/94). "Jacob's Journal" is in its way very indicative of the new directions in which T. V. Olsen took the Western story in his work, including late novels such as THE GOLDEN CHANCE (1992) that earned him a Golden Spur Award from the Western Writers of America and DEADLY PURSUIT (Five Star Westerns, 1995).

Jacob's Journal

June 8, 1886

Sarah is dead. I killed her with my own hands and buried her beneath tons of rock. I know she is dead. Yet this forenoon I saw her . . . alive?

I do not know. But I saw her as clearly as I see the page on which I indite these words.

I was crossing from the commandant's office to the agency house — a longish walk of perhaps two hundred yards — when I became aware of being watched. Turning my head, I saw her. A woman standing on the prickly pear-and-chaparral-covered rise a little south of the agency house.

At first I took only passing note, supposing her to be the wife of one of Fort Bloodworth's officers or enlisted men. But something in the way she stood, absolutely motionless and watching me, as I believed, arrested my attention. Leaving the well-worn path, I started across the intervening hundred or so yards of nearly barren ground toward her.

I was quite close before I recognized her, but, when I did, recognition came unmistakably. The sunlight lay full on her face and on the brightness of her red-gold hair.

It was Sarah.

I stopped, petrified with fear and incomprehension. Either I was experiencing an hallucination or I was a victim of some gigantic hoax. But the latter possibility, at least, seemed out of the question. None but I — I was positive — knew the truth behind my wife's sudden disappearance.

Screwing up my courage, I advanced slowly toward her. I was nearly to the rise when my nerve broke utterly and I shouted her name. Screamed it, more than likely.

Until that moment she had neither moved nor changed her expression by a hair's breadth. It was as severe and aloof as — damn her soul! — Sarah had so long been toward me.

Now I saw her smile. A lovely and alluring smile, one such as I had rarely seen on her face during our years together. And while she smiled, she slowly raised an arm and beckoned to me. Then she turned, not hurrying, and walked over the crest of the rise and out of sight.

When I had scrambled to its top, she was nowhere to be seen. She had vanished as if the rocky soil and scant vegetation had swallowed her up. Impossible! When I looked for any tracks which might help solve the riddle, I found nothing, not even the trace of a footprint. Still, the ground was so stony and impervious to ordinary sign that even a skilled tracker might have found nothing. Except. . . .

The fact comes to mind only now. As though, earlier, my mind had rejected the knowing. A hot wind was blowing off the desert, strongly enough to whip particles against my face. The woman on the knoll wore a voluminous dress with a wide skirt, identical to that in which I buried Sarah.

Yet in all the time I saw her, the woman's clothing, the drape of its fabric, was unstirring in the blast of wind. As though the wind could not touch her, could not have its way with her in any particular. . . .

With the last few sentences, the bold sprawl of Jacob Creed's rapid writing turned into a shaky, dashed-off waver. Then the entry suddenly ended.

Major Phineas Casement had been reading slowly aloud from the leather-bound journal he had slipped open at random, pausing often to squint at the words, swearing and muttering. Now he said a disgusted oath, slapped the journal shut, and tossed it on his desk.

"Good God, what a pack of nonsense! Sheer balderdash. The fellow must have been deranged."

"Possibly, sir," said Lieutenant Mayberly. "But every entry he made in that book, if you except this one persistent delusion, has proved out to a detail."

"I'm sure, Mister Mayberly, I'm sure. That fine probing intellect of yours would do its damnedest to ferret out the whole truth, no matter where it led."

Major Casement reached for the humidor on his desk, extracted a cigar, and offered the humidor to Mayberly with an impatient thrust of his hand. Politely, as Casement had known he would, the lieutenant refused a cigar.

Major Casement pushed his swivel chair back from his desk and rose to his feet, grimacing as the movement peeled his blouse sweatily away from his back and paunch. Arizona Territory — Christ! you'd think that after a dozen years of being stationed at one or another of its raw frontier outposts, a man would be used to the furnace heat of its relentless summers.

He lifted a foot onto the chair, struck a match on the heel of his high cavalry boot, and lighted the cigar, glancing enviously at the younger officer, seated at ease in the room's only other chair.

Mayberly looked as cool as a January thaw. His double-breasted blue miner's blouse and blue trousers, with the yellow cavalry stripe down the outseams, were hardly stained by dust, not at all by sweat. His black, neatly blocked campaign hat rested on the knee of his crossed leg; his dark hair was neatly parted above a sober, cleft-chinned face. The subaltern was only a year out of West Point; Fort Bloodworth was his first assignment. Yet he'd blended into this inhospitable land with the adaptability of a chuckwalla lizard. A leather dispatch case was propped against his chair.

Major Casement swiped a hand over his sweat-dewed, nearly

bald head, clamped the cigar between his bulldog jaws, and slowly paced his narrow office, up and down. "The fellow was a heavy drinker, I'm told. How much of that *persistent delusion* of his came out of a bottle?"

"There may or may not be a way of telling, sir." Lieutenant Mayberly leaned forward to take Creed's journal from the desk. He flipped backward through the pages. "In any case, the journal entries which are of main concern to us begin at a much earlier date. May I quote from them?"

Major Casement rolled out an irritable plume of smoke.

It would be his duty to write up a full report on the whole unsavory mess to the Secretary of War and file a duplicate report with the U. S. Department of the Interior, since Jacob Creed had been the agent assigned to one of the hellholes they called their Indian reservations. Before doing so, the major would need as thorough a briefing as possible from his ultracompetent aide, Mayberly, whom he'd ordered to investigate the almost simultaneous deaths of Agent Jacob Creed and Colonel Richard Dandridge, Fort Bloodworth's late commandant. Major Casement had been hastily dispatched here to replace Dandridge, and Mayberly had already given the major a sketchy report on his findings.

"By all means, Mister Mayberly," Casement said sourly. "The damned fellow's hand is so execrable I could scarcely make out the words. Read it aloud, if you please . . . ."

May 17, 1886

Today, after two months at this god-forgotten post, cautiously trying the tempers of the officers at Fort Bloodworth as well as those of the headmen on the adjacent reservation, I made my approach to Colonel Dandridge. Not only is he in the ideal position to abet my scheme, he possesses the requisite qualities to implement it.

90

Beneath his façade of an efficient and highly regarded career officer (President Lincoln himself bestowed a Medal of Honor on him during the late conflict), Dandridge is a savagely bitter and disillusioned man. This in consequence of his being several times passed over for advancement to a brigadier generalship, due to favoritism toward officers of far lesser qualification who were, nevertheless, politically well situated. . . .

The echo of taps died away in the gray twilight. Lamps winked out as darkness closed over the parade ground of Fort Bloodworth. From the Chiricahua reservation to the south drifted the lone, keening bark of a camp dog.

Jacob Creed had locked up his sutler's post. Standing on the porch, teetering gently back and forth on his heels, feeling mellow as all hell, he took an embossed whiskey flask from his coat pocket, uncapped it and took a small swig.

Creed was a bearded, thick-set man whose coarsened features and bloodshot eyes showed little of his genteel background. His belly was badly burning from the effects of intermittent drinks he'd consumed during a day of haggling with the Apaches who came to trade at his post. By now the damned siwashes should be aware that no one left Jacob Creed on the short end of a trade. Yet they never ceased trying. Born hoss-traders (as well as hoss-stealers) they were. All the bastards were.

Creed chuckled quietly. He treated himself to another pull at the flask. Things would be different from now on. A hell of a lot different.

As to bartering with him, the Apaches had little choice. Post trader Jacob Creed was also the Indian agent for the San Lazaro Reservation. In addition to his government salary, he received an allowance of federal funds to buy steers from local cattle ranches to furnish the monthly beef ration allotted the reservation Chiricahuas.

Behind the combination trading post and agency headquarters was a cattle corral. An issue chute was set up across the weighing scales adjoining the corral. And the steers were driven through the chute where the head of each family presented his ration ticket, had it stamped, and watched his cattle being weighed.

Colonel Richard Dandridge, as the fort C. O., was required to add his official presence to the weighing-out but, after their conference this morning, that would be a mere formality. Seething with his private bitterness, the aging career officer had been almost eagerly amenable to Creed's proposal.

For the hundredth time, Creed chuckled over the development.

It was simple. So damned simple. From now on he would buy up the poorest of the cull steers the ranches had for less than half the ordinary price, then pocket the balance of allotted moneys. A simple matter, also, to rig the scales so that the sorriest steer would be well within the minimum poundage allowed. One-third of Creed's swindled government funds would keep Colonel Dandridge's bitter-thin mouth silent. And the Apaches, unable to subsist on gaunt, stringy, possibly diseased beef, would be forced to trade at Creed's post for supplies.

Jacob Creed took another mild swig from his flask, capped it, and put it away. He took a step off the porch and damned near fell on his face.

Jesus! Was he that drunk?

Sure he was.

Why had he made the deal with Dandridge? Sold whatever dregs of gentle birthright he could still lay claim to for a mess of conspiratorial pottage?

Then, reflecting on Sarah and the miserable course his life with her had taken, he thought: *Why should I give a solitary shit?*

He straightened upright and lurched homeward along the sandy, thin-worn path to the agency house beyond the fort, considering (as he often did) ways in which he could repay her treatment of him.

Creed grinned crookedly. There was one sure-as-hell way. . . .

Even the most incorruptible man, when all his hopes and ideals have been repeatedly dashed by adverse fortune, may become approachable. . . .

"Damn the fellow's complacency!" Major Casement cut disgustedly into his subordinate's reading. "Did he fancy that *his* reason was any better or different from that of the man he bribed?"

Mayberly raised his brows. "Probably not, sir. I think it was Creed's wry, oblique way of telling himself as much. As I suggested earlier, his difficulty with his wife must have been a powerful goad behind all his actions."

"Hmm." Casement rolled the cigar from one side of his mouth to the other. "Powerful enough to drive him to murder. Go on, Mister Mayberly."

Again the lieutenant flipped back through the pages. "I think, in the light of subsequent developments, that this entry is a revealing one, sir. It was made on the day Creed arrived with his wife on the stage from Silverton to take over duties at the San Lazaro Agency. . . ."

March 12, 1886
 The conditions at our new post are not nearly as desolate as we had feared. The reservation itself is situated at a considerable height above the desert lowland to the south, to which

much of the reservation land forms a striking contrast. Numerous stands of giant pine lend a cool and indeed attractive aspect to our new home, although they are interspersed with terraced open flats which, I am told, have defied the sorry efforts of my reservation wards to farm them. As if we could, in a brief decade or so, transform a race of nomadic warriors, barely subdued by us, into tillers of the soil!

The agency house itself is a gratifying surprise to us. I do not know what we expected to dwell in — perhaps an oversized hut of baked adobe. However, the agent who preceded me at this post was James Montoya, a man — I was told — of pure Spanish descent and a true aristocrata. Clearly he chose to build after the fashion of his hidalgo forebears and, with all the splendid pine roundabout, found no need to build of stone or mud.

The squared giant timbers that compose both the inner and outer walls were hand-shaped by adze and draw-knife, fitted so beautifully together that one can hardly slide a knife blade between them, and the tiers of logs are fastened at all ends and corners with vertical iron rods. It must have cost him a pretty to import the highly skilled labor necessary to put up such an edifice. Most of the furnishings went with Montoya when he departed, but what remains indicates that they were opulent and costly. I was told, however, that his people have money. Of course the raw timber was free for the taking, and the rough labor (Indians and mestizos, no doubt) to cut the trees and trim the logs and transport them to the spot could be hired cheaply.

Salud, Don Jaime: Your family must have been a large one. (As is more often the case than not, of course, with these Papists.) There are no less than a dozen spacious rooms, including six chambers on the second floor, three to a side with a hallway dividing them. Of particular interest are the two

wide central balconies with their iron-wrought grillwork rail-
ings. Built off the center rooms on either second-story side of
the house, one faces north, the other south. Thus, I should
imagine, an occupant might enjoy sun or shade on almost any
day, according to his preference.

    Even Sarah seems delighted with the house and its piney
surroundings, and she is particularly taken with those charm-
ing balconies. Could this herald a change for the better in the
steady dissolution of our married life? One can only hope. . . .

"Obviously it didn't." Major Casement plumped himself
back into his chair, folding his hands over his paunch. "Eh?"

"No, sir." Mayberly turned a block of pages, going forward
in the journal now. "Here's his entry for June 4th. It reads
simply: 'Damn Sarah. Damn her soul to eternal hell. Last
night. . . .' "

"That's all?"

Mayberly nodded. "His temper reached such a passion that
his pen-nib slashed through the paper at that point, and a
scattering of ink blots suggests that he flung the pen down in
a rage. Whatever provoked the outburst apparently occurred on
the previous day or evening. From the shakiness of the writing,
I should say he was barely recovered from a monumental de-
bauch."

Major Casement unlaced his fingers, tapping them on his
paunch. "No entry for that date . . . June third?"

"None, sir. The journal is full of gaps and omissions . . . for
our purpose, at least. We can only speculate on the missing
parts. My inquiries among our own garrison personnel turned
up a few things that may help fill in the picture."

"Such as?"

"Well, it seems that Missus Creed *did* take a hankering to
those second-floor balconies. She loved to sit of an afternoon

on the one that faces north . . . on the side toward the fort."

"Is that where . . . ?"

"Yes, sir. Where Creed fell through the nailed-shut door."

Major Casement frowned. "I haven't paid a lot of notice to the agency house, but I'd assumed that it was a boarded-up window he went through. So there *was* a balcony there?"

"Until Creed had it torn off, sir. Lieutenant Verlain's wife told me that Missus Creed preferred the north balcony because it was cool and shaded in the afternoon. She was careful never to expose her creamy complexion, of which she was very proud, to the sun for any great time. In any event she would sit out and read or else let down her hair and brush it, a lengthy ritual." Lieutenant Mayberly cleared his throat. "Seems that some of our chaps at the fort . . . both officers and enlisted men . . . would get out field glasses and watch her from the barracks windows. It became a daily piece of business hereabouts."

"Did it now!"

"Sir, there's something mighty provocative in the sight of a beautiful woman brushing out her hair." Mayberly reached in his dispatch case and took out a photograph which he handed across the desk. "That is Missus Creed. A picture I found in her husband's effects. Missus Verlain verifies it is a recent one. You can't tell from this, of course, but her hair was very long and shining . . . like a waterfall of reddish gold, Missus Verlain put it."

Casement gazed long at the photograph. "A looker, Mister Mayberly. A looker, all right. Creed had reason to be jealous . . . if that is why he had the balcony removed."

"That's why, sir. And he had the door that opened out on it nailed shut. For a while after that, Missus Verlain claims, Missus Creed had recourse to the south balcony, holding a parasol against the scorching sun. But it was awkward and uncomfortable and she soon abandoned the practice. . . ."

* * * * *

Creed sat in the deepening shadows of his sutler's store, drinking and brooding. He was coatless, his single badge of dignity removed, and his shirtsleeves were rolled up. Now and then he hooked his thumb into the ear of a whiskey jug, tilted it on a thick, hairy forearm, put it to his lips and drank deeply, afterward wiping his mouth on the back of his other forearm. He was not drinking idly. He was drinking to get deeply and sullenly drunk.

Damn the woman! He'd never used to drink like this.

Where had it started? When?

Ten years ago and in Washington City, he supposed muddily, if you wanted to go back that long and far. To the beginning of a marriage. It had seemed an ideal match, everyone agreed. He was the young scion of an old New York family and, as the personal secretary of a U. S. senator, privy to secrets at the very pulse of power, destined for great things. She was the senator's lovely socialite daughter, and they were thrown often and naturally into company.

The engagement had been as brief as propriety allowed, the wedding lavish and festive, and the aftermath stained with acid. Sarah's ideas of perfect marriage were gleaned from the purported precepts of H. R. M. Victoria, discreet advice in *Godey's Lady's Book*, and murky tidbits from her mother ("A woman must learn *submission* to her husband, my dear, no matter how demanding he may seem.") All of this, along with too much festive champagne, had Sarah in a mildly hysterical state by the end of their wedding day. And Creed remembered his nuptial night vividly. The words she had screamed at him: "Oh my God, I never dreamed . . . *you hairy beast!*"

Words that still cut his memory like blades. Where could a marriage go from there except downhill?

Sarah had soon learned the submission that her mother had

97

recommended. It was all that was required of her and all that she damned well intended to give. Not bad if a man could pleasure himself by embracing a waxen statue, but Creed had found and taken his pleasures elsewhere. Along with a concomitant erosion not only of his married life but of his career in government service.

The pit of his descending fortunes had been reached two years ago, with his appointment as agent to the tiny blister patch of a Jicarillo reservation south of here. Granted, his new assignment to the big San Lazaro reservation was a step back up. But then, once you'd reached the lowest rung on a ladder, where could you go?

You could fall off it on your face, Creed thought with the humor of stark misery, and took another pull at the jug, draining it.

A trapped fly had been buzzing and batting monotonously against the fly-blown window beside his head. Suddenly furious, Creed took a backhand swipe at it with his right hand, shattering the glass.

"God dammit all to hell!"

He stared at his badly bleeding hand for a half minute, letting out a string of ripe oaths. Then, awkwardly left-handed, he bound the cut up with his handkerchief. It did little to check the bleeding.

He got off the petulant jag-end of his temper by smashing the empty jug on the packed-clay floor. Then he closed up for the night, not bothering to lock the door, and maneuvered foggily across the parade ground. Mulrooney, Troop L's bugler, gave him a bad start by suddenly sounding tattoo just a few yards away. Creed was barely sensible enough to curb his impulse to call the bull-chested Mulrooney a god damn bog-trotting mick.

He wove his way home along the narrow trail, barged into the agency house, tramped through the front and back parlors and into the kitchen, bawling: "*Sarah!*"

"You needn't shout. But as pixilated as you are, I suppose you wouldn't know the difference."

Creed hauled up in the doorway, glaring at her. Sarah was seated at the small kitchen table, picking at a plate of leftover chicken and biscuits. She gave him a radiant, meaningless smile and nibbled daintily at a biscuit.

"Where's my supper, god dammit!?"

"You've already drunk it, haven't you?"

Creed started to lurch forward, but the whiskey had caught up to him with a vengeance. He had to grab at the doorjamb for support. "God dammit. . . ."

"Don't tax your vocabulary, dear. If you have anything to tell me, you might be more at home, not to say lucid, with words of one syllable. Certainly not three."

Oh, Christ! Creed dropped his hot forehead against his bent forearm, braced against the doorjamb. *Ever since he'd had the damned balcony torn off!* Up till then, at least, they had always been tolerably polite, if cool, toward one another. He remembered her outraged cry as Miguel Ortez, the local handyman-of-all-trades whom he'd hired to demolish the balcony, had begun his work.

"*Please don't, Jacob! I didn't know those men at the fort were . . . were spying on me. You can't blame me! Please . . . I love that balcony!*"

Creed had felt a grim satisfaction in ignoring her plea. It was something to have finally broken through her cool and regal façade. All the years of his philandering and her silent knowledge of it had never touched a nerve. At least not so it showed. Now she was wringing her hands, pleading, driven literally to tears. And he'd grinned at her, unspeaking, while they'd listened to the shriek of pulled nails and the wrenching of boards as the destruction went on.

Afterward Sarah had locked herself in her room. Locked her door against him for the first time. Next morning, when he'd come down to breakfast, Sarah was composed and calm-eyed, even humming a little, as she set out a meal for herself alone. When he'd angrily asked where his breakfast was, she'd given him a gentle smile and said nothing as she began to eat.

It was pretty much how things had gone ever since. They never took their meals together. If Sarah chanced to fix more than she felt like eating, she'd leave the remainder on a plate for him. By the time he got home, it would be cold and marbled with grease: a more pointed sign of her contempt than when she left nothing at all for him. Always a meticulous housekeeper, she now abandoned any pretense at housekeeping except for keeping her own bedchamber tidy and washing her own clothes and sheets. Creed abhorred the notion of lowering himself to housework. Although he knew he'd be giving the garrison gossips a field day, he hired Dolores Ortez, Miguel's wife, to clean the place once a week, wash the stacks of dirty dishes, and launder his clothes and bedding.

Creed raised his head and stared at Sarah. She patted her lips with a napkin and rose to her feet. Lamplight ran a silken caress over the red-gold corona of her hair. Smiling faintly, she said: "Do try to be less casual, dear. Your hand is dripping all over the floor."

Somehow it tripped off the last cinch on Creed's temper. In all their years together, however angry and frustrated he'd become, he had never laid a violent hand on her.

Suddenly now, red rage sizzled in his brain. It was uncontrollable. With a throaty growl he surged forward, gripped the edge of the table between them in both hands and flung it aside. It caromed against the wall with a crash of shattering dishes.

As easily as if she'd been expecting this, Sarah slipped around and past him, graceful as a wraith. She paused in the doorway and gave a soft, taunting laugh.

"Temper, Jakey. Is that any way for a petty household tyrant to behave?"

Creed swung wildly around and after her. Sarah glided away, going through the back parlor and up the oak-balustraded staircase.

Creed's vision began to fuzz away as he stumblingly reached the staircase. Then everything tilted crazily in his sight. He wasn't aware of falling, but suddenly his chin crashed against the third rise from the bottom.

Befuddledly he lifted his head, waggling it back and forth, tasting blood. He felt no pain, but knew he had bitten through his tongue. Above him, Sarah stood at the head of the stairs. He had never seen a smile so radiant.

"Sweet dreams, Jacob. You'll have them exactly where you're lying now, I suspect. *Sic semper tyrannis.*"

She blew him a kiss and vanished into the upstairs hallway. Creed's head dropped; his chin hit the rise again. The three inside bolts on Sarah's door shot loudly, crisply into place as she secured them. Those were the last sounds Jacob Creed heard before he passed out. . . .

June 7, 1886

I have done the deed.

After several days of mulling over what further indignities I might inflict on that ivory-skinned bitch, I came to the conclusion that there were none. She was now armored in her mind against whatever I might do. There was no recourse left me but the final one. The most final of all.

The longer I mulled on how pleasant it would be to take that cool white throat between my hands, to crush it to jelly between my hands, the more forcefully the idea seized me. Sarah must die. And no way of encompassing her end could be more gratifying.

Yesterday I did not drink at all. I must be as keen and cold as steel to perpetrate the deed. I must make no mistake, leave no sign that might be traced to me. My only fear was that without the crutch of strong drink, my determination might waver at the last moment.

It did not.

I returned home at an early hour to be sure of arriving before she might retire behind the locked door of her chamber. I found her at supper. I throttled her in the midst of one of her tart and supercilious remarks.

God, but it felt wonderful. I could feel the strength coursing through my body into my hands, increasing momentarily, as I watched her face purple into death.

She scratched my hands rather badly, trying to tear them from her throat, but that is a trifle. The marks will soon heal. Let anyone, should I be suspect, prove how I came by them.

Making sure the body will never be found presented no great difficulty. I had already weighed the matter carefully. There was a place ideal for my purpose. Not five hundred yards east of the agency house is a deep arroyo lined with cutbanks of crumbling rock. At one spot was an overhang of massive rubble that, with a little assistance, would collapse in a slide of rocks so heavy that no flash flood would ever undermine them.

Accordingly, well after taps sounded, I left the agency house with the body across my shoulders, clinging to deep shadows against the light of a quarter moon. I laid her out (with hands folded on her bosom; peace be to her shade!) at the bottom of the arroyo beneath the cutbank. Ascending it, I struggled to pry loose a key rock that I was certain, if dislodged, would bring the whole mass of rubble crashing down.

It was quickly done and the evidence of my deed buried

102

forever. The pile of tumbled boulders looks as if it might have been thus for a thousand years. . . .

"The devil," muttered Major Casement. "And the story he gave out was that his wife simply . . . disappeared?"

"Yes, sir," said Mayberly. "No elaborate cover story. He was supremely confident. What was there that might prove otherwise?"

Casement shook his head slowly. "But to record the act with all incriminating detail in that journal. He *must* have been mad!"

"Well, sir, I've read that a madman may try to collect his scattered thoughts by writing them down. Of course, he had the journal well concealed and had no reason to believe anyone would see it while he still lived . . . in which assumption he was correct. I spent most of a day searching the agency house for clues, for evidence of any sort, before I located this volume. It was in a hidden compartment at the base of an armoire in his room."

"And it enabled you to look for . . . and find . . . the remains of Missus Creed?"

"Yes, sir. Had only the vague description he gives here to go on. As Creed mentions, there was nothing but tumbled rock to indicate the site, and that could describe almost any spot the length of the arroyo. Which is a quarter mile long, more or less. So I enlisted the aid of our garrison's chief scout, Joe Tana. He is full-blood Pima."

"Hmm. One of those fellows could pick up sign on the burned-out lid of hell. Which," the major added sourly, "a good piece of this country comes near to being. Go on."

"Lord knows how Joe Tana found the place, but he did. Then I assigned a half dozen of our troopers to dig through the rubble. After a couple hours of wrestling giant boulders away, they uncovered the body."

"It was identifiable?"

"Just barely, sir. The fall of rock had crushed it beyond facial or physical recognition. And it had been there for well over a month. Only the clothing gave indication of sex." Mayberly paused, looking down at the journal. "The only sure identification was the hair that both her husband's journal and Missus Verlain describe so . . . vividly."

"'Like a waterfall of reddish gold'?"

"Yes, sir. You can't imagine. . . ."

Major Casement grimaced. "Unfortunately, I can. Go on, Mister Mayberly."

"His entry for the following day records his first seeing the apparition of his wife." Mayberly flipped a few more pages. "Then a week later, this. . . ."

June 15, 1886

Came to an understanding with Colonel Dandridge today. Following Sarah's disappearance, which I duly reported, he ordered patrols out to search for her. When they turned up not a trace, he was inclined to feel that I knew more than I had divulged and bluntly told me so. Wherefore I told him just as bluntly that I have written a full account of our 'arrangement' anent the misappropriated government funds for the Apache beef ration and sent it under seal to my attorney in a city I did not name, with instructions that it be opened in the event of my death. I could as easily add a proviso that if I were to suffer imprisonment or detainment, or be held incommunicado in any way, it should be opened. In that case I would have nothing to lose. Dandridge . . . everything. . . .

Major Casement lifted a quizzical brow. "Was there such a statement?"

Mayberly shrugged. "Apparently Colonel Dandridge believed so, as there's nothing to indicate that he took any action then or later. However, Creed has been dead for weeks, the news widely published, and no attorney, no claimant to his estate, has come forward. I've found no will and no mention of any living relative."

Casement signed. "Then?"

"All the entries for several weeks thereafter . . . when he troubled to make them . . . deal with mundane, everyday matters. As though he had casually laid aside the very memory of his wife. Then" — Mayberly turned a section of pages to another marked place — "we come suddenly to the following. . . ."

July 20, 1886

The gradual cessation of heavy drinking has done wonders for the well-being of my mind and body. Indeed, my sexual vigor is far greater than it has been in years! Not only is this manifest in the state of my flesh, but my attention to comely females has intensified, at times almost to a frenzy I cannot control.

A liaison with one of the women of the fort, the wife or daughter of an officer or enlisted man, even if it could be managed, would be both difficult and dangerous to undertake. It is out of the question. Nor am I inclined, any longer, to cajole and flatter even a willing female. What god damned bitches women are. I shall never again make the least obeisance to gain the favor of any of them.

Another solution to my need has formed itself in my mind. I have examined it from every side and see no reason why it cannot be accomplished. In fact I shall implement it this very day. . . .

Creed squatted on his hunkers in front of the brush *wickiup* of Sal Juan, a leading headman of the San Lazaro Apaches. Facing him in a similar crouch, Sal Juan was a wolf-gaunt man whose barrel chest strained his calico shirt. His clean shoulder-length hair was streaked with gray, but the lines graven in his mahogany face told more of harsh living than of age.

Sal Juan's eyes were like obsidian chips, and they smoldered with hatred. He had reason to hate, as Creed was unconcernedly aware, and he knew that a few short years ago Sal Juan — one of the fiercest of Apache war chiefs — would have killed him without hesitation for what he had just proposed. But Sal Juan's war-trailing days were past. He had surrendered to the *pinda-likoyes*, the white-eyes, so that the pitiful remnant of his half-starved band might be spared a final annihilation.

Presently he lowered his eyes, scooped up a handful of dirt, and juggled it in his palm. "What will *Nantan* Creed give to take the daughter of Sal Juan as wife?"

"Horses. Goods." His years on the Jicarillo reservation had given Creed an easy command of the slush-mouthed Apache tongue. "What do you ask?"

Sal Juan raised his hate-filled eyes. "This thing you know as well as I."

"Cattle?"

"Fat cattle. For all the people of the *Be-don-ko-he*. From this time forward we will have fat cattle."

Creed dipped his head solemnly. "Fat cattle for all the people of the Chiricahua from this time forward. It will be as Sal Juan says."

Dandridge wouldn't go for his reneging on their bargain, he knew amusedly. But he wouldn't lift a damned finger to prevent it, either. He couldn't threaten Jacob Creed with anything Creed couldn't turn against him just as effectively. Not while he believed that a certain incriminating statement was in the possession of Creed's attorney.

What attorney? Creed laughed silently at the thought. Sal Juan again bent his head, his face a stone mask. Creed squatted patiently, letting him have all the time he wanted.

Creed shuttled his gaze past the headman to the girl. She was crouched on her heels grinding corn on a stone *metate* and her slim figure was lost in her shapeless camp dress.

But on other visits here he'd seen her moving about at one chore or another, walking graceful as a young willow, the lissome outlines of her body showing through the dress, letting you visualize all her tawny loveliness: gold-skinned, sweet-curving, secret-hollowed. Sweet sixteen and bursting with the just-ripened juices of her youth.

God. Just thinking of her was enough to make his mouth go dry, his hands grow moist. This close, even, seeing her ungracefully squatted at her squaw's work, set up a wild thunder in his blood.

"Sons-ee-ah-ray is a good daughter," Sal Juan said presently. "She is strong and works hard. She will breed strong sons."

Creed inclined his chin appreciatively. "This thing I believe."

"A young man called Gian-nah-tah has tied his pony before my lodge."

"Has the daughter of Sal Juan taken it to water?"

"Yes. It is her will."

"And Sal Juan's will? How many ponies can the young man give him?"

The headman held up all the fingers of one hand.

Creed spread the fingers of both hands. "I will give Sal Juan this number of ponies."

Supplementing Apache words with an English number, Sal Juan said flatly: "*Nantan* Creed will give seven times that number."

"Three times."

"Six times that number."

"Five times."

"Four."

"No. Five times that number."

Creed nodded. "Five times that number and fat cattle for all the *Be-don-ko-he* from this time forward. It is done?"

Sal Juan was silent. The gift of ponies weighed far less with him, Creed knew, than the welfare of his band. The burden of leadership outweighed even his hatred of Creed. Yet he hesitated.

Creed repeated: "It is done?"

"There is the chief of pony soldiers."

Creed let his beard part in a slow smile. "I tell you what, old man," he said in English. "You just leave *Nantan* Dandridge to me, all right?"

"You, him," Sal Juan said in the same language. "You dogshit. Both you dogshit. I spit on you."

Still smiling, Creed said mildly: "Uhn-huh. No you won't. You think your folks have had it bad up till now? You've hardly seen the start of how bad I can make it."

Sal Juan made a fist around the handful of dirt.

Creed said patiently: "It is done?"

The headman did not reply. Something else was troubling him, Creed realized. Giving up a hard-working daughter? Creed doubted it. Sal Juan had his share of women: two wives and a couple more unmarried daughters, neither of them a looker. But Apache standards of beauty were different from whites', and Sal Juan could easily spare one daughter.

"I have wealth," said Creed. "The daughter of Sal Juan will be treated well."

"It is another thing." Abruptly Sal Juan rose to his stocky height. "We will speak with *Skin-ya.*"

Creed got up too, hiding his irritation. Skin-ya, that dried-up old buzzard bait! But Apache life was colored with superstitions of every hue. Signs and omens dictated the Apache's choices and actions. Nothing important was undertaken against the wishes of the prevailing spirits. These spoke most trenchantly through the *izze-nantan*, the man of medicine. So Skin-ya, the local crucible of mumbo-jumbo, must be consulted.

As he and Sal Juan passed through the village, drowsing in the midday sun, Creed held the girl hungrily in his mind's eye. Sons-ee-ah-ray. Morning Star. That's what the name meant, and that's what he'd call her. He thought of the consternation he'd cause among the white contingent at the fort by taking a bride so soon after Sarah's disappearance. *A redskin bride!* The thought pleased him so much that he nearly laughed aloud.

As to the promise of a fair cattle issue he'd given Sal Juan, he would keep it for a while. As long as it suited him or as long as it proved convenient. You could never tell. The girl was a good worker; she'd fix his meals and keep that rat's nest of an agency house cleaned up. But she might go all to suet in a few years, the way a lot of these squaws did. In that case. . . .

They found Skin-ya seated cross-legged before his *wickiup*, head bent in meditation. Naked save for a breechclout, his wrinkled hide dyed to the neutral color of the arid land which had sustained him for eighty summers or more, he did not look up as the two men hunkered down, facing him. He seemed in a trance. At last, slowly, he raised his eyes. They sparkled blackly in his shriveled mummy's face.

"Sal Juan," he husked, "would know the will of the *chedens* in the matter of his daughter's marriage."

Creed stared. "How did you . . . ?"

Sal Juan cut him off with a chopping motion of his hand. "Will *Skin-ya* make the medicine?"

Skin-ya fumbled inside a buckskin bag and took out the accouterments of his craft, spreading them on the ground. A fragment of lightning-riven wood, a root, a stone, a bit of turquoise, a glass bead, and a small square of buckskin painted with cabalistic symbols. He sprinkled them with *hoddentin,* the sacred powder ground from maguey. He sprinkled *hoddentin* on himself, on Creed, on Sal Juan; he scattered *hoddentin* to the four winds.

The ancient shaman sat in silence for a long time, eyes closed. He opened them suddenly, eyeing Creed. "There is a smell of *tats-an* about the *pinda-likove.* Also he walks with a ghost."

Sal Juan said, "What of Sons-ee-ah-ray?"

"Would Sal Juan wed his daughter to one who is *tats-an*?"

"I am alive," Creed said harshly.

"Soon you will be *tats-an.* You will not be present."

Jesus. These siwashes had such a damned polite way of saying you'd be dead before long. "*How?*" he spat.

Skin-ya struck his own neck sharply with the edge of his palm and let his head hang grotesquely to one side.

"You lie," Creed said coldly.

"The white-eyes walks with a ghost," Skin-ya repeated imperturbably. "The *cheden* of a woman."

He raised a scrawny arm and pointed.

Sarah stood on a barren rise not thirty feet away. Heat danced on the flinty slope, and he could see its shimmering waves *through* her body; they made it shimmer and waver, too.

She smiled and beckoned to him.

With a hoarse cry he lunged to his feet and stumbled toward the rise and up it. The loose soil cascaded away under his driving feet and sent him plunging on his belly. He lay unmoving and stared. Before his eyes the smiling form grew dim and slowly faded and was gone. . . .

. . . *Sarah. Then I did not imagine the other time. But that*

110

was on the day after the night I killed her, well over a month ago.
Why has she come back? What does she. . . .

"Balderdash!"

Major Casement's cigar had gone out some time ago. He took the wet stub from his mouth and eyed it distastefully. "You've questioned these Apaches, of course?"

Lieutenant Mayberly nodded soberly. "Sal Juan says he saw nothing. But he believes Skin-ya and Creed did."

Casement snorted. "And I suppose the old charlatan *insists* he did?"

"Well . . . ," Mayberly nodded at the photograph of Sarah Creed on the commandant's desk. "I showed that to Skin-ya and asked if he had ever seen the woman. He said that was *her* . . . the ghost that walked with Creed."

"Preposterous! Do *you* . . . ?"

"Sir, I've merely reported what I was able to find out."

"All right . . . all right!"

"There's a little more. For the next day. His last entry."

"Very well." The major gestured resignedly with his cigar stub. "Get it over with, mister. . . ."

July 21, 1886

After yesterday's experience in the village, I had no taste for returning home. I dreaded the prospect. What might I now encounter in the very house where I killed her?

I cannot doubt that I actually saw the abomination, for Skin-ya saw it first and directed my attention to it. Badly shaken, I returned to my store and steeped myself to the eyebrows in booze. It gave me the courage to return to the house where, in drunken hallucination, I might easily have seen the apparition again.

But I did not.

111

I have only the vaguest memory of getting out my journal and recording my second entry of the day, a lengthy and rambling one to be sure. Now, looking back over what I wrote at the time, I have tried to determine how much of it is fact, how much of it fancy.

I can no longer tell. My thoughts are too confounded.

Tonight I must not drink. I must go home cold and clear of head and confront whatever is there, surely and finally. I know something is there. But I must have the truth —

Creed scribbled the last words with an impatient flourish. He was standing at a long counter of his sutler's store, the journal spread open before him. For a moment, pen poised in hand, he glanced over what he had just written. By now it was dark enough so that he had to squint to make it out.

What more was there to say?

Impatiently he thrust the pen back in the inkstand, closed the journal, and thrust it into his coat pocket. Then he skirted the counter and headed for the door, preparatory to locking up.

Creed paused. A sly tongue of thirst licked at his belly.

Liquid courage. Why not? He could use some. He turned quickly back to the counter, reached under it, and pulled out a bottle of Old Crow. The best. Saved for a notable occasion. Perhaps now.

No, god dammit!

Resolutely he stowed the bottle back out of sight. It was a time of reckoning. He had to be certain. No false courage. And no drink-inspired delusions.

Creed locked the door behind him and tramped hurriedly across Fort Bloodworth's parade ground. It was long after tattoo; all lights were out. The path to the agency house was paved by moonglow. Creed kept his head bent, not looking at

the dark masses of brush to either side, as though he feared
what he might see.

*Is it all a damned trick? Couldn't it be a god damned trick of
some kind?*

Those god damned Cheery-cow Apaches hated his guts.
They'd like to see him dead, Sal Juan most of all. Suppose that
Sal Juan and that shrunken bag of bones, Skin-ya, had rigged
all this between them. Mesmerized him into thinking he was
seeing something that wasn't? Planted a fear in his mind that
might trip him to his doom.

That was it, sure. A lot of god damned hocus-pocus.

The only trouble was, he didn't believe a dust mote of his
own rationale. . . .

The house loomed ahead, a flat black oblong against a cobalt
sky. Creed's steps slowed. But he had to go in. Had to face
whatever was there.

He opened the front door and left it open to the stream of
moonlight as he crossed the room to a lowboy where a lamp
reposed. He lifted the lamp's chimney, struck a match, shook
it free of a sulphurous flare of sparks, and touched it to the
wick.

Suddenly the door slammed shut.

Creed started and wheeled around. The tiny spoon of lamp-
flame faintly picked out familiar objects of the room. Nothing
else.

No wind at all. No draft. Why should the door . . . ?

Now the lamp-flame was guttering in the sudden stir of air
from the slamming door. Heart pounding wildly, Creed cupped
his hands around it, cherishing the flame. God, if it went out!
If he were isolated in total darkness. . . .

The flame held and became steady again. Carefully he replaced the chimney and turned the lamp up high. Carrying it
with him, treading with a slow care, he walked from the front

parlor to the back one, where the staircase was.

Creed halted at the bottom step. The lower rises were picked out in a waver of shadow and saffron light, but the top of the stairs was lost in darkness. He sleeved away the cold sweat from his forehead. He started up the stairs, making his feet move independently of the congealed fear in his brain and belly.

It is up there. God! It's waiting. I can run from it, but it will still be with me. It will always be with me. I must face it out now, or. . . . Go on, god dammit! Don't think about it. Just go on. . . .

He reached the top of the stairs and advanced into the hallway. It smelled musty and unused, like an exhalation from the tomb. He came to the door of his room, a central one whose one window faced south, along with a door that opened on the still-intact south balcony.

Creed opened the door, peered cautiously about, and went in. He set his lamp on the commode and crossed the room to the armoire. Squatting down, he slid back a small panel at its base, exposing the hidden compartment. He took the journal from his pocket, placed it in the compartment, and pushed the panel back into place.

"*Ja-cob.* . . ."

The murmurous whisper froze him where he was, crouched on his heels. Creed did not want to look around. The blood thudded sickly in his temples. And then he looked.

She stood in the open doorway, appearing as real as if she were still flesh. Creamy flesh. Tinted as if the rich blood of life still pulsed beneath it.

The smile formed; the arm raised and beckoned.

Creed let out a mad roar. He surged at her, his hands lifting to grasp and crush. He plunged through her as if she were smoke. Momentum carried him on through the doorway. He crashed against the closed door opposite him.

114

The door of Sarah's room.

He swung around, wildly. His own doorway was empty now, framed by lamplight and nothing else.

"*Ja-cob. . . .*"

Where? He froze, straining his ears. No other sound. But he was sure. The cajoling whisper had come from behind Sarah's door.

He wrenched it open and flung it wide, the door banging against the inside wall.

She was in front of him. Smiling still, the arm beckoning. Moonlight from her room's one window, as well as lamplight from his back, picked her out, but more faintly now.

She was transparent. *Again.*

With a howl he dived at her, reaching and closing his hands, seizing hold of nothing at all. And when he wheeled around again, she was gone.

"Jacob. To me. Come."

Sarah's voice. Unmistakably hers. Not ghostly at all. Just words spoken in a calm, quiet tone. Yet firm and commanding.

She was standing close to the window and both her arms were outstretched now. She was not smiling any more. Only positive.

"*God damn you to all hell!*"

Creed shrieked the words as he dived at her. His hurtling weight smashed against a solid wall. Almost solid.

It yawned open abruptly with a snarl of ripped-out nails, a sound of splintering wood. Jacob Creed plunged on and out into a cool rush of night air, his arms flung wide to embrace nothing.

Falling, he had one last impression: the trailing sound of a woman's laughter. . . .

Lieutenant Mayberly closed the journal and laid it on the

commandant's desk beside the photograph of Sarah Creed.

"What happened after he made that last entry, we can only surmise. When he didn't show up at his store the next day, Corporal Higgins of L Troop . . . who'd gone to the sutler's to purchase some tobacco . . . was curious enough to stroll over to the agency house and investigate. What had happened was plain. The door that opened on the north balcony . . . the door that had been nailed shut after Creed had ordered the balcony torn off . . . was split nearly in half, dangling from a single hinge. Creed's body was on the ground beneath. Obviously he had smashed through the door. . . ."

"And died of course," Major Casement said irritably, "as that old shaman had divined he would? Eh?"

Mayberly gave a noncommittal nod. "Incidentally, sir, he did. Yes. Of a broken neck."

"Balderdash," the major said wearily. He nudged the journal with his thumb. "For God's sake, Mister Mayberly, I don't doubt that you've investigated this matter with your usual thoroughness and efficiency. But how in hell can I assemble a report to the department that will make any sense of it all?"

"Sir, I'd simply relate what we've been able to tell for certain. Higgins immediately reported Creed's demise to Colonel Dandridge. I've checked Higgins's story. He says the colonel seemed apathetic, almost indifferent to the news and then dismissed Higgins with a disconcerting abruptness. Five minutes later Sergeant-Major Carmody, at his desk in the outer office, heard a shot. He hurried to the inner office and found the colonel slumped across his desk, his service revolver clenched in his fist. He had shot himself through the head. No doubt because revelation of his complicity with Creed in cheating on the Apache beef issue would have wiped out the last remnant of his career."

"All that is clear enough, Mister Mayberly," snapped Casement. "What concerns me is this blather about spectral apparitions. I don't see any way to avoid alluding to it if I'm to submit a complete and truthful report on the business." He scowled, tugging at his underlip. "Suppose I can hazard a speculation that Creed was suffering from a massive delusion brought on by feelings of personal guilt or whatever . . . ?"

Mayberly cleared his throat. *As he always did when he found something difficult to communicate,* Casement thought irritably. "Out with it, mister!" he barked.

"Perhaps you'd better see for yourself, sir." The subaltern cleared his throat again. He nodded at the journal. "It's in there. The last entry."

Casement's patience was worn to an edge. "You said you'd read off the last entry in that damned thing. What . . . ?"

"*Creed's* last entry, sir. But there's another one after it. See for yourself."

Major Casement picked up the journal and flipped impatiently through its pages to the end of Creed's almost indecipherable writing.

He stared at the place.

The short hairs at the back of his neck prickled; his throat felt stuffed with phlegm. He managed to clear it with a couple of mild *harrumphs*, trying not to let Mayberly know that he was doing so.

"Hmm. Isn't it possible, mister, that somebody . . . for whatever odd reason . . . added this final entry later on?"

"I doubt it, sir. I found the journal in the base of Creed's armoire, his own place of concealment. The handwriting, as you can see, is crisp and clear, in a backhand script. Quite different from Creed's broad, forward slanting scrawl. Too, as nearly as I can tell, it's a woman's hand."

"Preposterous," the major said in a fading voice.

"One more item, sir. . . ." Mayberly reached in his dispatch case, pulled out a piece of paper and slid it across the desk. "I found this in Missus Creed's room. It is a letter she had begun to write to a sister in Boston, but never got to finish."

Mayberly paused, wrinkling his brow. "Don't ask me to explain *this* one, sir. I'm no handwriting expert. But I needn't be one, nor do you, to perceive that the hand which indited this letter and the one which made that final entry in Creed's journal are absolutely identical."

Major Casement stared at the letter. Then his gaze moved with a slow, dreading reluctance, back to the journal spread open on his desk. To its brief and final entry:

Poor Jacob. His fancies overcame him. He fancied that he saw a ghost. Sic semper tyrannis.

In December, 1961, after having lived most of his life in the north woods of Wisconsin, Olsen made his first trip into the Western states. He would do so again in subsequent years but always as a tourist. When it came to a vivid recreation of an historical period or a Western terrain, Olsen found that research was of more value than physical proximity to the scene of the events, although the latter remained vital when it came to providing a distinct sense of place. Only in a "town" Western is the land of less importance in what happens to the characters. "Center-Fire," appearing here for the first time, is one of the few "town" Western stories T. V. Olsen was to write.

Sheriff Jim Renford stood with folded arms on the boardwalk on the east side of El Cañon's single dusty street, leaning against the weathered siding of the bank. He was a high, lean figure in the morning sunlight that caught highlights from his dark-bronze face, dressed in worn and faded, albeit clean, overalls and calico shirt. The sun-bleached hair at his temples was visible below the low, flat-crowned, gray Stetson. He was young, a hard-riding, saddle-trim sort of lawman. At his side was a holstered Colt's Frontier Model .45.

This, he decided, was a typical morning. The townspeople were going about their errands, and an errant breeze whipped up a fine spume of dust from the street. Even Sheriff Renford, leaning there leisurely, appeared to be entirely at ease. But his pale blue eyes were hard and alert in the shade cast by the brim of his hat. His gaze was fixed on the saloon doors of the Golden Spurs gambling house and saloon just across the street. A single, restless horse stood at the tie rail outside.

Now it comes, he thought bleakly as the doors parted and a tall, thin man with drooping black mustaches and dressed like a cattleman stepped out, strode heavily across the boardwalk, ducked under the tie rail, and caught his horse's bridle roughly, swinging into the saddle.

Renford's resolution faltered as he saw the man's red and fevered face. *Crandall's been drinking*, he thought, *and there is no talking to him like that.*

Still, he had to try. It was a duty of the office to which he had been only recently elected mostly because of his splendid war record. He had to show them that he could perform as was expected.

He stepped resolutely off the sidewalk, walked between the tie rails, and strode across the street. A cautious instinct pulled him up a few yards short of Crandall's skittish horse.

"Crandall," he said mildly, "what are you trying to prove?"

Crandall turned in his saddle to face him, face livid and ugly and plainly showing the influence of liquor. Renford's mouth went dry as he realized the futility of argument.

"What the hell's your business?" Crandall said irritably.

"Your wife told me to keep you out of Bayard's place," said Renford levelly.

"I know she did . . . damned meddling female. A man's affairs are his own."

"As long as they don't hurt someone else." Renford took a step forward. "Man," he said earnestly, "can't you see what you're doing to yourself? You had a good name . . . a fine ranch. What have you now? Where do you think this'll all end?"

"My God, now he's giving a sermon," jeered the rancher. "I heard you was under McDowell at Bull Run, Renford. You're good at bull, all right . . . and you was probably running."

Renford's gaze went bleak. "For your wife's sake, I'm trying to be nice to you, Crandall," he said quietly. "Don't push me."

A wicked light danced in Crandall's eyes. He spurred his horse around to face the sheriff. "Damn, can't abide a nosey sheriff," he murmured, "especially when he's a snotty kid!"

He spurred his horse straight at Renford, then pulled him up to rear back on his hind legs, and came down. Renford had to throw himself to one side, barely escaping from flailing, iron-shod hoofs. He rolled over once and sprang to his feet to see Crandall, tugging at his gun.

He thought for a fleeting instant of the .45 at his own hip, but he didn't pull it. He wanted to avoid that as long as possible. He hadn't had to use it except to bluff, and he didn't want to.

He saw Crandall's gun was stuck in its sheath and lost no

time taking advantage of the opportunity. He lunged forward and caught the gun just as the rancher finally succeeded in yanking it free of the stiff holster. With a twist he pulled it away from Crandall and hauled him out of the saddle.

Crandall pulled himself upright. He was blind with rage and whiskey, but he was not drunk — at least not drunk enough to impair him physically. His long sinewy arms shot around Renford and his driving feet carried them both backward into the tie rail. It splintered beneath their weight and both fell with a crash onto the edge of the boardwalk.

The board ends caught Renford in the small of the back, and the pain momentarily paralyzed him. But Crandall was through. Although Renford had taken the impact, the older man's dissipated body was unable to sustain itself. The wind was knocked from him. He sprawled there, gasping. Renford pulled himself slowly and painfully to his feet, hauling Crandall up with him. He held him upright with his left hand while he threw his right fist in a long sledging blow into the rancher's face.

Crandall twisted around and fell limply on his face. He did not move. Renford straightened slowly, setting his teeth as the throbbing pain in his back subsided gradually. The moiled dust settled about his feet.

Men came running up from all directions. Renford ignored their frantic queries and said: "One of you give me a hand with Crandall. I'm locking him up."

Something in his face stopped any objection — the look of a man already pushed too far.

With Crandall jailed, Renford stared back down the street. He stepped, hesitating, as his eyes fell upon the door of MacGunn's General Store. His heart sank. Nell MacGunn stood there in the doorway of her father's store, watching him quietly. He veered toward her, removing his hat as he approached.

"Come inside, Jim," she said, her voice toneless and low. "We can talk there. Dad's in back."

He followed her into the front of the store. It was cool here, smelling of leather. She turned to face him. She was little and wore a dark dress, immaculate in its plain severity. Her black, smooth hair was parted primly and not a strand was misplaced. The slim-chiseled contour of her face was cold and white.

"I watched it, Jim. What did you do to him?"

"Put him in jail," Renford said curtly. "You needn't worry. His wife's behind me, and she does all their buying here. You won't lose any business."

He had seen her antagonism and was deliberately baiting her. A tide of angry red started in her cheeks, then receded quickly. Nell never permitted an emotional display.

"I'm not worrying about Crandall's patronage," she replied quietly. "I am talking of us. Where will it stop, Jim?"

"That's what I asked Crandall," said Renford humorlessly. "He thought I was preaching."

"So you started a brawl."

"If you saw it, you know who started it."

"But you locked him up," she pursued stubbornly. "How long do you think you can hold him?"

"Until his trial comes up for assaulting an officer. Then he'll be locked up again, and that'll keep him out of trouble for a month anyway."

"And who will take care of Missus Crandall and the children while he is serving his sentence?"

"I'll do what I can for them. That's better than letting Crandall drink away what little they have left."

She bit her lip and looked away. He took her by the shoulders and turned her gently back toward him. "Nell," he said quietly,

124

"there's a point where words and diplomacy have to stop, and action begins."

She put her hands on his arms and looked up at him, a suggestion of color again entering her cheeks. For a moment at least her face held a vibrant warmth.

"Drop this job, Jim. Drop it before it's too late, and you have to shoot someone or be shot yourself. Dad would give you a bookkeeping job here at the store. . . ."

"Bookkeeping!" He laughed coldly. "You're asking me to sit pinned down behind a desk. You ought to know me better, Nell."

Her hands fell, and her hazel eyes were now cold and remote. "Yes . . . I should know you better. Is it asking too much? Would it be a signal weakness to do that for me . . . to get a respectable job and wear a suit . . . ?"

He interrupted her, saying softly: "A month ago, Nell, I asked you to marry me, and you said yes. Have you decided it was a bad bargain?"

She stood like a tiny frozen statue. "It's only that I want a man . . . not a street brawler."

He laughed bitterly. "You don't want a man, either, Nell. You want a damned clothes dummy!"

He whirled around and started for the door. He heard her call after him, low and sharp. "Jim!"

He hesitated at the doorway. Her tone was imperative, but there was not the merest suggestion of softening in it. He slammed the door behind him as he went out, clamping his hat back on his head.

A street brawler! He knew her mind now. His jaw clamped hard, and a boiling-up anger found expression in swiftly decisive steps that carried him toward the false-fronted Golden Spurs saloon. He pushed the doors wide and stepped inside, pausing a moment to accustom his eyes to the dim interior that was

125

commodious and garishly furnished. There were tables and chairs and a long polished bar at one side. At the back was the gambling room. Its entrance was a high archway, flanked by beaded black curtains.

The only occupant of the barroom was the fat barkeep, Wes Kessler, who was busy placing merchandise on the depleted shelves. He paused as Renford entered.

"Where's Bayard?"

Kessler jerked his head toward the rear.

Renford nodded, and walked into the gambling room, threading his way between deal tables toward the thin-paneled door marked **Office** in large black letters. He knocked.

"Come in," said a voice.

Renford pulled the door open and went in, closing it behind him as he advanced toward the desk. The office was windowless and small with white-washed plaster walls.

Bayard, proprietor of the Golden Spurs, was sprawled in his swivel chair, feet on the desk, displaying his fine boots of hand-tooled leather. He was black-haired and thin with a small waxed mustache and sleepy, heavy-lidded green eyes.

"Sit down, Sheriff," he murmured. "It's been a long time since I've had the . . . er . . . pleasure of a visit."

"I'll stand, thanks. Crandall was out front a few minutes ago. He was drunk. He tried to pull a gun on me."

"Well, well," said Bayard gently.

"He's locked up now, Bayard. I'm just telling you . . . lay off him."

Bayard spread his slim, effeminate hands. "Really, Renford, if people are going to come here to drink my poison and gamble, it's their business. I'm not twisting anyone's arm."

Renford's eyes narrowed to gleaming slits. He leaned forward over Bayard's desk. "If there's anything that turns me sick," he said slowly, "it's a two-legged viper like you who preys on human weaknesses. Only a few months ago, Crandall was a well-to-do and respected rancher. He had a big spread. He was running a big herd. He had a fine, healthy family. But he had the gambling fever, and your place opened. He couldn't keep away from your crooked faro tables. After you took all his money, his cattle, land, and everything else followed. Then he began drinking. Now he's a damned sot with a sick wife and kids, living in an old line shack. Ruined by your damned greed."

Bayard yawned. "I resent your calling my faro tables crooked, Renford," he said mildly.

"I call a horse by its name," replied Renford, somehow fighting down his rage.

"Well spoken," applauded Bayard. "You are an intelligent and educated man, Renford. It is ridiculous for two such as we to tangle horns. If you wish to take cards in this game, I strongly advise you to play on my side. The stakes are high. . . ."

"In other words, it would be handy to have a friend in the sheriff's office?" murmured Renford.

"I said you were an intelligent man," chuckled Bayard. "Of course, you can't touch me in any event. I'm inside the law. My games of chance are quite in order, my dealers likewise, although . . . er . . . they are proficient at their games."

Renford stood erect and spoke levelly. "Here's the straight of it, Bayard. The town is up in arms at you as it is. The first time anyone's hurt by you again, I'll get a gang of men together with axes to cut your place down, law or no law."

He spun on his heel and left the office, departing the saloon swiftly. As he once again stood on the boardwalk, an aching twinge inwardly forced his gaze toward the general store. He thought he caught a momentary glimpse of a face looking from the window, then it disappeared.

It was a mistake, Nell, he thought sorrowfully. Yes, it had been a mistake. He had thought that Nell MacGunn's quiet, gentle ways were what he wanted in a woman. He saw now that this rough frontier town was hell for such a prim, sheltered girl. *It was his life but not hers,* he thought with pity. She couldn't live with it, couldn't understand it, and didn't want to. She didn't understand him, either, so it would never work. He thought with bitterness of the plans they had made together.

Reluctantly he approached the general store. He had to buy the supplies he had promised Crandall's family. To his relief he found that Nell was not there. Her crippled father, John MacGunn, was just hobbling behind the counter on his crutch. He was a wiry, white-haired Scotsman.

"Hoot, mon, she saw ye coming, yelled fer me, and run in the back of the store," chuckled MacGunn. "What'll it be, lad?"

These cheerful words were like a stab in the heart. Nell loathed even the sight of him now!

As he was leaving with his purchases, MacGunn said in a low voice: "Dinna be too hard on the child, James. It hae be somethin' she kinna help."

"It's all over, John," snapped Renford, and walked quickly out the door.

It was late afternoon before he rode back into El Cañon and left his jaded pinto at the livery. The new looks on the faces of the Crandall family and Mrs. Crandall's thankfulness at his jailing her husband for his family's welfare had warmed his cold feelings. As he entered his office, he was surprised to find MacGunn, Quarrie, the banker, and other influential townsmen waiting for him.

"Jim," said Quarrie, a portly man, in his characteristic bluntness, "Crandall has been murdered."

Renford stood motionless.

"Aye, Jim, murdered," put in MacGunn. "It appears he was shot through the little barrel window of his cell about fifteen minutes ago." He regarded Renford with shrewd narrow eyes. "This empty cartridge was found by Milt Jergen who came to investigate when he heard the shot. Aye, he found *this* . . . !"

He held out a cartridge shell, and Renford took it wonderingly. A thin chill lanced his vitals. It was a center-fire shell.

"Lad," said MacGunn, "we all know ye're the only one in El Cañon who has one of these new center-fire Forty-Five pistols. It's probably the only one in the whole county, an' all others who carry sidearms carry rim-fire Forty-Fours. Also, ye had no cause to love Crandall."

"I shot Crandall this way when I could have killed him this morning after he threw down on me," murmured Renford, "then left the expended cartridge for some bright son of a bitch to find?"

The solid citizens looked at each other sheepishly. Renford turned the shell over and over in his hand.

"There's one man in town," he said slowly, "who stands to gain by fixing Crandall's murder on me. It's pretty weak evidence . . . he probably wouldn't be convicted, but he figured it would scare me enough, so I'd lay off him."

The others stared at the sheriff now as they caught the significance of his words. He didn't have to name names.

"Well," drawled Milt Jergen, the lanky bank teller who had found the body, "seems to me now I saw Wes Kessler, the barkeep over at Bayard's, hurrying inside the Golden Spurs just as I came out after hearing the shot. Struck me funny that Wes should be running inside when everyone else in town was running outside on hearing the shot. . . ."

"Thanks, Milt," cut in Renford in a quiet voice. "Gentlemen, I'll have your murderer within an hour."

With that, he turned and stalked from the office, almost colliding with Nell MacGunn just outside the doorway. For a brief moment he stopped, looking down into her eyes. They were very wise, and by her pale face he knew that she had heard the entire conversation. Abruptly he turned from her without a word, and walked with rapid strides across the street directly toward the Golden Spurs. He pushed through the swing doors, halting just inside. The usual nightly influx had not begun, and the place was still empty except for Kessler behind the bar.

The corpulent barkeep's flaccid form was sprawled in a chair. He was reading an old newspaper, and he glanced up, his eyes becoming narrow and wary as he saw Renford.

The latter advanced slowly toward the bar. "I want to see your gun, Wes."

Kessler came nervously erect, laying down his paper. He coughed to clear his throat. "I don't own one of them things, Sheriff."

"Don't stall, Wes."

"What's the trouble, Renford?" murmured the gentle voice near at hand.

Renford, tilting his head the slightest bit to the right, saw Bayard's slender form, slouching at ease in the archway, leading to the gambling room.

"Bayard, I'm placing Kessler and you under arrest for his murder of Crandall on your orders," said Renford briefly.

"Oh, really, Renford," said Bayard with a bored, heavy-lidded gaze.

Renford's glance included both men as he bluffed: "Milt Jergen saw Kessler running out of the alley adjoining the jail block just after the shot."

Wild terror and consternation showed in the fat barkeep's face. Even Bayard's bored mask was shattered. The saloonman grew rigid like steel while his sloe-like eyes, no longer sleepy, regarded Renford watchfully.

"In that case, Sheriff . . . ," he began, then his hand streaked inside his waistcoat.

Renford palmed his .45, swinging it up, his first shot breaking Bayard's arm as his hand tensed out with a Derringer. Bayard staggered and fell against the wall, trying with fierce concentration to draw a bead. Twice more Renford's Colt crashed out. Bayard slumped slowly down against the wall, then pitched forward into a table that careened wildly and toppled over on its side.

Kessler had been groping under the bar and came up with a pistol, firing just as Bayard's body struck the floor. Renford felt a savage pain sear through his right shoulder, even as the bullet whirled him toward the barkeep. His right hand, still holding his gun, fell uselessly to his side. His shoulder shattered, he could not command his muscles.

He saw the savage gleam in Kessler's eyes as he drew a careful bead on Renford's heart. The fat man was hesitating just a split second, savoring the moment gloatingly.

"Drop it! Drop it, or I'll shoot!"

Renford's gaze turned, astonished, toward the doors. Nell stood there, both small trembling hands tight around the butt of a heavy six-gun, trained on Kessler. Her hazel eyes flashed, and her lips were set.

Kessler half turned toward her, hesitating as he saw that it was a woman who faced him. Then he grunted, and the pistol in his hand swiveled around toward her.

In that one fleeting second of terror Renford realized that Nell's tiny form could never handle the recoil of her heavy weapon. It was desperate energy that forced Renford's forearm up. It was a superhuman effort that steadied the wavering muzzle on Kessler's heart. Then he pulled the trigger. Through the thin line of smoke he saw Kessler twist forward across the bar, then slide backward with a crash that jarred the floor.

The next thing Renford knew was, men were peering into the saloon, then they were all around him, supporting him, plying him with questions. Nell was sobbing on her father's chest. There was a terrible ache in his right shoulder of which he was only hazily aware.

Somehow, he pushed away from the restraining, solicitous hands, pushed his way around the bar, holding to its edge for support, and dropped down beside the body of Kessler. He pulled the gun from Kessler's nerveless fingers and held it up for all to see.

"Your proof, gentlemen! Guess this is all we need," said Renford, swaying dizzily from weakness. Kessler's gun was a Colt center-fire Forty-Five.

Renford grinned and drifted into oblivion.

Shafts of morning sunlight cut through the window as he awoke. He blinked and looked around for a moment before he realized where he was. He was lying in a bed in a room over MacGunn's General Store. His head ached a trifle, and his shoulder was heavily bandaged, as he found when he tried to move it. The door opened, and John MacGunn peered in.

"Aye, ye're awake," he muttered.

He sat down in a chair at the bedside, leaning his crutch against the wall.

"For heaven's sake, John, tell me what's going on?"

"Weel, nothin' much. We toted ye up here fer the time."

"Nell?" asked Renford quietly.

MacGunn's eyes smoldered with a soft fire. "We can both be proud, lad. When ye entered the Golden Spurs, she was over to the store and got my gun. I hobbled after her, cussin' her, when she run into the saloon, but me with my jerkin' foot I couldna move nae faster than a snail."

"She saved my life," muttered Renford. "Where is she, John?"

"She's sleepin' . . . late. She sat up by yere bed near all o'

132

the night. In the wee hours I made her go to sleep." The Scotsman sighed. "But I reckon ye won't wait. I'll fetch her."

MacGunn hobbled out of the room. In a minute Nell appeared in the doorway, where she stopped. She was wearing a fresh blue dress. Her eyes glowed warmly. There was a faint color in her cheeks. She smiled almost shyly.

"Hello, Jim."

"Hello."

There was a brief, embarrassed silence. Nell stammered: "The townsfolk have agreed to provide a fund for Missus Crandall and the children."

"That's fine." Renford was tongue-tied a moment, then he blurted: "Nell, what happened?"

"I . . . I can't say, Jim. I only knew I suddenly saw you were right . . . after you left me. It doesn't matter a bit, a person's station. Fine feathers don't make what really counts. You wouldn't be you . . . if someone tried to make you over . . . but I was ashamed to face you afterward." She stopped, blushing. "Can we start over?"

"Come over here, and I'll tell you," he grinned.

T. V. Olsen's stories, as his novels, work on two levels — the gnawing question of what will happen next is combined with a profound emotional involvement with characters about whom a reader comes to care deeply. The events may be those of an action/adventure narrative, but the characters provide such a rich texture to the stories that they carry forward the plot as readily as do the events. Above all, T. V. Olsen's West is one where reason does not prevail, and, therefore, all that happens is unpredictable, as it is so often in life. All that remains to Olsen's battered and struggling protagonists, male and female alike, is their commitment to decency, to loyalty, to friendship, in a word to each other. The losses are great and irretrievable, but the ordeals form a school for character that alone becomes decisive in an individual's life even if, as sometimes happens, he loses it.

His Name is Poison

The sun was already mounting in a blue-white sky as Vinnie Todd left the weather-beaten cabin she called home and walked down to the spring, pausing under the pleasant shade trees that bordered it. At this early hour the air might be already uncomfortably warm to another — but not to Vinnie. She'd grown to young womanhood here on the desert, and to her this was the drowsing coolness of a new day. Humming, she dipped the bucket she carried to the spring, lifting it easily in spite of her size. She was a small, honey-haired girl who looked even smaller in a man's rough trousers and hickory shirt.

As she straightened, her eyes came level with the brush on the opposite side of the stream. She dropped the bucket and stood with her eyes and nostrils dilating like a hunted creature's — but she made no sound, simply froze to the spot. The man whom she'd seen crouching in the brush straightened, sheathing the revolver he'd been holding on her. His sly, raffish face broke in a smile, revealing a prominent gold tooth that flashed in the sun.

"Sorry, missy. Didn't mean to scare you."

The man circled the spring and stopped two yards from her. He was tall and built like a beanpole. Vinnie now noticed the dust-filmed lawman's badge that glinted on his vest.

She found her voice, full of spirited resentment. "What are you doing here, mister?"

The man grinned again. "You live here alone, missy?"

"My father and I live here. He prospects for gold. If a visitor wants grub or a bunk, he can come to the door and ask like an honest man. No need to skulk in the brush, mister."

The man made a deprecating gesture. "The name ain't

137

important. You've a sharp tongue, missy. You're right, though." He nodded approvingly. "You can't be too careful, you and your pa, livin' alone way out here." He saw the impatience mounting in her face and added quickly: "Sorry to sneak up on your place this way . . . but I got to be careful, too." He threw a quick glance around and rubbed his chin, black whiskers rasping stiffly. "I been trailin' a man south for three days. Figure he'll try to get over the line into Mexico. Figured he might have stopped here for grub and water."

"What'd he look like?" Vinnie asked, watching him closely.

There were too few people who came this way, reason enough in this wild land to be suspicious of everyone — even a man who wore the badge of a deputy U. S. marshal. There was a long break of hesitancy in the man's expression, and Vinnie's suspicion quickly mounted. She took a step backward. She wished she had Pa's big Henry in her hands. Then the gold-toothed grin came again.

"Why, sure, missy, couldn't identify him less'n you knew how he looked, could you? Hmm, he's 'bout my height, built some bigger, though . . . blond, gray eyes, considerable younger than me . . . mebbe twenty-four, twenty-five. Name's Johnny Lapham." He added — almost with a trace of smugness, Vinnie thought — "Government wants him for tryin' to seize gold an' murderin' a Land Office surveyor in a range war . . . too far north for you to've heard of it, I reckon."

"I haven't seen him," Vinnie said curtly. "We haven't seen anyone through here for weeks."

"Why, now, is that so?"

The man pushed back his hat — a headgear too narrow-brimmed for desert travel, Vinnie thought contemptuously. Then she saw that his eyes were red-rimmed with heat-glare and his shoulders stooped with exhaustion.

"Too bad," he went on. "Hoped he might've stopped over

here. Good water, shade, place to sleep, grub." He grinned and winked at her. "Pretty girl, too."

Vinnie's eyes were cold.

The man abruptly changed his tone. "Missy, I'm dog-tired. Been in the saddle three days, most of three nights. Figure you could fix me with a bed, food, maybe some bait for my horse?"

Vinnie bit her lip. Lawman or not, she felt an instinctive recoiling from this fellow. But the unwritten law of the desert ingrained into her from childhood demanded open-handed hospitality for whoever asked it; indeed, it should be offered before requested. Her father would be glad of the company. Too, he could see the spring from the house. If he were watching now, and she turned this man away, she would be severely scolded, and she hated that.

"Come up to the house," she said shortly.

She filled the bucket again and led the way to a makeshift two-room shack that was the only home she could remember. Her father was sitting just within the doorway, swaying monotonously backward and forward in a creaking rocker. He was a big, snowy-maned lion of a man who took his pipe from his mouth and briefly surveyed the visitor with fierce eagle eyes before extending a thick horny hand.

"Welcome, sir, welcome. You'll pardon me if I don't get up. This damned gout. . . . Vinnie, set another plate for breakfast."

The stranger flashed his expansive grin again and pleaded to be excused, saying the only blamed thing he could think of right now was sleep.

"Certainly, sir," old man Todd beamed. "Vinnie! Make up my bed for the gentleman. Be quick about it, girl."

Vinnie, do this, Vinnie, do that, she thought crossly as she went into the next room. She straightened the blankets and plumped the pillows with angry movements and returned to the other room, feeling a twinge of remorse for her feelings.

139

Resentment was wrong — but so was their whole life here. How could you learn common decency when you didn't see another human being for months on end?

When the man had retired, pulling the soiled curtains over the door between the rooms, Vinnie set about making breakfast, aware of her father's fierce gaze following her.

"Daughter," he said at last, "can't say I like your attitude."

She set two plates on the puncheon table with an angry clatter and wheeled to face him. "And I can't say as I like inviting this man under our roof. He's too sly in his looks and too oily in his talk. And he didn't give his name."

"Man can't help the face and voice the Lord give him," her father said irritably, "and the name's his own business. Reckon you've been in this wild country too long. No female softness left in you."

"And whose fault is that?" she retorted furiously and was instantly sorry. Her father's great form seemed to crumple and shrink in the chair. "Oh, Dad," she whispered, going down on her knees beside him.

He put a big hand on her bright hair. "No, daughter," he said musingly, "you're right. You got all your ma's common sense, and you're right. No place for a girl. You need a bit of town life to meet some young fellows your age."

Strangely, that thought frightened Vinnie. She'd grown up alone and in her way as untamed of mind as a savage. Only in the last few years had she begun to feel an aching loneliness for the company of people. Vinnie Todd was eighteen now.

"No, Dad, I didn't mean it. I want to be with you."

He waggled his shaggy head. "Reckon that can't be for much longer, daughter. I was past forty before I married your ma and settled down . . . and you was born. Then she died, and all I could think of was to get as far away from people as I could. Thought of no one but myself all these years. That was wrong.

140

Should've thought of how you'd be taken care of when I'm gone."

"Oh, Dad."

"Be still, now. There's still plenty of vinegar in the old horse. I been givin' this some thought, daughter. I've salted away plenty of gold in my secret cache over the years . . . and I've thought it would be fine to go back to my home town in Ohio and finish out my years there. My younger brother . . . told you about him . . . runs a dry-goods store there. I could throw in with him on shares . . . have a steady income."

"Dad, that would be. . . ."

Vinnie broke off as a floorboard creaked in the next room. She threw a quick glance at the curtained door. Was the stranger sleeping — or listening just beyond the curtains? Her father saw the direction of her gaze and gave an understanding nod. He said no more, and they finished breakfast in silence.

It was on toward mid-morning, as she was sweeping the rickety porch, that Vinnie saw the second man approaching, coming across the desert on foot at a broken footsore pace. This time she was not to be caught unaware. She went into the shack and came out with the old man's Henry, then waited on the porch. As he came nearer, she could pick him out clearly in the heat-shimmer: a tall, saddle-trim man with bleach-streaked blond hair under his hat's shadow. She remembered the marshal's description of Lapham the killer, and her fingers tightened around the rifle. The man came to within a few yards of the porch and showed no sign of stopping.

"Don't come any closer!" she warned sharply.

He stopped dead, his gray eyes flickering with sardonic amusement. There was a blood-stained bandanna tied around his forehead. "Lost my horse a ways back, miss. I wonder if . . . ?"

"You get those hands up . . . high, now!"

He whistled softly, then smiled almost good-naturedly at her businesslike vehemence. "I kind of hoped for hospitality. Seems, though, there's precious little. . . ."

"Don't you try to soft-talk me!" Vinnie said angrily, centering the rifle on his chest. "I know your kind. Now, get those hands up and come over here."

She heard her father, gently rocking in the doorway behind her, say: "Good work, daughter."

The tall young man shrugged, still smiling through dry-cracked lips, and moved to the porch till the gun muzzle nearly touched him.

"That's close enough!" Vinnie said, and moved the rifle dangerously. "Quick, now . . . your name."

"Johnny Lapham," the man smiled negligently — then his eyes widened at the way her face paled beneath its tan. "Appears," he said, "that that name is pure poison around here. I wonder . . . ?"

He'd spoken to divert her attention, Vinnie realized too late — for his hand snaked suddenly up, closed over the barrel of the Henry, wrenched it sideways, and twisted it from her hands. Vinnie cried out, once, then faced him unflinchingly. She heard her father swear furiously.

"Damn it, daughter . . . I told you a hundred times, never get close to a man when you got a gun on him!"

Johnny Lapham turned the rifle in his hands, regarding it with the latent amusement that had not yet left his face, then lifted his twinkling gaze to her. "Well, miss, I guess it's my play. You'd best get inside . . . and you can keep your hands down."

He was laughing at her, Vinnie knew furiously, and she bit back a retort and reëntered the shack. Lapham was behind her.

Old man Todd shifted his considerable weight, the rocker setting up an angry creaking. "By heaven, young man, you'll regret . . . !"

142

"*Shh*, Pop." Lapham lifted a finger to his lips. "Bad for a man your age, all this shouting."

Todd turned apoplectic, but Lapham's attention had already left him, and his gray eyes probed the curtained doorway to the other room. Vinnie's heart skipped a beat. Maybe the marshal was awake and was waiting for Lapham. This hope fell flat as she heard the loud sleep-sunken snore when the sleeping man turned on his cot.

"I figured old Rufe might have beat me here," Lapham said.

He tiptoed to the curtains, pushed them aside, and moved cat-footed into the bedroom. Vinnie could see through the doorway that the marshal was sleeping heavily on his side, fully dressed except for his boots and his gun belt, which he'd flung over the back of a chair. Lapham quietly lifted the gun belt and buckled it on, then, without disturbing the sleeping man, he snaked a pair of handcuffs out of the marshal's left-hand hip pocket, snapped one cuff over the man's lean wrist, and the other to the wooden frame of the cot that was nailed to the wall. He only stirred in his sleep — and snored on.

"Guess that'll hold Rufe," Lapham said as he came from the bedroom. "Might as well let the poor old duffer sleep a mite longer." He slacked into a chair, laid the rifle on the floor close by, and gingerly eased off his boots, groaning with relief as he massaged one foot with the other. "Nothing like a ten-mile desert walk in the morning to make you appreciate a horse," he said. He winked at Vinnie. "Bet I'm an inch taller with blisters."

Vinnie stood by her father's chair, hands on his shoulders. The old man was hunched forward, fierce old eyes burning at the young man. Both father and daughter held a stony silence, but Vinnie's thoughts were chaotic. She couldn't keep her eyes or her mind off Johnny Lapham. He was young and good-looking — a far cry from the grizzled, bearded prospectors, old or of middle age, she'd seen most of her life. She had never been to a town. All their supplies were packed in by a friend of her father's, paid by a small sack of gold dust for each trip he made. There was no need for old Todd to leave his oasis retreat in this trackless desert, and Vinnie had accepted this without question — though she could not help wondering about the outside world. Young Lapham, with his carefree manner and quick tongue, was the first fresh breath of that other world to touch her life.

Carrying the rifle, Lapham walked outside, unself-consciously stripped off his shirt, poured water from the bucket into the basin on the wash bench, and began to wash the dust and grime from his upper body. *Sputtering like a winded horse*, Vinnie thought wonderingly — for she'd never seen a young man wash up. His chest and shoulders swelled with the latent power of a young bull — "built some bigger than me," the man called Rufe had said — *and so he was*, she thought admiringly.

Suddenly she wanted to talk to Johnny Lapham, wanted it with all the unnaturally pent-up impulses of a growing girl. His features were clean-cut and harmonious — certainly not the face of a killer. And evidently he meant them no harm — no doubt just meant to make a brief stayover, to rest up at their place. Only memory of Rufe's indictment — that Lapham had murdered a man in a range war — and her father's repeated warnings never to trust a man for appearance's sake held her mute.

Lapham reëntered the house, buttoning his shirt, and ramming the tails into his pants. Already he was recovering with a youthful animal vigor from the beginnings of heat exhaustion he'd shown.

"That's a real prime," he said. "Now I'll thank you for a bit of grub, ma'am. Don't go to no trouble. Anything you got left over. . . ."

With a stony face Vinnie served him at the table, then retreated to a corner of the room and sat stiffly in a chair, her arms folded. Finally Johnny Lapham pushed back his plate and set about unloading and cleaning the pistol. This he did methodically, taking his time, paying only careless attention to his prisoners. He talked most of the time, addressing his comments to old man Todd who unbent with a few curt comments.

After he'd finished the pistol, he began to clean the rifle, saying good-naturedly: "A small return for your hospitality."

"Right neighborly of you," old man Todd said acidly, "especially since you'll be taking it with you."

"Now what gave you that idea? No, the rifle's yours. I'll just sorta rather keep it outa your reach long as I'm here, that's all." He chuckled, finished up his work on the rifle, laid it on the table, and rubbed his hands briskly. "Well, how about another bit of grub?"

"You just et," the old man said peevishly. "You aiming to eat us out of house and home?"

Johnny laughed. "Friend, that was three hours ago."

Vinnie was surprised at how the time had passed, watching and listening to this man. The sun had mounted to almost high noon. She got out the big Dutch oven and began to whip up bacon and *frijoles*. Then she walked out to the porch and picked up the bucket.

"Where're you going?" her father demanded sharply.

"To get more water. Our guest managed to dirty all we have."

Johnny Lapham rose from the table. "Powerful sorry, miss. Naturally, I'll have to accompany you . . . seeing as you might have a gun stashed outside."

He was mocking her again, Vinnie knew. She flushed and headed for the spring, walking as fast as she could, but he kept at her side with long easy strides that matched every two of her own.

At the spring Vinnie started to bend with the bucket when he reached down close beside her and gently grasped the handle.

"Let me," he offered gallantly. "Little gal like you might strain her back."

His shoulder briefly pressed the curve of her hip as he reached for the bucket handle, and she sucked in her breath and then was unaccountably angry with herself. She relinquished the pail and stood back as he dipped up the water.

Sweat darkened the back of his blue shirt. He straightened and turned, set down the bucket, leaned the rifle against the big boulder, bordering the spring, and grinned at her. "Let's talk," he said with disarming candor.

"I think," Vinnie said tightly, setting her small fists on her hips, "we had better get back to the house."

She could have picked up the bucket and walked away, but she didn't. She knew guiltily that she wanted to stay here a while and listen to a young man talk.

He eased himself down on the boulder with a grunt, pulled out a long, thin cigar, and chewed on it, looking reflective and half serious. "Must be pretty lonely out here."

"I like it," Vinnie said tightly.

"Bet you never been to a party. Or a town dance. Bet you don't even know any young fellas," he said with mock gravity.

"Well, and what of it?"

He stood up, looking down at her from his towering height, smiling in disbelief. "You mean to say you never been sparked?"

"*Sparked?*" She turned her tongue cautiously on the word.

"Oh sure," he gestured vaguely. "One fella, one girl. Buggy ride, moonlight, that sort of thing. And sometimes. . . ."

He grinned unabashedly, looked at her with a bright impulse dancing through his eyes, then stepped close, snaked an arm

146

around her waist, and kissed her hard.

Vinnie made a small sound of protest and pushed away. Strangely, she didn't feel angry, only exhilarated. She said, her breath quick: "Do you do that to all the girls you *spark*?"

"Some," he admitted. The amusement had suddenly left his face, and he looked disturbed. "You . . . ah . . . ?"

"Vinnie," she prompted softly.

"Vinnie, I. . . ." He reached out to grasp her arms, bare and golden-tan where she'd rolled her sleeves high above her elbows. She waited expectantly. He seemed to be struggling for words, then said lamely: "You're a pretty girl, Vinnie. Better be getting back, like you said."

He let go of her, picked up the bucket and the rifle, and trudged up to the house, Vinnie following with her feelings in a puzzling tangle. The old man's angry gaze struck sharply at her as they entered, and she knew he'd been watching. Flushed with shame, she stared at the musty window squares of sunlight on the faded rug by the door. Johnny put the bucket down and without a word went outside again, walking off a little way from the shack and staring across the heat-dancing flats.

"Now," old man Todd exploded, "just what the hell you mean by that crazy play? Talking to that damn' killer, then letting him . . . ! Have your wits gone addled, girl?"

"I didn't do anything," Vinnie protested. "He just. . . ."

"You liked it all the same," the old man snorted. "I ain't shocked none, daughter. Just mad. If it wasn't for my gout, I'd tear that young rascal apart. Keep away from him now . . . you hear?" He added, almost to himself: "Funny . . . he don't look bad, act bad. Fact, he's been mighty decent so far. Just a kid, straddling the fence now, and don't know which way to jump." He lifted a fierce look to his daughter. "All the same, you keep away from him, Vinnie!"

They heard an angry, startled grunt in the next room and

knew that Rufe had awakened — to find himself shackled to the bed frame with his own handcuffs.

"Go talk to him, daughter," old man Todd said thoughtfully. "Tell him his man's here . . . and has run a sandy on all of us. Just now I'm gettin' an idea."

Vinnie went into the bedroom and explained the situation to the marshal in a low voice. She was not certain what reaction she had expected — but certainly not the blank, staring fear that paled the lawman's face.

She was about to speak sharply, to shock him out of it, when her father's low-hissed whisper reached her. "Come here, daughter."

When she stood by his chair, the old man said: "I been thinkin', I can't get on my feet to reach Lapham . . . but, if I could get my hands on him . . . just for a second. . . ." Rapidly, he told her what she must do.

"I . . . don't know if I can," she faltered. What she meant, she knew guiltily, was that she did not want to try — she wanted Johnny Lapham to have his chance.

"You can do it, all right. He's comin' back to the house. Remember now. Talk . . . get his back to me."

As Johnny came through the doorway, she laid her hand on his arm, making her voice sound impulsive and eager: "Johnny . . . can't you tell Dad and me why you're running? Is it so bad as that?"

A frown touched his eyes then altered into laugh-crinkles at the outer corners. "Why, ma'am, I'm just a poor misguided lad."

He turned as he spoke, swinging his broad back toward her father who rocked lightly back and forth in his chair, as though half asleep. Smiling, Vinnie lifted both hands to Lapham's chest and shoved with all her strength. Caught off-guard, off-balance, Johnny fell backward on top of her father, and the dozing old

148

man galvanized into sudden motion, wrapping his massive arms around the young man, pinning him briefly in thrashing helplessness. The Henry slipped from his grasp and clattered to the floor.

"Grab his gun, girl!" old Todd shouted, almost carried out of his chair by Johnny's struggle. "I can't hold him!"

Vinnie moved two steps, hauled Johnny Lapham's gun from its holster, and brought it to a level, cocking it in both hands. Johnny became motionless, staring at her, and the old man released him. Lapham came to his feet, ran his hand back through his hair, and regarded her bitterly.

"In my trade, you learn early . . . never trust a woman. Trouble is, you forget."

"You'll have plenty of time to think about it where you're going," Todd said grimly. "Here . . . give me the gun, Vinnie girl. Now, mister, where's the key for them handcuffs?"

Still looking at the girl, Lapham dug the key out of his pants pocket.

"Good. Hand it to my daughter . . . slow, now. Girl . . . go free the marshal."

"You got him . . . you got him?" Rufe pressed her in an almost frenzied voice, as she unlocked his cuffs.

"Yes," Vinnie said quietly, contemptuously, "we got him."

Law or no law, she knew now where her sympathies lay. She hesitated in turning the key, fighting a desire to throw it through the open window, leaving the marshal helplessly chained, then getting the gun from her father and giving Lapham his chance for escape. But she had made her choice, no matter if it went against her womanly instincts in the matter. The cuffs fell from Rufe's skinny wrists.

He almost scrambled through the doorway to reach the next room. "Good work, Mister Todd," Rufe said. "I'll take charge now."

Old Todd silently handed him the .45, and Rufe took it and cat-footed nervously around the chair to face Johnny Lapham, chuckling.

"Well, Johnny . . . it's been a long trail."

Lapham smiled faintly. "For both of us, Rufe."

Rufe's gold tooth flashed gaudily in his yellow-fanged grin. "Why yes. But mostly for me. Because I was scared. Nothing much scares you, does it?"

"Just women." Johnny slanted a wry glance at the girl.

"You got anything I can tie this fella up with, Mister Todd?" Rufe asked. "Rawhide, preferably. I don't trust hemp . . . or handcuffs."

"Man in your position has a sort of mutual distrust of those, doesn't he, Rufe?" Johnny murmured.

Rufe darted a quick glance at the girl and her father, licked his lips, then turned back to Johnny, his mouth snarling. "Shut up! How about it, Mister Todd?"

The old man directed Vinnie to dig out some deerhide he'd sliced into lengths to braid a riata. She hauled it from under the bunk and brought it to Rufe. The avid gleam in his eyes made her uneasy. She thought of Johnny's strange last words, and Rufe's snarling reaction, and felt suddenly caught in the grip of paralyzing fear that had nothing to do with the attraction she felt for Lapham or her instinctive repugnance toward the man who wore the marshal's badge.

Rufe tied Johnny Lapham hand and foot, then turned to the waiting father and daughter, tilting his gun almost casually to cover both of them. "All right, folks . . . suppose we get down to cases. Just before I dropped off to sleep, I heard a certain gold cache mentioned."

Old Todd sputtered explosively then found his voice. "What the hell is this?" he bellowed.

Vinnie shot a frightened glance at Johnny Lapham, bound

helplessly on the floor, his back propped against the wall.

He gave her the wriest of smiles without a trace of anger. "It's fairly simple. You want to tell them, Rufe . . . or shall I?"

"You take it, son," Rufe grinned wickedly. "Give you a chance to use your voice . . . you won't be usin' it much longer."

Johnny Lapham sighed. "That's my badge on Rufe's vest. I'm a deputy U. S. marshal, trailing Rufe . . . or was, up till yesterday. Rufe knew I was following him, so he just laid up in ambush and killed my horse under me with a long rifle shot. Then he shot at me as I got up and knocked me cold. I reckon then that he ran over to me. . . ."

Rufe grimaced. "Thought my bullet had split your skull. There was blood all over your face."

"Nope. Just creased my scalp . . . enough to knock me out. When I woke up, I was layin' by my dead horse and my sidearm and saddle carbine were gone . . . along with my badge, credentials, and handcuffs. Guess you figured they might come in handy before you reached the border."

"Somethin' like that," Rufe said equably. "They did, too, as witness your position now and mine. About three hours after I left you, my own horse give out on the desert, and I had to leave him. Had to get rid of all excess weight, so I got rid of yer hand gun, yer carbine, and my own saddle gun. Buried 'em."

"I set out to track him down on foot," Johnny continued, "knowin' it was pretty useless, him on horseback. When I found his dead horse, I figured there might be a chance, if I could outlast him."

"You would've, too," Rufe said. "I ain't young any more. Lucky I found this place. Lucky, too, I give these folks your name and description as a killer I was trailin' . . . jis' for a

151

private joke. Didn' know how much help it'd be."

Old man Todd gripped the arms of his chair and stared at Johnny Lapham. "Why the hell didn't you tell us, boy?"

"Waste of breath. I saw that right off. No reason for you to believe me."

The old man thought a moment. "Reckon not. It would have sounded too pat, but it would've put us on your guard. Now . . . ?"

"Now" — Rufe swung the pistol in a semi-arc — "let's get to the matter at hand. The gold. It'll start me off with a good stake down Mexico way." His tone became abrupt. "Where you got it stashed, old man?"

Todd said stolidly: "You could burn all my fingers and toes off, and I still wouldn't tell you."

"*Your* fingers and toes?" Rufe said musingly. "How about missy's, instead?"

"Lord alive!" breathed the old man. "You wouldn't . . . !" His words choked off.

"You'd be surprised, mister," said Rufe softly. "I'll give you . . . say, about five minutes to think it over." With his free hand he pulled out a brass-cased watch on a leather cord. He glanced at it, chuckled, and put it away.

Vinnie could almost hear the seconds ticking off in the harsh silence that followed — broken only by her father's strained breathing. She put a hand to his shoulder and felt the muscles, braced and rigid.

Johnny spoke suddenly. "I got a bad dry, Rufe. Think you could see your way to handing me a dipper of water?"

"Why, sure, Johnny boy." Not taking his eyes or leveled gun off the other two, the bogus marshal drew a dipper from the full bucket Vinnie had set by the doorway. He backed over to Lapham, and Johnny lifted his hands, bound in front of him, to reach for the dipper — a quick, too eager reach that knocked it from Rufe's fingers and cascaded water over Johnny's hands and arms.

"Why you damned clumsy fool," Rufe said pleasantly. "Now you can try sucking it out of your sleeves." He turned and moved back toward the rocker, still watching his prisoner out of the corner of his eye. He looked at his watch again. "I'll give you two more minutes, old man."

Again the heavy cottony silence, rolling like a thunderclap against Vinnie's ears. Once Johnny gave her the faintest smile and nod. Strangely, it calmed her.

Time was up when she saw Rufe glance once more at his watch, take a step forward, saying genially: "All right, missy. Tie your daddy to that rocker." He nudged the remaining strips of deerhide on the floor. "Don't want him gettin' violent when. . . ."

His attention had momentarily left Johnny Lapham, and Vinnie saw everything that followed in sharp clarity. She saw Johnny's hands, suddenly free, brace against the wall at his back then give a hardened backward thrust that aided the lift of his legs, carrying him to his feet. She saw Johnny bend at the knees once more and lean forward, and, as he leaned, straighten his legs into a dive that thrust him with lowered head and slugging arms into Rufe's back. Rufe gave one last, helpless wail as he plunged face down under Johnny's weight, his gun blasting into the floor. His head banged against the concrete-hard, dried-clay floor.

Immediately Johnny Lapham was cutting the thongs on his feet with Rufe's knife. He did not glance up or say a word until he'd tied Rufe hand and foot, hands at his back and feet drawn up in back and tied to his hands. Then Johnny was on his feet, rubbing his wrists. His hard face altered to the old boyish smile.

"Clever, son!" boomed old Todd. "Stuff stretches like hell when wet."

"Yeah," Johnny said dryly, "so I've heard."

Vinnie's dark eyes were candid and searching on his face. There was a trace of hurt in them. "Can you forgive me for failing you?"

"Failing me?" Johnny asked in surprise.

"Yes. I knew I was making the wrong decision when I tricked you. I *felt* it. But I went through with it. I let Dad decide for me. And I went through with it, knowing it was wrong."

Old man Todd snorted heavily. "Woman's intuition!"

"Never laugh at a woman's intuition, sir," said Johnny Lapham, his young eyes at once grave and humorous. "As I see it, Miss Vinnie, your choice was based on a moral issue, not on personal feelings. You thought I was a killer, and Rufe was the law. You did what you figured was right morally, and you'd have done that regardless of what your dad thought, or what you felt personally. What I'd have done myself."

She smiled at him for the first time. "Would you? Really?"

Johnny smiled down at her. "Right now," he said, "I've got to be taking Rufe back. But I'll come back, and we'll talk about it."

Vinnie and Johnny laughed together.

T. V. Olsen frequently wanted to break with the time-frame of the 1880s so commonplace in the Western story when he came upon the scene. Eventually he ventured back into earlier periods, and in one instance, "The Strange Valley," collected in WESTWARD THEY RODE (1976), he even introduced the notion of a time-warp into a Western story where 19th-Century Sioux warriors are suddenly confronted by a modern semi-truck in a valley known and feared for its magic. "Five Minutes" is the only story Olsen wrote set in the north woods of Wisconsin, circa 1956. When he could not sell it, he revamped it, setting it in the West in the 1880s with the title changed to "Journey of No Return." In that guise it was his second published story, appearing in *Ranch Romances* (3rd April Number: 4/20/56). The original text, as T. V. Olsen intended it, appears here now for the first time.

Five Minutes

It was late afternoon of a bleak fall day when a man stepped into a small, deserted clearing in the north woods and looked about with bright, feverish eyes. This man was young, perhaps twenty-five, dirty and unshaven, with equally disreputable clothing — worn, ragged canvas trousers and shirt. He might have been handsome beneath his weeks' beard and dirt, for his features were strong and regular and his clear blue eyes, despite their feverish fixity, were intelligent. He was tall, although his big frame was slumped with weariness as happened to a man who had caught scarcely an hour's sleep in two days and nights of almost steady travel. He was sick, too, for he had been cold and wet for nearly all that time. The urge to drop to the ground and rest was overpowering.

But it was not in him to rest. Seemingly his flight was without purpose or direction, yet his set features held a purpose.

Now, as he stopped at the verge of the little clearing, he thought: *Why, this is where it happened — it was just a year ago — a fall day just like this.*

He leaned against a tree as a qualm of weakness surged through him. Before his feverish eyes the whole scene which had changed the course of his life was reconstructed vividly. He turned away, with a sickened intake of breath, and staggered on across the clearing. He could not afford to hesitate a moment.

A rifle cracked out just ahead of him, and his canvas hat was torn from his head and flung away. Without a moment's hesitation he lunged on into the bushes from which the report had issued. He plunged directly at the marksman, where he stood concealed behind the bushes.

He heard a strangled yelp of astonishment from the diminutive figure as he lunged into it and knocked it sprawling. He bent and tore the rifle roughly from the grasp of the fallen marksman with one hand, while the other caught the small figure by the front of its jacket and yanked it to its feet. In an instant he was staring into the frightened blue eyes of a girl.

"A kid!" he gasped hoarsely.

She struggled to free herself. "I'm no kid!"

He let go, and she stepped back a few paces, facing him defiantly. Even in his anger he observed that she was wearing overalls and a canvas hunting jacket, and that her hair was light gold.

"Agreed," he said, "but why shoot at me?"

"I . . . I mistook you for a deer."

This obvious lie infuriated him. "A deer? Why, I was standing right in plain sight, you trigger-happy . . . !" He broke off, seeing that her fright was genuine. He smiled faintly. "And besides, it isn't deer season."

She nodded as though in relief. "I was rabbit-hunting. When you came across the clearing, I thought you might be. . . ." She laughed nervously. "I thought you might be that convict that escaped from prison a couple of days ago. . . ."

"You're pretty smart," he murmured. "I am."

She recoiled. "You . . . you're . . . ?"

"Frank Quinn, the convict." He laughed without humor. "Don't worry. I've got nothing against you . . . not even your trying to part my hair."

She shook her head, a little angrily. "I could have killed you if I wanted, believe me. You were coming right toward me. I thought you saw me. I . . . was trying to scare you off."

"I'll buy that. What's your name?"

"Amy Gordon. You're not . . . going to hurt me?"

"I said I wasn't. Any relation to Sheriff Gordon?"

"He's my father."

Frank pondered that a moment. "Which way's the closest highway?"

"Five miles east . . . on G."

His laugh was again humorless. "You can go, then, Amy. You can't get your old man before I. . . ." He left the statement incomplete.

"Before you get Reuben?" she asked hesitantly.

Frank looked at her. "You know . . . then?"

She nodded. "I read about your trial in the paper. The whole county was excited about that trial. Halloway was a big man . . . and. . . ." She looked up at him with widened eyes. "Why, the murder must have taken place right around here."

Frank smiled thinly. "It did. Right in this very clearing, in fact. Funny, isn't it, Amy? They say a murderer always returns to the scene of the crime."

He searched her face disinterestedly for some sign of fear, but she faced him unflinchingly.

"And did you murder Halloway?" she asked.

Again that humorless laugh. "The jury said I did."

"And what do you say?"

"Does it matter . . . to a sheriff's daughter?"

She shrugged, estranged by his apparent indifference.

His gaze traveled over her head to the trees beyond. He said quietly: "No, Amy, I didn't murder Halloway. Mat Reuben did, though. That's why I'm going to kill him."

"His testimony sent you to prison?"

He nodded, and turned to resume his trek in the direction he had been traveling. She ran along beside him, trying to match his long steps.

"Slow down, you long-legged galoot!"

He glanced at her, frowning. "You better toddle along home."

"You still got my gun!"

He glanced down and saw that he was indeed still holding the rifle. "That's a heavy gun for such a little girl," he murmured. "Maybe I ought to relieve you of it."

Amy seized the barrel and held it.

"You're not using my gun to kill Reuben!" she told him, looking him steadily in the eye.

He laughed. "When I work friend Reuben over, I won't need a gun, Amy."

She tried to pull it from his grasp. "Then give mine back."

He laughed and held onto it, even while he admired her nerve. "I think I'll hang onto it for safety's sake . . . *my* safety."

She released her hold on the gun, and he saw the hurt in her eyes.

"Oh," she said slowly, "so you think that I'd. . . ."

"I don't know," Frank returned. "But I'm not taking any chances with a sheriff's daughter. I'll make you a fair trade. All your bullets for the gun." He shot the breech open and took out the cartridge in the chamber. "Give me your jacket," he commanded.

Silently she removed her hunting jacket and handed it to him. In both pockets he found a number of cartridges which he transferred to his own pockets. Then he handed jacket and rifle back to the girl.

"New shells are cheaper than a new rifle," he grinned.

Her lips compressed reproachfully. "You might have trusted me."

"Why?" he asked. "Would you want to help me?"

"I'm beginning to wonder."

He laughed mirthlessly and continued on his way. After a

160

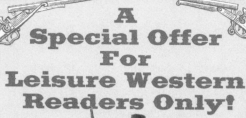

A
Special Offer
For
Leisure Western
Readers Only!

Get FOUR
FREE*
Western Novels

Travel to the Old West in all its glory
and drama—without leaving your home!

**Plus, you'll save
between $3.00 and $6.00
every time you buy!**

GET YOUR 4
FREE* BOOKS NOW—
A VALUE BETWEEN
$16 AND $20

Mail the Free* Book Certificate Today!

FREE* BOOKS
CERTIFICATE!

YES! I want to subscribe to the Leisure Western Book Club. Please send me my 4 FREE* BOOKS. Then, each month, I'll receive the four newest Leisure Western Selections to preview FREE* for 10 days. If I decide to keep them, I will pay the Special Member's Only discounted price of just $3.36 each, a total of $13.44 ($14.50 US in Canada). This saves me between $3 and $6 off the bookstore price. There are no shipping, handling or other charges.* There is no minimum number of books I must buy and I may cancel the program at any time. In any case, the 4 FREE* BOOKS are mine to keep—at a value of between $17 and $20!

*In Canada, add $5.00 Canadian shipping and handling per order for first shipment. For all subsequent shipments to Canada the cost of membership in the Book Club is $14.50 US, which includes $7.50 shipping and handling per month. All payments must be made in US currency.

Name _____

Address _____

City_____ State_____ Country_____

Zip_____ Telephone_____

Tear here and mail your FREE* book card today!

Get Four Books Totally F R E E* – A Value between $16 and $20

Tear here and mail your FREE* book card today!

PLEASE RUSH MY FOUR FREE* BOOKS TO ME RIGHT AWAY!

LeisureWestern Book Club
P.O. Box 6613
Edison, NJ 08818-6613

AFFIX
STAMP
HERE

few paces he stumbled and fell. Amy ran to his side and helped him up.

"You're sick."

"You're damned right I'm sick. That's why I want to get Reuben now...while I'm still able."

He staggered on, then was arrested by Amy's voice. "Frank."

He stopped but did not turn to face her as he heard her soft footsteps on the sodden carpet of fallen leaves as she hurried to his side.

"Why do you want to kill Mat Reuben?"

He shrugged, still not meeting her eyes. "Because it's been riding me every night for a year while I rotted in that prison. Because they'll catch me, and, before they do, I've got to get him out of my system. Because it's all I've been living for. You can take your pick."

"You'd be making a terrible mistake," she replied quietly.

"I made my mistake long ago," he said bitterly. "I trusted Reuben. That's why I'm where I am now." He whirled on her abruptly, almost angrily. "What do you care?"

She placed a hand on his arm. "I believe you. I want to help you."

For a moment he stared at her, trying to interpret the expression on her face. "You want to . . . ? Forget it. You're a nice girl, Amy. You don't know how life can be. If your folks knew where you were now, they'd. . . ." His voice slowed, and he looked gently toward her, responding to her sympathy and friendliness. Their eyes met momentarily. "I wish . . . ," Frank resumed huskily. Then he paused. "Good bye," he said quickly, and hurried on.

Once he glanced back and saw her looking after him, appearing small and forlorn. Then she turned quickly and disappeared from sight.

He really hurried now. His head was clearer, and he quickened his pace as though to escape his thoughts. Occasionally he would stumble over a root or trip on a fallen branch, but he regained his feet and drove himself mercilessly onward. His brain had room for but one thought. Ten miles ahead was Mat Reuben's hunting lodge where the big political boss stayed every fall vacation. He knew where Reuben would be — in his study, his small, thin form crouched behind his big desk. *Waiting for me to kill him,* thought Frank with a cruel smile. He flexed his fingers, almost feeling them closing about that scrawny throat.

He stopped to rest briefly against the bole of an oak, and his thoughts turned to Amy Gordon. He closed his eyes to visualize her big, earnest eyes and the small, piquant face. She was goodness. *Oh, God,* he thought, *if I had only met someone like that a year ago instead of the damned false hussies I fell in with.* It was easy now to dream of what might have been.

He opened his eyes to the bleak sky, the stark tree trunks, the gray, wet mist that was descending to dampen his upturned face and add to his discomfort. The cold, saturated air seemed to chill him to the marrow.

He moved on doggedly between the towering boles of oak and maple rising on every side of him, ghost-like in the mist. Then he emerged from the confines of the forest into an open field.

Fierce, triumphant energy was instilled into his veins. This was the ancient pasture behind Reuben's hunting lodge — and Reuben would be here this year as every year. He recalled reading in the newspaper a week ago that Reuben would be up from Chicago for his usual fall vacation.

He broke into a run across the pasture. He knew exactly where the house was, although he could not discern it across the mist-laden landscape. How many times he had crossed this area with Reuben and Halloway on hunting forays!

His brief burst of adrenal power expired quickly, and, as he

162

drew up beside the thicket at the rear of the lodge, he was gasping for breath. He paused there, fairly certain that the mist had covered his approach from the view of anyone in the lodge.

He stole swiftly to the corner of the lodge and edged his way along the half-log pine siding toward the front. There was a small window through which he peered cautiously into the living room. Seated there at ease in a wicker chair was a huge bold figure in sweatshirt and slacks built on the order of a pugilist — which he probably was, to judge from his battered features. He was leafing through a magazine. A revolver rested on a table at his elbow.

Frank ducked back from the window, thinking swiftly. The man's presence meant one thing. Mat Reuben had heard of Frank's escape, had deduced that he would make a try to get him before he was re-captured, and had hired a bodyguard. He considered briefly his chances. There was room for little more than one thought in his fevered brain: to get the man he hunted, no matter what the odds. He heard footsteps entering the room.

"I'll have my coffee in the office, Martin." That was Reuben's voice. "I have precinct reports to study. You stay here."

"Sure you'll be all right, Mister Reuben?" Martin's voice had the nasal quality typical of the south side of Chicago.

Reuben laughed indulgently. "There is only one window opening on my office. I have a gun, and I can watch one window, don't you think? I'll call you if anything happens."

Frank waited till he heard the door to the office close, then with painstaking caution he raised his eyes just above the level of the window sill. Martin, he saw, was still sprawled in the comfortable chair, smoking now, one foot propped over the arm while he continued to leaf through the magazine.

Frank sank down in a quandary. He had to take Reuben by surprise to keep him alive. But how could he do it with Reuben watching his office window and Martin guarding the front room onto which the office door opened? The sick blood pounded through Frank's temples as he restlessly quested out what he knew of the layout of this lodge. There was a kitchen and a pantry to the rear, for Reuben liked to do his own cooking, a large bedroom and, up front, the living room and Reuben's office. Thoughtlessly Frank's hand brushed his trouser pocket and the handful of Amy's shells there. The suggestion of a crystallizing idea, a scheme in embryo, touched his mind. It would be a tall chance, but there was no time to consider alternatives.

He moved at a low-crouching run to the rear of the lodge, eased the back door open, and stepped inside. He stumbled on the door sill and almost fell. He leaned against the wall for a moment. *Take it slow*, he thought numbly, *take it easy. Get him first, then it won't matter.* Fighting down the nausea that gripped him, he moved to the iron stove in the corner and lifted the stove lid with infinite care. He set the lid down silently to one side, seeing, as he had hoped, a banked layer of glowing coals. He worked quickly to stir up the coals with the poker. Then, selecting a thin, narrow strip of kindling wood from the wood box by the stove, he emptied out his small handful of Amy's shells and laid them down in a row on the wooden strip. He lowered them delicately onto the surface of red coals.

He returned silently outside and went swiftly to the front-room window, crouching there, listening tensely over the heavy strike of his heart, feeling a rising excitement mount his tight nerves. When the crash of fire-touched gunpowder came from the kitchen, he heard Reuben speak over it loudly. "What's that?"

Martin left the front room to investigate. *Now*, Frank thought. He opened the window, slung a leg over the window-sill, and stepped into the room. Nine fast steps took him to the office door. It was unlocked, and he stepped quickly inside and closed it noiselessly behind him. Only then did Reuben, behind a desk of expensive walnut, look up. His hands, on the desk, moved.

Frank said in a voice of steel: "Don't."

Reuben became motionless, watching as Frank walked toward the desk. His mouth fell open — his jaw moved, but no words came out. His eyes widened slowly as recognition dawned in them, then terror! There was a gasp of fright from his lungs. Then he moved.

His hand darted down to snatch open a drawer of his desk. He yanked out a small pistol, but Frank reached him at the same moment. He caught the scrawny wrist in one big hand and twisted. Reuben started a wild bleating sound for help which Frank choked off with his other hand. Reuben kicked and wrestled, but he was far from a match for his young opponent, even though the latter was in a sickly condition.

With the gun in his possession, Frank threw Reuben back in his chair, coughing for breath, and seated himself on the edge of the desk. All was silent then except for the ticking of a big clock in the corner and the muttering bodyguard as he returned to the living room and hammered on the study door.

"You all right in there, Mister Reuben?" he called loudly. "I've checked on them shots. Somebody must've gotten into the stove. I couldn't find nobody in the rooms or outside."

Frank held the muzzle of the little pistol an inch from Reuben's forehead which was glistening with sweat. Reuben looked at the gun with bulging eyes and wheezed out in a high voice: "Yes, I'm fine. Go back and sit down."

There was the sound of retreating footsteps outside the door, then silence. Frank said softly: "All right, Mat. Don't raise your voice."

Reuben gesticulated frantically with his trembling hands.

"Frank, it was a mistake," he quavered in a choking whisper.

"Who made it?" sneered Frank.

"P-please, Frank. . . ."

"Shut up," Frank interrupted deliberately. He paused for a moment, blinking as dark spots seemed to obstruct his vision. He was getting sicker and wearier by the minute, but there was still time. He continued: "Reuben, this is my game, and I'll call the plays. You keep your mouth shut."

He shifted on the desk, still holding his pistol at the other's head. Reuben sat rigid with fear.

"You got five minutes to live, Reuben," said Frank in a soft, cruel voice. "Keep your eyes on that big clock in the corner and listen to it tick away while I talk. You're going to die in just five minutes, Mat. I wonder how it feels? I wonder if I can crowd into that time as much agony for you as you made me go through for nearly twelve months. I lived all that time just for this, and I'm in no hurry to end it." Frank's voice was gentle with hate. "I had a lot of time to think in prison, Mat . . . but it didn't take much thinking to figure how you worked it. Your system was smooth. All you had to do was find an unknown young fool like me who wanted to start a pulpwood business of his own . . . who wanted to get up in the world fast . . . who needed good friends . . . big shots like you to get next to the right people with capital and backing. I remember when it was, Mat. You took me to big parties . . . dances . . . all the glitter of high-hat society . . . took me into your confidence . . . and finally . . . you took me on a hunting trip."

The room was chill, but Reuben was sweating copiously. For a while there was again only silence except for the fateful tick-tock of the clock. Then Frank went on, his voice low.

"I thought you were the best friend I had in the world. I was a lucky guy. Nothing out of the way about a little trip to your hunting lodge . . . just you, me, and Halloway. We hunted . . . for rabbits, partridge. We didn't know you had bigger game in mind . . . what you'd been leading up to all this time . . . what you'd planned for.

"On the third day we were walking down the trail, Halloway ahead of us. When Halloway entered a little cleared space, you raised your rifle casually and shot him through the head . . . and, while I just stood, too shocked to know what was happening, you clouted me over the head with your gun.

"I woke up in jail with a cracked skull. It was simple and perfect. You switched guns with me, gave the law a story about my quarreling with Halloway and threatening to get even. There were no fingerprints, no clues . . . just that the rifle that had killed Halloway was by me.

"The trial was quick. No jury would believe my word against a big politician's about what happened. It wasn't till after the trial that I heard that you came into a big hunk of Halloway's timber holdings through his death. He'd mortgaged them to you as security for the loan of some money for a little speculating. If that debt wasn't paid in three months, you'd get the timber. You made sure he'd never pay by killing him, and, when the debt reverted to a poor relative he'd named as his heir, that heir, of course, couldn't pay the mortgage. You've since been doing a land-office business. I hear there's a lot of talk about it, but no one investigated . . . you had so much influence."

Reuben forced a sneer. "You . . . you were a ready-made sucker, Frank."

"Sure I was," replied Frank with a gentle grin, "but I'm not the goat in this deal. You've still got three more minutes to sweat, Mat."

Tick-tock-tick-tock-tick-tock.

Perspiration exuded from Reuben's every pore. "Look, Frank," he whispered hoarsely. "You'll just go back to jail, killing me. I'll give you money, help you to escape. . . ."

Frank stared at him dully.

Reuben's voice was agonized. He bleated: "Frank, you don't have to trust me . . . you're holding the gun. You can take me with you . . . take me as a hostage till you're safe from the law. . . ."

Frank wasn't listening now. His brain was reeling again. Dark spots obliterated his vision. He set his teeth, trying to fight it back. *Just for three minutes*, he prayed silently. *Just for three minutes.*

But he knew vaguely that it was useless. The constant strain and hardship of the past two days, the lack of food and sleep were no longer to be resisted. He was sitting still, too. That was bad. And here was Reuben, who had now stopped talking and was watching him intently. Understanding glittered in his eyes.

Frank tried to pull himself erect. He had to walk — had to keep on his feet. But he couldn't. His limbs felt like jelly. He couldn't even hold the gun steady.

Reuben was on his feet now. Frank tried to level the gun, tried to pull the trigger. It was useless. He was slipping slowly to the floor.

He felt Reuben snatch the gun from his lax fingers as he fell. Roaring, pounding blood seemed to clot his ears. Dimly, in an almost detached way, he saw Reuben leaning over him with evil exultation on his face as he raised the pistol.

Frank heard a shot, then sank into a pit of soft blackness.

When he again knew consciousness, his eyelids seemed stuck shut. He forced them open, his sight immediately encountering a half-open window beyond which the waning sunlight of an autumn afternoon cast its mellow glow on tri-colored treetops, stirring gently in a soft autumn breeze. He felt alert yet at peace with himself. He found, now glancing about, that he was in a small, white-walled room, lying in an iron bed.

His mind and vision were clear, while his body was still weak, and he sensed that a considerable length of time had elapsed since his last memory. Despair filled him. He had been balked out of his vengeance. Reuben had gotten the upper hand and, instead of mercifully killing him, must have turned him over to the law so he might suffer for the rest of his days behind iron bars. Frank neither cursed nor wept over his future. Months ago in prison a deep, irrevocable bitterness had settled in him. That made him now accept stoically the reverse of fortune.

The door opened, and he heard a woman's voice say: "You can see him now, Sheriff. Perhaps he's rational. He's been conscious, as you know, but delirious."

"Thanks, nurse."

Frank turned his head to see a big, stoop-shouldered man with a gray mustache enter the room, closing the door behind him. He advanced to Frank's side.

"How are you, Quinn?"

"Fine, Sheriff Gordon," murmured Frank calmly.

"Remember me?"

"Sure, I was in your jail a year ago before they transferred me to the prison."

The sheriff chuckled. "Good. Now let me talk and don't interrupt till I finish. Three days ago I'd just parked my ole car in the garage when my daughter came running out of the woods an' began babbling a story about meeting convict Frank Quinn in the woods, that he was going to kill Mat Reuben at his hunting lodge, but that Frank had told her he never killed Halloway. After I got the whole story straight, I told Amy to git home and then headed for Mister Reuben's lodge.

"I parked my bus a ways from the lodge and sneaked in close. I was hidin' in a thicket close by the house when you came. After you got into Reuben's study, I slid over to listen by the window which he'd fortunately neglected to shut tight an' was about to close in when you began to talk. Amy had said she was sure that you were in the right. That made me thoughtful, so I listened an' I heard the whole story. It was better'n a confession. I walked in just as Mister Reuben was fixing to plug you, and I shot him in the shoulder.

"I phoned the hospital an' headquarters, and it wasn't long before Mister Reuben was in jail, waitin' fer trial, an' you was in the hospital here in town with Amy comin' to visit you half a dozen times a day . . . only you didn't know it, since you was flat on your back, delirious and a mighty sick boy."

"I think I'm still delirious," Frank muttered in a dazed, unbelieving voice. "And Reuben?"

"He got what he intended for you . . . and I sorta found it convenient to forget why you went to see him."

"Amy?"

"I'll fetch her."

Sheriff Gordon paused at the door. "My girl saved your life, Frank. I reckon you owe her more than a vote of thanks."

When he was gone, Frank settled back, staring at the ceiling, finding it strange to accept all this as reality. With a sudden contentment he realized that he had been living the last twelve months in a dream from which he was just awakening.

It was a very few moments before Amy entered the room softly, and it took some seconds for him to recognize her. She seemed very small in a yellow blouse and skirt that rustled when she walked. Her soft, honey-tinted curls fell to her shoulders.

She sat on the edge of his bed, smiling shyly. He felt a little in awe of her.

"Thanks sounds pretty cheap," he said quietly.

She looked down at her hands. "You know what Dad said, Frank? That it took a lot of nerve and brains to do what you did. He . . . he admires you."

Frank had to think about that for a second before he realized what she was trying to say, then a halting smile broke over his face. "I guess I've been looking the wrong way a long time."

"And now, Frank?"

"From where I am now . . . well . . . things look pretty good, Amy."

T. V. Olsen's protagonists, men and women alike, are frequently loners, those who generally live, by necessity if not by choice, on the outskirts of society. This is certainly the case for Sara Carver in THE STALKING MOON (1965), a white woman who has been living with an Apache warrior and raising their children before the U. S. Army separates them, and for Gage Cameron, the mixed-blood protagonist in THE GOLDEN CHANCE (1992) and the woman he comes to love, Opal Bedoe, a former slave. It is no less true for Ad Standish in this story.

Bandit Breed

When Standish picked out the light wagon approaching the seep from the northeast, he left the height of the sun-scorched limestone outcrop and walked down to the others, waiting in their camp in the cottonwoods. Standish was a nearly gaunt man whose dark-burned face often curtained his feelings as it betrayed his Indian blood. His walk held the stiffness of a man cramped too long in unceasing, unmoving vigilance — while the others slept through the hot midday hours. They roused out now, the three of them on their feet as Standish came up.

Renshaw said: "Keller?"

"There's a wagon coming," Standish said. "If it's Keller, he's got someone with him."

Renshaw shoved his hat back from his thick, curly, iron-gray hair. He was a heavy-set man with a kindly, reflective face. He was the leader and looked it. He said authoritatively: "Gentlemen, Keller was to come alone. Will you take your positions?"

Simm Keena smiled, his brooding and deep-sunk eyes brightening at the thought of trouble because it was all he understood or even cared for. Moving like a lean wolf, he headed farther into the stream-created bog where the camp lay and sank noiselessly down behind a willow clump. Leach, a tall angular half-wit of a man who never spoke and who made up in animal awareness what he lacked in intelligence, headed upstream and flattened on the ground behind more willows.

Renshaw and Standish took up similar positions around the camp so that to all outward appearances, it was deserted — though the four men from their strategic places of hiding could see anyone who entered it without being seen themselves. Stan-

175

dish was standing in sunlight-mottled immobility behind a cottonwood so that he merged as one with it. He thought with a still-faced amusement how very methodically Renshaw built dream-plans on a grand scale, but for one reason or another they rarely crystallized. He and his men were rat-poor, living like hunted animals, and it was only the force and weight of Renshaw's personality that had so far held the gang together. Today the meeting with Keller might determine the future of Renshaw's sway over his men who were restive, mutinous, and tired of promises.

Standish could hear the wagon nearing camp, and presently it drew up within the glade of cottonwoods. Watching from the gold-flecked shadow of this giant cottonwood, Standish felt a thin backwash of surprise at the sight of the other rider on the high seat of Keller's buckboard.

Renshaw left the cover of a willow stand and walked to the wagon with a drive to his massive stride that told Standish of the leader's angry impatience. Renshaw's voice, when he spoke to Keller, was of a deceptive gentleness. "A woman?" he said.

Linc Keller stepped down from the buckboard. He was a slight young man of average height whose movements held a wiry, nervous energy. Keller wore a black business suit, town shoes, and a fawn-colored Stetson. He brushed at nonexistent dust on his trousers and didn't meet Renshaw's gaze. "My wife, Renshaw," he said slowly.

"Fine," Renshaw said with cold anger. "But why bring her here?"

"Damn it, I had to! She was in the next room listening when your Indian came to my house with your message to meet here. She heard everything, and I had to bring her. She wouldn't listen to reason."

Standish, with Leach and Keena, had now moved from cover

into plain sight. They watched the tall, red-haired young woman of slender and stately form, heightened by her dress of soft gray material.

"We can keep her here until the job's over," Keller was saying placatingly. "No reason why trouble should come from her being here."

"As to that, I can answer for me, but not for my men," Renshaw said dryly, flicking a glance at the steady interest in the faces of his men. Then he glanced back at the young woman. "Your husband is a damned fool, Missus Keller. But I reckon you know that. Permit me to help you down." With a certain courtliness native to him, Renshaw swung the girl down, gave a curt nod to her murmured, "Thank you," and turned back to Keller.

Standish gave her a full, curious appraisal. At the very least she was a quiet, soft-voiced lady. There was a bruise on her left cheek where her husband must have struck her in forcing her to come here with him. For no particular reason Standish felt a sudden quiet hatred toward Keller — maybe because he was part Indian, he admitted this honestly to himself.

Renshaw was saying to Keller in a hard voice: "I'm not gambling for a pig in a poke. You said there's big money in your bank. There better be."

Keller nodded swiftly, a feverish gleam in his eyes.

Ad Standish knew that gleam. His earliest remembrances were of a father who had reaped a small fortune running guns and liquor to the embattled tribe of Standish's own Indian mother. That, Standish knew, had been a marriage of convenience for his father to facilitate the liaison of his gun-and-whiskey-running to the Sioux. The motives of the white man's insatiable lust for gold had never been apparent to Standish himself who was only half Indian. But the red blood ran deep in him, as Renshaw often remarked, and for this reason the leader often had Standish do the jobs requiring great patience or stealth or woodcraft. The tedious watches, the tracking, the message-bearing — such as taking a message yesterday to the home of Keller (who had mistaken him for a full-blood Indian) in the very heart of the Wyoming cowtown of Indian Grove — were always assigned to Standish.

"There's money, all right," Keller was saying now. "I haven't been cashier there ten years for nothing. With the inside information I can give you on the bank, you can take out enough to make us all rich and without much risk."

"Yeah. Especially for you," Renshaw said. "You know . . . you're hungry, Keller. You're real hungry. I figured as much when you went to all that trouble to get in touch with a wandering bunch of bad actors like us. So we can knock over the bank that's given you a living for ten years."

Keller eyed the leader with a faint repugnance. "At least, I don't intend to make my living knocking over banks. It's a stinking business."

"But a business," Renshaw said softly.

"Just talking," Keller said quickly.

Standish arranged his blanket coat on the ground beneath a tree, then walked silently, still-faced, over to Keller's wife. "Ma'am, I've fixed a place for you under that tree. You best sit down."

Mrs. Keller looked up in surprise at him, and her blue eyes swiftly searched his face. Standish braced himself for the cold denial of a white woman's scorn. Instead, she murmured, "Thank you," with an unforgotten dignity and walked to the tree to sink onto his folded coat. *In her time she was treated like a lady*, Standish thought. *But that's long gone.*

Keena hadn't missed this by-play. He chuckled and, lounging over to Keller, said: "If I was you, I'd watch my wife around that noble Injun."

A remote, cold wrath stirred in Ad Standish, but his face did not change.

Keena went on amusedly: "He's the spawn of a whiskey runner and a Sioux squaw. The blood's bad, Keller."

Standish felt the taut strain in his own face. For weeks he'd endured Simm Keena's random insults and had kept his place. He'd found that all people touched with Indian blood were tainted in white eyes. The offense of an Indian striking back at a white man was unendurable, unforgivable. But so were Keena's small cruelties.

Standish came slowly up to Keena. He said softly, "Shut your rank mouth," and slashed the back of his hand across Keena's face.

Keena gave way a step, lost balance, and back-pedaled to keep on his feet. He came up against a small deadfall and fell over it to the ground. Mouthing a savage curse, he was on his feet serpent-quick, reaching for his holstered gun.

Renshaw was at Keena's side and ready with an iron grip that immobilized Keena's arm before he could clear the holster. To Standish, Renshaw snapped: "Take it easy," and to Keena: "Sit down."

Keena was shaking hotly. "I'll kill him!"

"Sure. Now sit down." Renshaw glanced at Standish who still stood warily, poised on the balls of his feet. "You hear me? I said, take it easy."

"I don't give one little damn what you said," Standish responded.

"Don't be funny, Ad," Renshaw snapped, not conceiving a serious rebellion on his hands.

"I don't feel funny, Bart," Standish said slowly. "I don't feel funny at all."

Renshaw frowned. "You looking for trouble?"

"No. But I can take all you want to hand out."

Renshaw and Keena faced Standish stiffly, and Keller and his wife were watching apprehensively. Even the shambling Leach, in the act now of turning supper bacon in the spattering skillet above the small fire, stopped in mid-motion and carefully laid down his fork, ready for what might come. Renshaw and Standish watched each other warily.

Ad Standish thought sinkingly that he was pushing too far. And thought then, in a sudden prideful resolution: *No! Have it all out at once. There's just so far they can push a man.*

The wintry fury in Renshaw's face became tempered with uncertainty. After a moment more of hesitation Standish could see him deciding to let it go at that.

The leader said now in a lesser tone that made some token effort to salvage authority: "There'll be no more of this between you."

Renshaw turned away then with an air of no more than a faintly ruffled irritation. But Standish wasn't deceived. He thought with a calm fatalism: *He hates my guts now because I faced him down. And he knows I know it.*

They ate an early supper in a harrowing silence, Mrs. Keller sitting off by herself. Afterward her husband brought her a plate of food and she refused it — fifteen minutes later accepting a plate brought to her by Standish.

Keller went off to sulk by himself, and this time Keena said nothing. He found a bottle of whiskey in his saddlebag and nursed it along until Renshaw, cursing him roundly, took it away and broke it on a rock, saying they were doing the job tonight. And, by God, they were going to do it right.

Renshaw squatted against a tree smoking in the lowering dusk, brooding at the ground as though wrestling a knotty problem. Finally he knocked the dottle from his pipe, stepped over next to the fire, and directed the others to gather around.

"Pay attention now."

He smoothed out about two square feet of ground and with a stick began sketching lines and squares on it to represent the streets and buildings of Indian Grove, Wyoming. Plying Linc Keller with questions, Renshaw built up a detailed scheme in which each man knew his place. With Keller's first-hand help the leader went over names and locations of buildings, descriptions of key townspeople, roads to travel in case they became separated. He minutely timed and placed every move down to where to tie their horses and who'd watch them.

Keller raised an objection that Renshaw scratched without lifting his voice. "We need you with us, Keller. Need you to handle things inside the bank, once we're in there. You work there. You know where the biggest money is kept, how we can get at it quickest. Don't worry about your wife. I'm leaving Ad Standish here to take care of her."

Keller looked wildly at Standish. "But . . . ?"

"Maybe you'd rather I left Leach or Keena, huh?"

Keller looked at Keena's depraved face and at the vague-eyed Leach, and shook his head slowly. "It's as you say," he said almost inaudibly.

In the near darkness the men broke up to find their hobbled horses and saddle them. Standish remained by the fire, staring into its red-glow heart, wondering why Renshaw should be concerned about Mrs. Keller and could find no certain answer. He thought: *The old fox is getting devious.*

Standish could see Keller approach his wife who hadn't moved from her position by the tree. She looked up without speaking.

"You won't be sorry, Doris," he said. "We'll leave this place. You'll have wealth, fine clothes, everything you deserve. Everything I couldn't give you as a petty cashier."

"That you can as a petty thief? I am not going with you, Linc," Mrs. Keller said quietly.

"You will, Doris. No matter what you think of me, there's nowhere else you can go."

"And I tell you that I will not," she said in an iron voice.

"Don't try my patience," Keller said harshly. "I mean what I say." He abruptly switched to another tack. "I've slaved and sweated to give you a good home. Now I want to give you something better. And this is my thanks!"

Mrs. Keller showed him a sudden thin and withering contempt. "Don't shoot at the stars, Linc. They can't hear you."

"Please," Keller said wearily, almost pleadingly. "Consider it, Doris." As though seeing that there was no more to be said, he went over to the others to mount the horse that Leach had brought for him.

Settling easily into his saddle, looking like a gray-haired centaur, Renshaw wheeled his mount out of camp, lifting a hand to Standish in parting. "Take care of the little lady, Ad. Don't worry. You'll get your share. Even if you're not in on the job."

Renshaw's gaze settled briefly on Mrs. Keller. Then he rode out, flanked by Keller, Keena, and Leach.

Standish stood, rolling a cornshuck cigarette, watching Mrs. Keller, sitting listlessly against the tree and staring at the ground. She was a really beautiful woman. Thinking of Keller, remembering how he'd vacillated from overbearing to pleading against his wife's unwavering resistance, Standish thought: *The man's an empty barrel.*

The night was moving down over the grove. A stormy night wind stirred blackly through the high cottonwood boughs. Standish cupped his hands around the flaring match to light his cigarette. He looked up to see Mrs. Keller, watching him.

She said quietly, without preliminary: "You're a gentleman."

Standish shrugged. "Maybe I'm a gentleman. They call me an Injun."

"You are not really an Indian, then?"

"My ma was. My old man was white. Renshaw always says I may be only half Injun, but it runs deep. Maybe he's right. Keena says Indian and white together makes bad blood, and maybe *he's* right."

"There is one man who would not have agreed with that last," Mrs. Keller said quietly. "My father. He was a fur trader in the early days. He used to tell me that many Indians are of an inborn integrity that place them above all but a few whites."

Surprised at the easy and natural way he had fallen into conversation with this woman, Standish, usually reserved, said: "Your father was rare. Not many think that way."

"No, they don't." She added with surprising candor: "But I'm thinking you're very like my father. He had taken on some Indian characteristics from many years of living with them. You walk and talk much like him."

"Reckon your father was an honest man. But . . . no, Missus Keller, it has to run deeper than the skin. If I'm not bad blood, why'm I here?"

"Why did your leader leave you here to guard me, if he thought you were not to be trusted?" she countered. "Why not one of those other men?"

He said nothing, looking at her.

"I think," she said at last, "that you had little choice to begin with."

"Maybe," Standish said slowly, never having thought of it just this way. "Lived till I was ten with my mother's tribe. When the tribe went on the reservation, an officer's wife from the nearby fort adopted me. She raised me and educated me. I knew the white man's ways but still looked like and moved like an Indian. I lost half a dozen jobs because lots of white men won't work side by side with an Injun. Thought outlaws might accept a man on his own merit, if solid citizens wouldn't. Been

183

with Renshaw a year now."

"You see," she said. "You had no choice. Far less than I did when I made my mistake."

Standish knew she meant her husband. He said nothing.

"He's a coward," Mrs. Keller said quietly, then was silent a moment. "Maybe that's not right. It was as much my fault as his. When my father died, I married Linc because I thought I saw in him something that never existed. Waiting for a knight in shining armor. Then finding the armor was tarnished. So I never was a wife to him as I should have been. Probably that's much of what made him as he is now. Selfish and dishonest, as well as cowardly. When I overheard the message you brought him . . . telling him to meet this outlaw, Renshaw, here to plan a bank robbery . . . I knew that Linc had taken the last step down the ladder. I wondered for a long time what to do. To say nothing, to notify the sheriff. Or try to talk Linc out of it. I tried the last. When he found out that I knew, well, there was no talking to him. He went almost crazy. And here I am."

"What about when he comes back? Will you go with him?"

"I said I wouldn't," she said wearily, "but, of course, I will. I'm the only one that can save him from himself. Perhaps . . . I can persuade him to return the money. . . ." Her voice trailed off.

Standish said gently: "You can't make heaven into hell, ma'am. Can't make your husband more than what he is by painting him with rainbows."

"But that's only part of it," Mrs. Keller said hesitantly. "I owe this to him for not being a good wife before. Don't you see? I *have* to pay."

Standish nodded. Any Indian would understand. An Indian fiercely castigated himself for a fault. But Standish was only part Indian. He knew that a person should stop paying when payment was no longer of value.

"You think you can help him now?" Standish asked.

She bit her lip. "I have to try. You think I'm a fool."

"No. I admire loyalty. Rare thing."

She lifted her head and said: "Thank you," in a voice that only hinted at the unvoiced gratefulness in her face.

Seeing it, Standish felt something which touched a depth in him. He felt it move powerfully between them for one timeless moment. "Better try to sleep," he said.

Moving off in the grove a way and throwing out his bedroll under the trees, Standish stretched out tiredly, wondering if he should have told her his suspicions about Renshaw's designs on her. Still, why alarm her if he wasn't certain?

A lonely man all his life, a man of two races who was acknowledged by neither, Standish had found a rare understanding in a woman. It had fostered an odd, settling sadness in him. And a harsh decision, too. If Renshaw made a move to harm Mrs. Keller in any way, he'd have to reckon with Ad Standish first. Oddly calm now, and readied for what might come, Standish relaxed in his blankets and slept.

The outlaws returned when the first dawn stain touched the eastern horizon. Standish was roused out instantly by the tinkle of bridle chains and went forward to meet them. Renshaw, Keena, and Leach. It was as Standish had half expected. They were leading Keller's horse, but Keller was not with them.

The way Renshaw told it, they'd ridden into town at midnight and gotten into the bank without a hitch. It was as they were leaving that a townsman spotted them and shot Keller out of his saddle. The others had gotten away untouched and even shook the posse that tried to follow them down.

"They'll never trail us over the country we rode," Renshaw said, finishing. "Sorry about your husband, Missus Keller," he added blandly, "but it's all in the game."

Standish glanced at Mrs. Keller, standing with a stunned horror in her face. She hadn't loved her husband, but he'd been her husband.

Standish's jaw tightened. He thought: *Maybe the posse couldn't follow your trail, Bart. But I can.* Unnoticed by the others who were too occupied with the gold they'd gotten, Standish found and saddled his own horse and rode quietly from the camp. He followed the neatly covered trail the outlaws had made in returning. There was something he had to know.

It was much later when he returned to camp. As he rode in, Standish warily gauged the odds. Leach was sitting at the far side of the clearing, cleaning his rifle. Renshaw and Keena were squatted on the ground, playing two-handed stud with bank money. Mrs. Keller was sitting apathetically by her tree and barely glanced up as Standish dismounted.

Renshaw threw his cards down and stood, half smiling. "Where you been, Ad?"

"Picking up your back trail to find out what really happened to Keller," Standish said and watched the slow, poised stiffening of the three men.

It was all Standish needed, and in a fluid movement he drew his gun and cocked it, leveling it on the three. Mrs. Keller was looking up now, staring at him, and it was to her he spoke.

"Your husband wasn't killed in town, Missus Keller, and he wasn't killed by a citizen of Indian Grove. I didn't think so. Back-tracked the trail they made coming here. Your husband got out of town all right, but between town and here I read sign where one of the boys reined behind him and shot him in the head. I found where he'd fallen from his horse, then he was dragged off a way and buried under about a foot of sand. Where I found him."

"We covered all that," Keena said thinly. "We covered it good!"

"Why, Simm," Standish murmured, "you ought to've remembered. You reminded me often enough."

"Reminded you of what?"

"I'm half Injun. You don't hide things like that . . . even from a half Injun." Standish looked at Renshaw now, easing his gun around to settle squarely on the leader. "Why don't you tell Missus Keller why you killed her husband, Bart?"

A fine sweat-gleam covered Renshaw's face. "You letting a woman come between you and your friends, Ad?" Then in sudden anger: "Take that damned gun off me!"

"Friends?" Standish said. "You shot Keller in the back of the head. You . . . or Simm here . . . would need a lot less reason to shoot me first time you got the chance, after the way I faced you down this afternoon."

"What'll you do, then?" Renshaw asked.

Standish recognized the ultimatum in his tone. He felt the stir of an angry anticipation, thinking: *Now the fat's in the fire.* "I'll take you . . . and the money . . . to the sheriff in Indian Grove and leave it to him."

Renshaw said in a violent whisper, "Be damned if I'll give up to you! Take him!"

Keena's gun was out first, and Standish shot once, blindly, without really aiming. Keena dropped his gun and sank down on his knees with the pain as he clutched his thigh.

Renshaw snapped a shot at Standish, then ran for the shelter of the cottonwoods at the north end of the clearing. The bullet threw up dirt far to Standish's left, and then Standish ran, bending for the shelter of the limestone outcrop, shouting to Mrs. Keller: "Get down on your face!"

He saw her flatten herself on the ground and then went for the cover of the outcrop, just as Renshaw's second shot spanged harmlessly off the rotting limestone. Standish could see now only that Leach had taken up a position behind one of the biggest cottonwoods. For a while a wary silence hung over the seep except for Keena, groaning in the pain of his wound.

Standish heard the crashing of brush back in the grove, moving off to his left. Renshaw was trying to circle to get him from behind, knowing that Standish was trapped behind the isolated outcrop. And Leach was waiting to pick Standish off when he moved from its shelter.

Then the crash of a rifle split the air and drowned all other sounds. Standish saw that Mrs. Keller, lying flat and inching herself along, had reached the tree where Leach had leaned his rifle. Now she was shooting at Leach with his own rifle to keep him pinned behind the vantage point he'd chosen — so that he dared not show himself to shoot at Standish.

Standish left the shelter of the outcrop then, cutting wide in a low-crouching run to head off Renshaw in his circuit to get behind Standish. He saw Renshaw suddenly as the leader moved into a break in the cottonwoods. Surprise was on the man's face at seeing Standish, running to meet him. Renshaw swung his pistol up in a tight, desperate arc. Standish dropped in his tracks, pointed his own gun before him, and shot once by instinct. Renshaw, unable to aim in his pell-mell rush forward, plunged down on his face and did not move.

Standish moved over the fallen man, turned him over, then straightened, looking down at Renshaw. Here, at least, it was finished.

Standish circled back to the camp by the same way Renshaw had come, so that he was almost upon Leach before the man saw him.

"Don't bring that gun up, Leach" Standish said in a low voice. "You haven't a chance."

Leach let the gun fall to the ground in a mute token of surrender. Standish scooped it up and motioned Leach ahead of him into the clearing. Mrs. Keller came slowly to her feet and walked to meet them.

At mid-morning three riders paused near the residential outfringe of Indian Grove. Keena was tied into his saddle, only half conscious. Standish had let Leach go on his promise not to come back to this country. Keena needed a doctor's care, and Standish had no inclination to let him go free, knowing that Keena would never forget.

Pausing now on the edge of town, Doris Keller said to Standish: "Where will you go?"

Standish lightly slapped the heavy bags of stolen money slung from his saddle. "I'll give these . . . and myself . . . up to the sheriff. In view of that a jury might go easy. I'll try another start. Somewhere. Maybe this time, I can do it. You?"

"My uncle has a farm about fifty miles north. He'll let me come and keep house for him until I work something out." She looked steadily at Standish now. "I'm sure the law will be lenient with you. Perhaps you could come up there, too. The territory is still open to homesteading. You . . . well, you might start as your own boss on a place of your own."

"Would you want that?"

"Yes."

"I'll come," Standish said.

As T. V. Olsen continued to write, his horizons continued to broaden. Increasingly his male and female protagonists could only succeed when they pulled together, varying strengths in the one compensating for weaknesses in the other. He must have believed that to love God truly is to love change. Certainly the theme of change — so profoundly indigenous to the frontier — is aptly expressed by Mike Rhiannon in BLOOD RAGE (1987). Bernal Rubriz declares that men do not change just as a rattlesnake does not change when it sheds its skin. " 'A rattler ain't a man,' " Rhiannon responds. " 'A man can change . . . aye, change his whole life quick as an eye can wink. He can if he's got a reason.' "

Outcast's Chance

Johnny Ring stepped off the Redrock stage, gave the two young women, who were the only other passengers, a hand down, and then, no longer curbing his impatience, had his long hungry look around the town. It wasn't much — a dusty street flanked by false-fronted frame shacks — but to Johnny Ring this was home with all that meant.

It had taken a year of wrecking his health in long-working hours in an Eastern mill to show him that he belonged to this country. Some men could live in cities; some could not. Twenty now, and orphaned since the time he was twelve, Johnny Ring had lived from hand to mouth over most of the United States and its Territories.

One ordinary day, a few months ago, at a factory in Connecticut the picture of this dry mesa country where he'd lived long ago had come to his mind, and suddenly, of all the places he'd ever been, this seemed the best to him. He knew where he wanted to put down roots and live out the rest of his life.

A gnawing hunger and a growing tiredness from long sleepless hours on the stage drew Johnny Ring's gaze to Redrock's single hotel across the way. He picked up his valise and started obliquely along the street toward it, a tall, leaned-down boy with a gaunt and angled face that showed he'd become a man too early — by experience.

Johnny stopped in his tracks, hearing a woman's voice, low-pitched and angry, behind him. Glancing around, he saw that two cowhands had intentionally accosted the young women he'd helped off the stage. Johnny Ring dropped his valise. In five quick strides he reached them.

"You boys have lived long enough to know ladies when you see them," Johnny Ring said quietly.

The bigger cowhand stared stolidly at Johnny with no change in his sleepy, crafty face.

The slighter cowhand's gaze brightened with a spark of delight. He was a small, nervous, ferret-faced man, chewing restlessly on a straw. He said with a liquored slur: "You want trouble?" He shifted the straw to the other side of his mouth. "You got trouble."

The small man stood, hands on his hips, and waited, and Johnny knew that he intended to make him force the action, if any. Johnny Ring saw only one way to finish it decisively. He rushed the small man, who sidestepped and gave Johnny a teeth-jarring clout in the jaw as he plunged by. As he came dazedly about to face the small man again, the cowhand placed a hand against his bony chest and shoved, sprawling him hard in the dust of the street.

"Atta boy, Cope," the bigger cowhand said.

Johnny Ring got to his feet, breathing carefully against his aching chest, knowing with a bitter certainty that city life had left him too physically inept to handle even a man half his size. Still, he moved doggedly back in toward the small 'puncher. Then he stopped, seeing a gaunt man who had just stepped off a spring wagon drawn up on the opposite side of the street. The man came across.

The two young women had stepped onto the board sidewalk out of harm's way. Now one of them ran toward the gaunt man and caught his arm. "Cass," she said breathlessly, "thank heaven you're here."

"I'm here, Kit," he said gruffly. "What's the trouble?"

"Those two men insulted us. The young one tried to help us."

Cass nodded, and walked purposefully over to the two

cowhands. "You lads wouldn't be knowing who the young ladies are, would you?"

"I don't particularly care," the bigger 'puncher said sleepily.

"I'd care if I were you, Tolliver," Cass said. "They're the Maylin sisters, old John Maylin's daughters. Your boss won't be awarding you hearts and flowers for molesting 'em."

Tolliver's sleepy gaze flickered to alertness, then shaded warily. "A man can make a mistake."

"Especially a drunken man," Cass said. He waited, watching, as the two men left, going their way down the sidewalk.

Johnny glanced curiously now at Kit Maylin. She was a tall woman in her late twenties whose erect regal height gave her an aloof, inaccessible beauty. Her sister was about ten years younger, a slight, sunny-haired girl whose blue candid eyes had hardly left Johnny since his attempt to face down Tolliver and Cope.

"Hello, Julie," Cass said very gently to this girl. "You've grown up."

"You haven't changed, Cass Reno," Julie said shyly.

Kit asked: "Who were those men, Cass?"

"Hands from Payton's Blackjack spread," Cass answered. "The big one's his foreman."

"So George Payton still owns Blackjack," Kit said softly.

"I'm afraid so," Cass said wryly. "You've come home to trouble, Kit."

Without answering, Kit looked at Johnny Ring. "Are you hurt, boy?"

Irritated by the form of address, Johnny said curtly: "No." He added with constrained courtesy: "Thank you."

"Thank you for what you did."

"What I tried and couldn't finish, you mean, ma'am." Johnny bent to pick up his valise, then turned downstreet.

"Wait." Kit Maylin's voice stopped him. "Are you looking for a job?"

"Yes'm. Ranch work."

Kit turned to Cass. "Can't Doubletree use another hand?"

"I reckon Ray and I could stand some help. But this kid's not strong. He couldn't help you just now."

"That's not important," Kit said. "He tried." She looked at Johnny Ring. "Will you work for me?"

Johnny Ring looked at the girl, Julie, and wondered at his own thoughts. He said: "I reckon."

Late that afternoon, having ridden to the Doubletree spread with Cass and the Maylin sisters, Johnny Ring unpacked his valise in the bunkhouse. When he finished, and was washing up, a 'puncher about his own age entered the room. "Hi," he said. "You're the new man, I guess. Cass told me about you. My name's Ray Mack."

Johnny told Mack his, and they sat on their bunks, talking casually. Mack was good-humored and friendly as a pup.

Johnny knew that, if he wanted information, here was the place to get it — not from tight-lipped Cass Reno. He said idly: "Do the young ladies own this spread?"

"Yeah," Ray said. "The old man . . . that was John Maylin . . . died a couple of months ago. His two girls inherited everything. Missus Maylin's been dead for ten years. The girls have been in Boston for the last five years. This is the first time they've been home, the first time I've met 'em. Old Cass has been ramrodding Doubletree for thirteen, fourteen years. He and I have been holding it down alone . . . not that it's much bother holding down a vest-pocket spread."

"Who's this Payton I hear tell of?"

"Payton owns Blackjack. It's a fair-sized spread next to ours. There's a long-standing feud between us and Blackjack. Payton

would have run right over us a long while back, except. . . . "
Ray hesitated.

"Except what?" asked Johnny.

"I talk too much. Maybe, though, you ought to know, if
you're staying on here. I hear talk, just rumors, mind you, that
Payton used to cut a fancy loop around Miss Kit. He courted
her for years. The talk is that the reason she went East while
her sister was in school there was to get away from Payton. Say,
don't you quote me on this."

"I won't," Johnny said, and glanced at the doorway. He saw
Cass Reno standing there with his stern eyes sharply on them.
Johnny wondered how much he'd heard. He wouldn't care to
run afoul of the man.

Cass was in his forties, but his gaunt frame seemed tough
as jerky, and his face looked like rough-hewn granite. All Cass
said was: "You boys better get something to eat, then go to
bed. You'll be digging post holes tomorrow."

The three of them were up with the dawn, loading cedar
wood posts into the wagon. Ray grumbled and groused as he
slung a roll of wire on top of the posts, adhering to the traditional hatred of cowhands for post-hole digging. Cass overheard
him.

"Bring your rifle along, kid," Cass said. "Maybe you'll get
a chance to shoot off something besides your mouth, for a
change."

"On a fencing job?" Ray asked puzzledly. "Are you expecting
trouble, Cass?"

"We're fencing off Indian Spring," Cass said grimly. "You
boys ride the wagon, and I'll get my horse."

Ray got his rifle from the bunkhouse. With Johnny Ring
beside him on the seat, he rode out toward the east. Johnny
asked: "What's important about Indian Spring?"

197

"Both Doubletree and Blackjack use it to water stock," Ray said, "only it's a dry season, and Cass figures there's not enough water for both of us. He told Payton so. Payton didn't listen. So Cass is fencing it off."

The spring was a tepid water hole, lying in a sage-fringed bowl of sun-cracked mud. Cass caught up with the wagon as it reached the spring, and the men set to unloading it with a tacit need for furtive haste, quickening their movements. Johnny Ring saw why when the two horsemen rode up from the west.

Cass and Ray stopped work. Cass wiped his brow and settled onto a log to await their arrival. The horsemen stopped at the rim of the natural bowl where the spring lay. One was the small Blackjack 'puncher, Cope, the other, a big, bland-faced man in his middle thirties. He cast a musing eye over the three men, then said: "Cope told me he saw your post wagon heading for the spring, Reno."

"And what follows from that?" Cass asked dryly.

"That you're not fencing anything," the bland-faced man said gently. "Move your stuff out of here."

Cass came stiffly to his feet, his long arms hanging loose. "I told you, Payton . . . there's water and graze for your cattle north, behind the big mesa. It's a lot closer for you than for us. But there's not enough here for both of us."

Payton started to answer, then stopped, his gaze shifting away as another rider, following the Doubletree wagon tracks, came toward the spring. It was Kit Maylin. She pulled her horse up near Payton. She was very good to look at in her gray riding suit.

"Hello, George," she said coolly.

"Hello, Kit," Payton said. "It's been five years. You're more beautiful than ever, I see."

His tone was casual. Johnny Ring thought that, if the gossip

198

about Payton's roughshod courting of Kit were true, the man hid his feelings well.

"What are you doing here, Kit?" Cass asked.

"Riding," she said. "What are you doing here, Cass?"

Cass reluctantly explained why he was fencing the spring, and Kit said thoughtfully: "Why, that sounds reasonable, George. There's no valid reason for you to hog this water hole when there's other water accessible to you. We have no other source."

"I wanted to talk to you about that, Kit," Payton said, "and this is as good a time as any." He pulled a folded paper from his pocket and handed it to her.

"What's this?" she said, frowning.

"A quitclaim," Payton said smoothly. "A deed of release to me of all claims on water rights on this section . . . signed by your father and witnessed by my foreman, Tolliver."

"Don't smudge it, Kit," Cass said dryly. "The ink's probably still wet."

Kit looked stunned. Her face was white as she looked from the document to Payton. "I can't believe this, George. Dad must have known that Doubletree couldn't continue operation if it lost possession of Indian Spring."

"He knew, Kit," Payton said. "Your father wanted you to sell out."

"But why?"

"He was afraid of your dying an old maid as long as you had the independent ownership of your own ranch. He didn't want to make the whole decision for you, but he did want to prod you toward a decision. When he knew he was dying, he sent for me. By giving me all claim to Indian Spring, he thought he could force you to sell Doubletree and prompt you to marriage with a man who could provide for you."

"Preferably you?" Kit asked scathingly.

"That's how I wanted it five years ago, Kit," Payton said. "I still do."

"I think this paper is a forgery, George," Kit said coldly, handing it back to him. "Dad was a hard man, not a cruel one. He would never force me to a thing like this."

"I'm afraid he would, my dear. Hadn't he always pressed you to get married?"

"Well, yes."

"And despite our professional differences, hadn't he always regarded me as a prospective son-in-law?"

"Yes, I'm afraid he did," Kit said quietly.

"Then, why argue? Even a small ranch is too much responsibility for a woman. If you and your sister will sell to me, you can have a home for life on my ranch. You'll have all the comforts, and you can let me worry about how to pay for them."

"But what about Julie? And Cass? He couldn't leave Doubletree after all these years."

"Your sister would live with us, of course. And there's a lifetime job for Cass on my crew."

"Oh, no, there isn't," Cass said dryly. "When I leave Doubletree, I leave the country."

"Suit yourself," Payton said. "What about it, Kit?"

She bit her lip, looking from Payton to Cass, then said suddenly: "I can't, George. I'm going to hang on. I don't know how, but I will."

Payton nodded, his face empty, unconcerned, perhaps faintly irritated. "Can you, Kit?" he murmured. "Can you hang on now?"

"We're going to try, mister," Cass said. "That fence is still going up."

"No, Cass," Kit said in a troubled voice. "We don't want trouble." Her voice trailed into almost a plea as she looked at Payton.

The rancher said in a kindlier voice: "Use the spring anyway, if you've a mind to, my dear . . . at least until you've made up your mind for good and all. Come on, Cope." Payton turned his horse, and he and his man left.

Kit remained unmoving on her pinto, staring at the ground. Johnny Ring saw that she more than half believed the quitclaim was authentic. In allowing her to use the spring when her legal right was gone, Payton had made a cleverly diplomatic gesture of open-handedness that had deeply impressed the woman.

Cass's dry voice was startling in the silence. "Come on. We might as well get these posts back on the wagon."

Kit smiled wanly. "I'm sorry, Cass, but I think that would be best for now." She began to turn her horse on a sharp rein, then stopped, and swung back. "Cass, did you ever hear mention of Dad's releasing his claim on Indian Spring . . . before now?"

Cass prodded his hat to the back of his head, his frosty gray eyes bleak. "Not a thing. And I doubt that your father ever heard of it, either."

There was other work to be done, and Johnny Ring threw himself into it with a will. He felt a slow return of his weight and health. There were rides now and again with Julie Maylin. A frail girl, she needed exercise and fresh air, but Kit would not let her sister ride unescorted on the open range.

Sometimes it was Johnny who accompanied Julie, sometimes Ray Mack. It became a friendly, light-hearted rivalry between the two young men. But Julie preferred Johnny Ring, and she let it be known to him in the occasionally serious talks they had during the course of their rides.

Johnny tried to steer away from such talk, though the attraction of this girl was half the reason he'd first come to Doubletree. If he began to court Julie, there would be trouble with Kit Maylin whose influence over her younger sister was too strong — almost domineering.

For a time Johnny Ring went with the tide of things, carefully minding his own business. But it could not last. On an afternoon ride two weeks after he had come to Doubletree, he and Julie spoke seriously of their past experiences. Johnny's life had been a hard one, and he said so.

"It won't always be that way, Johnny," Julie said softly. "You'll see."

There was almost a suggestion of promise in her voice, and Johnny Ring knew that he was reacting to it without wanting to. Back at Doubletree he assisted Julie out of the saddle. When she swung down, she came easily, naturally, into his arms. He kissed her swiftly, then stepped back. He saw only half-hidden pain in her face.

"Johnny," she said softly. "Johnny, I thought you meant it."

"I mean it, Julie," Johnny Ring said dismally. "I mean it more than anything." Then, being too honest not to have it all out at once, he said: "I want to marry you, Julie. It's been that way with me since the first."

"Oh Johnny, that's what I want!"

"And Kit?" Johnny Ring asked quietly.

"I know," she said soberly. "I know, Johnny."

"I'll talk to her."

"It won't help. We'll run away."

"No," Johnny Ring said flatly. "I've been running all my life. It's no good. I know. If we start running, we'll be running all the way to the end of the line. I'll talk to Kit."

Johnny went up to the big house and found Kit Maylin in her father's office. The door was open. Johnny saw her toying with a pencil on her desk, while she stared moodily out the window.

He tapped at the door, and she glanced up. "Come in, Johnny. I suppose you want to marry Julie now?"

Johnny stiffened, then relaxed resignedly. "I reckon you saw us from the window."

"I did, and I'm vexed. I've seen it coming, but I gave you credit for having sense enough not to become embroiled."

"That being so . . . about all my sense . . . you shouldn't object to that marriage you mentioned."

"Don't bandy words with me, Johnny," Kit snapped. "I'm in no mood for it. How old are you?"

"Well . . . twenty."

"Twenty," she said dryly, "and Julie is not quite seventeen."

Johnny Ring was becoming nettled by this cold-faced, cold-voiced woman. "Ma'am, my father married when he was seventeen, my mother just turned fifteen. This is the West, not Beacon Hill."

"That will do, Johnny," Kit said stiffly. "And what does Julie say?"

Johnny Ring shifted uncomfortably. "She said we could run away."

"To where? You're penniless, and Julie can't touch what little Dad left her until she's twenty-one. I can see you and Julie trying to eke out your living as a pair of nesters in some tumble-down line shack. She's a frail girl. How long do you think she'd survive those conditions?"

Johnny knew Kit's argument made sense. Yet, because he'd been hurt, he wanted to hurt back. "I don't think you're worrying about Julie," he said slowly. "I think you're trying to hurt her because she's got more'n you could ever give a man."

Kit winced as though she'd been struck. Her lips tightened to a white line. But she stood her ground. "Perhaps I am a cold woman, Johnny, but I would never make Julie suffer for it. I can't let you hurt her, that's all. You'll have to leave Double-tree."

Feeling that he was tasting the full measure of defeat, Johnny went directly to the bunkhouse without even seeing Julie. His valise was packed in five minutes. At the corral he found a catch-rope and dabbed it on a bay gelding which Kit had told him he could take. He had swallowed his anger and pride and accepted the horse with thanks, knowing he'd not get far in this country without a good mount.

As he was tying his valise to the saddle, he heard Cass's gruff voice behind him. "Where're you riding, son?"

"Out. I'm through."

"Kit gave you your walking papers, eh?" Cass murmured, and added shrewdly: "About Julie?"

"Something like that."

Cass rubbed his chin, scowling. "Look, it's none of my business, but why not let me talk to Kit?"

"Like you said, it's none of your business."

"Don't play the long-suffering hero with me. Get a cinch on that temper. Don't go off like this."

Johnny swung into his saddle and then, looking down at Cass, said: "I wouldn't have to, if some man had taken Kit in tow long ago." He paused, adding wickedly: "Why not you, Cass, seeing how you feel about her?"

Cass was neither angry nor surprised. "It's obvious, eh?" He shook his head slowly, a kind of tired pain showing through his granite-hard features. "I'm too old and too rough, Johnny. It's too late for me. I've known that for the last ten years and more."

Watching Cass's towering, unbent form moving off toward the bunkhouse, Johnny Ring felt a brief stab of remorse for his gibe at the man. And then, because there was nothing more to do, he rode away from Doubletree without seeing Julie. Before he saw her again, he must prove to her that he intended to stay in this country and fight for her. Suddenly he knew how he could do it.

A short time later he pulled up his horse in the cottonwood-shaded yard at Blackjack in front of the squat frame ranch house. Payton, with his foreman, Tolliver, came out on the porch, idly talking. Both stopped when they recognized Johnny.

Tolliver picked his teeth and said sneeringly: "Here comes the gallant protector of ladies, children, and three-headed monkeys. I hear you're working for Doubletree."

"I was."

Payton noted the valise on Johnny's cantle and nodded toward it. "Did Kit give you the rush?"

"That's right," Johnny said. "Are there any jobs open here?"

"That depends," Payton said. "What was your trouble with Kit?"

Johnny Ring hesitated, then decided to tell the truth. "I wanted to marry her sister. She didn't like it."

Payton's beginning frown altered to a tolerant chuckle. "She wouldn't. I know how it is with Kit and marriage." He glanced at Tolliver. "How're we fixed for hands, Les?"

"Barney quit last week. That left us short-handed. We could use this man."

"Good," Payton said. "You're hired."

Johnny settled easily into the routine at Blackjack. The day following his arrival was Saturday, and that evening he decided to ride to Doubletree and see Julie. He was heading for the corral and contentedly picturing the surprise at Doubletree once they saw him, when Payton's voice hailed him from the house.

"You, Johnny Ring . . . come here."

Johnny walked up to the house, and Payton led the way to his study. Here he motioned the younger man to a chair, then sat behind the desk from him.

Presently the rancher asked: "How would you like to help teach Kit a lesson?"

Johnny's eyes narrowed. "Depends."

Payton leaned forward confidingly. "I want to kidnap Kit and hold her until she agrees to have done with this foolishness and marry me. She wants to, you know. She's just playing coy. I've waited for ten years, and I'm not going to wait any longer."

Johnny knew now that Payton's bland surface hid a hard-handed and coldly bigoted man who would take what he wanted regardless of who was hurt. Suppose that Payton carried through this plan, that he abducted Kit and held her? What might he do to her when Kit still refused him?

On the very verge of a flat refusal to help, Johnny was caught up by a sobering thought. He knew of Payton's intent, and the rancher was in no position to let him refuse. A glance at Payton's face — with narrowed eyes that held a warning glint — was a confirmation.

So Johnny covered his first impulse by saying: "Where'll you keep her? They'll search everywhere."

Payton relaxed and smiled at Johnny's indirect acceptance of his proposal. "There's an old line shack back on my land, by the mesa. We could hold her there indefinitely, and no one'd find her."

Johnny nodded casually. "That sounds good, sir. But what with losing her water supply to you and all, I reckoned she'd give in without this."

"Some day, perhaps," Payton said. "I forged her dad's name to that quitclaim, you know, but it doesn't seem to have been worth it. She still keeps me dangling. I figured abducting her might help her make up her mind quicker."

Johnny Ring glanced at the carelessly crumpled and discarded papers littering the floor about Payton's desk, and a thought came to him. He couldn't follow it up with Payton sitting here.

"We have to plan this," Payton continued. "You worked at Doubletree. You must know Kit's habits. When does she usually leave the house?"

Johnny told him that Kit's habits were irregular. She might ride all day or stay in the house for a week at a time. Payton considered that for a moment, then said they'd have to kidnap Kit right out of her room — and tonight was as good a time as any.

"There'll be a bonus for you for this night's work, Johnny. And don't worry, you'll get your girl. Once I break some of the sass and vinegar out of Kit, she won't be of a mind to stand in your way. Now, go over to the bunkhouse and tell Tolliver and Cope that I want to see them. You come back, too."

Leaving the house, Johnny had an impulse to run for the corrals, get his horse, and ride to warn those at Doubletree of Payton's plan. But he knew Payton could see him from his study window, and that he could never rope and mount up a horse before Payton had the whole crew on his back. The only thing he could do now was to wait, to play along, and look for his chance.

The four riders paused near the Doubletree outbuildings, sitting their horses in the moonlit night, watching the lighted house and bunkhouse.

"Get this," Payton whispered. "Les, you cover the south side of the house, in case anyone at the bunkhouse gets curious. Cope, you cover the north side of the house. If you do any shooting, shoot to scare. Got it? Johnny, you know the layout of the inside. You'll help me get Kit out."

Johnny wished for the hundredth time that he had a gun. He alone was weaponless. Payton was trusting a fresh recruit only so far.

It was a matter of waiting now, watching the lights wink out one by one until Doubletree lay in darkness. When Payton glanced at his watch and said it was time, they ground-hitched the horses and moved in toward the house. Tolliver and Cope took their stations. Johnny Ring and Payton moved silently onto the verandah and let themselves in the front room through the one door that Johnny had known would be unlocked.

Moving ahead of Payton through the dark front room, guided by familiarity, Johnny knew that, if he were to break up Payton's plan, he must do it soon. Payton was behind him, and Payton was armed.

From the front room, they moved into a corridor off which lay the girls' rooms. It was here that Johnny made his gamble. He stopped dead in his tracks so that Payton, at his back, was brought up hard against him.

"What's wrong?" Payton whispered harshly. "You said her room was the last door."

"I'm not sure," Johnny whispered. "It might be one of these side rooms."

"You're handy as hell," Payton said cuttingly. "Get outside. I'll handle this by myself."

Johnny hesitated, wondering whether to jump the rancher now and try to get the gun. Then he thought: *He's too big for you. Get to the bunkhouse and rouse Cass and Ray.*

Johnny moved swiftly back through the front room, and paused there. Tolliver would be watching this side of the house, would see him if he crossed the open space between here and the bunkhouse, for he'd be silhouetted by moonlight all the way. *Play it bold,* he thought then, opened the door, and stepped swiftly onto the verandah.

He could see Tolliver's hulking form, standing stolidly by the corner of the house. As he walked silently over to the big man, Johnny briefly toyed with the notion of trying to argue Tolliver out of this — an idea he discarded as swiftly as it came, knowing it would be useless.

Reaching Tolliver, he spoke swiftly. "The boss said I should

208

stand guard by the bunkhouse, just in case. He thinks Cass might be watching for something like this."

Without waiting for an answer, Johnny started boldly across the open space to the bunkhouse, walking leisurely but feeling the cold crawling of his back muscles, expecting any moment to hear Tolliver call after him to stop. But Tolliver must have been satisfied because Johnny reached the shadow of the bunkhouse in safety. The Blackjack foreman could not see him once he stood within the inky shadow. Moving swiftly around to the side, Johnny fumbled the doorlatch open and stepped into the bunkhouse. He struck a match in the darkness.

As the flickering light probed through the room, he saw Cass on his bunk, propped up on one elbow, blinking at the light. He recognized Johnny immediately.

He stared, then said: "Hello, bad penny."

Johnny told him about it in a few taut words. Cass was on his feet in an instant. He always slept fully dressed, except for his boots. He yanked a drawer of the battered dresser open, hauled out his old Remington, and started for the door. He muttered: "Ray went to town. He probably won't be back till morning. It's up to you and me."

"Wait," Johnny said. "I need a gun."

"There's a rifle on the wall," Cass said and was out the door, running for the house.

Johnny wasted precious seconds striking another match to locate the rifle, then he followed Cass. He saw dark figures flitting away from the rear of the house and knew that Payton had gotten Kit out through the window of her room and was running for the horses. Johnny veered in that direction, shouting to Cass to follow, but his voice was drowned in the blast of gunfire as Tolliver sighted Cass, coming for the house, and started shooting. Johnny caught only a glimpse of bright spears of flame in the night as Tolliver and Cass traded shots, and then Johnny was gaining swiftly on Payton as he dragged the struggling woman toward his horse. The slight form of Cope moved directly behind Payton, covering his retreat.

Cope sighted Johnny and fired at him. Johnny felt the whining fan of the slug past his temple and couldn't shoot back, for Cope was in line with Payton and Kit. He flung himself sideways to the ground, rolled over once, and lay prone, skylining Cope over the sights of the rifle. Cope shot again, and Johnny, seeing the bullet spew up dirt far to his right, knew that the man was shooting blind, unable to pick him out against the shadows on the ground. Johnny squeezed off a shot at Cope and saw him fall.

On his feet again and running for Payton and Kit, Johnny heard hoofs sounding a sudden pulsing beat. Then he saw Payton's horse with Kit across the saddle cutting away from the other horses. Payton must have had his hand across her mouth before. Now her sudden scream slashed the night like a naked blade, spurring Johnny to decision.

Working the lever of the Winchester, he took careful aim at the horse's forequarters. With the roar of the shot he saw the animal crumple, his hind legs lifting and cartwheeling him on his back, throwing both Kit and Payton far out of the saddle.

Payton was on his feet immediately. Johnny saw the upswinging pistol in his hand, even picked out his rage-distorted features, and knew there was no time to waste. He swung the Winchester to a level at his hip and pulled the trigger.

Payton buckled at the middle and collapsed slowly to the ground like an empty sack. Kit lay unconscious where Payton's falling horse had thrown her. Johnny thought she was unhurt but knew he'd better not move her until he could get Cass here — if Cass himself were all right. Then he heard Cass shout his name and saw him standing by the rear of the house.

Johnny called: "Over here."

Cass ran toward him. Johnny could hear Cope on the ground, groaning and swearing in his pain. Payton was lying utterly still, where he had fallen.

The next day in the big sitting room Johnny explained to Cass, Kit, and Julie that he'd gone back to Blackjack early that morning and searched the litter of papers on the floor of Payton's office. He'd found several crumpled sheets on which Payton had practiced old John Maylin's scrawling signature — the one he'd forged to the quitclaim for Indian Spring.

"Those practice sheets ought to convince any court there was a forgery, in case any heirs of Payton's want to contest ownership of the spring," Kit reflected. "Johnny, can you ever forgive me? You've handled all this like a much older man."

Julie, at Johnny's side on a window seat, squeezed his hand.

"I suppose you'll be wanting that marriage soon." Kit smiled. "But I wish you'd both do me one favor. Stay on at Doubletree."

Johnny Ring glanced at Cass who was sitting uncomfortably, rubbing his bandaged left arm, where Tolliver had scored one hit before Cass had brought him down.

Johnny said: "On one condition."

"Condition?"

"Yes'm. Cass's wanted to say something to you for a long time. The condition is that you listen."

Kit smiled and her face softened as she looked at Cass Reno. Johnny knew then that Cass's unspoken mind had been known to her for a long time — and that she'd done a lot of thinking in that time.

"I've always depended on Cass for advice," Kit Maylin said softly.

During the years when he was writing primarily short fiction, T. V. Olsen did produce two short novels. "Lone Hand," which appeared in *Ranch Romances* (2nd December Number: 12/13/57), was one of them. There is no question that this story, with Trace Keene's attempt to live down his past as a gunfighter, was influenced by Jack Schaefer's Western fiction, especially his most notable novel, SHANE (1949), although in Trace Keene's case he has become demoralized by the effort. This only points up once again that, however much action there might be in one of T. V. Olsen's Western stories, he never wavered in his awareness of the deeper psychological dimensions of his characters.

Lone Hand

I

More than most white men Trace Keene knew the habit of patience. He had hunkered for two hours in the tall grass, waiting with the patience of an Indian for the horses to graze nearer. He was leaned down and hungry-looking. He hadn't shaved in two weeks; a thick black beard gave him a tough, raffish look. His hands played idly with the coils of his catch-rope.

While he watched, the horse herd began to drift farther away. He swore under his breath and eased stiffly to his feet. He took the cigarette from his lips — tight-set, wind-chapped lips in a thin sunburned face.

His throat was parched with thirst, and the acrid dry taste of smoke wasn't helping. He ground the cigarette under his heel, mashing it deeply into the earth. Trace Keene was a saddlebum who hadn't an acre of land to his name, but the scruples of a better past made him take care against starting a fire on this sweeping expanse of New Mexico grass.

There were fifty head in this bunch, that was now due east of him. It was late afternoon, and the sun was in the horses' eyes. There was little or no wind to carry the man's scent, so maybe he could approach nearer. He left his saddle in a clump of grass and began to work in. When he was as close as he dared get, Trace squatted again, shook out his loop, and waited.

In a half hour the herd began to shift again, this time in his direction. The man's muscles trembled, partly from tension, but also with the quivering weakness of thirst and a belly-knotting hunger. Unless he could rope one of these horses, he'd be stranded. He was miles from any habitation and too exhausted to go ahead on foot.

The horses were so close now that Trace could make out the brand mark on the hip of the nearest. It was a curious design, unknown to him. Not that he cared who owned the animals. His legs were already cramped from miles of unaccustomed walking.

After a day of it he'd found that a man used to the saddle — even one who had the ingrained hatred of a Westerner for a horse thief — could be restrained only so long. Though he intended only to borrow an animal, it was an act which could easily be misconstrued.

Holding his breath, Trace inched to his feet, then lunged toward the herd, whirling his loop wide for the throw. Seeing him, the horses snorted and began to bolt. Trace had already singled out a big buckskin, toward the flank of the herd. Now he made his cast. It settled true as a die.

Trace came to a stop, his heels clinging hard at the earth as he braced himself for the moment when the buckskin's rush took up the slack. The rope whipped to a taut line; the horse reared high and began to plunge wildly. Trace hung on as the animal bucked himself out, finally coming to a lathered, blowing standstill.

Talking low, soothingly, Trace began to walk toward the horse, coiling his rope. The animal stood motionless, save for a quivering of muscles as Trace laid his palm on its neck. It was not new to ropes or to men.

It was a good horse for a broke, ragged drifter. Wry bitterness curled the corners of Trace Keene's mouth. Well, he could dicker with the owner when he located the ranch headquarters. He could at least get a feed there, and maybe he could keep the horse, if the rancher would let him work out its price.

Trace, always short on optimism, thought it was more than likely that the rancher would be enraged at his presumption. Borrowing another man's horse, no matter what the circumstances, was not a healthy business.

He led the horse back to where he'd left his saddle, saddle blanket, and bridle. He cinched on the rimfire rig, bridled the buckskin, and then removed the rope. When he mounted, the animal pitched a little, but he got it under quick control and set it north at a brisk pace.

Trace pulled up as he mounted the shoulder of a steep rise and came face to face with four riders just ascending the opposite slope. The leader reined in, raising his hand to halt the others, then cantered forward to meet Trace.

Trace judged him to be not past twenty, a man with the wiry slenderness of youth and a cocky set to his shoulders. He wore Mexican *taja* leggings and a fancy *charro* jacket. His young face was darkly handsome in a sharp-etched way. His richly-tooled saddle was decorated with silver conchos. His horse was a splendidly built blue roan with the same strange hip brand the buckskin wore.

The man's eyes glinted, almost with a wicked anticipation. "Stranger, that's a Skull horse you're riding."

"Sorry." Trace's voice came huskily from a parched throat. "I had to borrow it from that herd. My bronc' broke its leg in a pothole this morning. I had to shoot it. I've been on foot all day. I figured I'd never make it to a town or a ranch without a horse."

The youth turned to one of the three men who now moved forward to side him, his grin wolfish. "He said he borrowed it, Trask."

Trask Ermine rolled a dead quirly between his lips. "I heard him."

Trask wore his sun-bleached hair collar-length; he wore his

gun low. He was wide-shouldered but with the pared hips of a horseman. His cold, pale eyes bored into Trace's. He gave no sign of recognition, nor did Trace.

Yet they knew each other of old, from Texas trail days. Trask Ermine hadn't changed a bit, but Trace knew that he himself had changed considerably. He could see Trask's curiosity behind the opaque mask of his face.

"I heard him, Chad," Trask repeated. "Funny, isn't it?"

"Funny," agreed Chad, still grinning. "Stranger, this is Skull range, and that's a Skull horse. You'll have to do better than that."

Trace said patiently but with a sinking feeling: "I told you, it's just a loan. I was looking for the ranch headquarters."

"North? With headquarters due east?"

"I'm new to this country."

Chad undid his lariat from the pommel. Idly he shook out a coil. "You must be. You have a few things to learn about it, such as that horse thieving is frowned on."

"Now hold on."

Trace's words were jerked off as Chad's noose snaked out, settled over his head and shoulders, and tightened, pinning his arms. The buckskin shied in fright, and Trace was dumped off and dragged to the ground.

He grabbed the rope, tried to pull himself up along its straining length. But Chad had taken his dallies by now, and he simply spurred his animal sideways and dragged Trace for two yards on his face and belly. Trace rolled on his back but made no effort to get up.

"You're learning already," Chad said. He stepped from his saddle and sauntered over to Trace, who said nothing, only eyed him with cold fury.

"You'll swing for this day's work, friend," Chad said. "But, right now, it's that cocky-drifter look of yours that's gotten under my skin. It bothers me. Get up."

He pulled his pearl-handled six-shooter and balanced it in his hand.

Trace climbed slowly to his feet, bruised and sore, his mouth clotted with rage. He knew that Chad meant to pistol whip him, and he didn't intend to stand still for it. He lowered his head suddenly and drove in low, slamming Chad in the pit of his stomach.

The youth gasped and went down, jack-knifed with pain in the grass. Trace used the brief slack in the taut rope to lift off the noose, then swung to face Chad.

It was Trask Ermine who reacted first. He wheeled his mount in close to Trace and swung low in his saddle to slam the barrel of his pistol along Trace's skull. Pain burst in Trace's head as he fell, but he held onto consciousness. With his ear to the ground, he picked up the hoofbeats of other horses approaching.

When he was able to focus his eyes, Trace saw that a towering man with gaunt, ascetic features had joined the group. He was dressed like a prosperous cattleman in fringed leather *chivarras*, polished knee-length boots, a white broadcloth shirt with a string tie, and a newly blocked gray Stetson. His white mustaches bristled like sabers above a thin mouth bracketed with severe lines. His question carried harsh anger.

"What's going on here, Trask?"

His gun sheathed, slouched easily now in his saddle, Trask lifted a lazily remonstrating hand. "Why, we found this drifter on a Skull horse, Mister Breakenridge. He claims he just borrowed it, that he was trying to find Skull headquarters."

"I suppose it wouldn't occur to you . . . or to Chad . . . that he might be telling the truth?"

It was a girl's voice, and now she reined into view from behind the others, her gaze fully on Trace Keene. She wasn't

219

more than eighteen, slim and lithe in a yellow silk blouse and brown riding skirt. Thick-clustering auburn curls flowed past the restraint of a narrow-brimmed felt hat.

"Let me handle this, Paula," Breakenridge told her in the tone of a man who brooked no opposition. He glanced now at Chad. "Are you all right, son?"

"Good enough to finish what I started," Chad said hotly. "Pa, this damned drifter. . . . "

Breakenridge cleared his throat authoritatively. "That will do, Chadwick." His tone was noncommittal, but he glowered hatred at Trace. "You," Breakenridge said, "what's your name?"

Trace climbed to his feet, swiping at his dusty knees with his battered hat, and met the man's chilly stare. "Trace Keene. Did you train your whelp to pistol whip a man with his arms tied?"

"Drifter," Breakenridge barked, "keep a civil tongue in your head!"

The girl laid a placating hand on his arm. "Please, Uncle Dock. May I talk to him?"

Dock Breakenridge frowned. "Need I remind you, my dear, that I'm manager of this ranch till you're of legal age? At any rate, this is not a woman's affair. You'd better go back to the ranch, Paula."

There was a half smile on Trask Ermine's lips. "He might even be one of the bunch that's been hitting your cattle from the hills, Miss Harper."

The girl's color was high. "You men seem to have reached a verdict without even a token trial. But I *will* talk to him, Uncle Dock. And I'm not leaving till I'm satisfied."

There was a stubborn light now in the blue eyes that met her uncle's unflinchingly.

Breakenridge's face was dark with anger; his spine was stiff

220

with it. His iron will was matched by that of a young woman. Then he settled back, his saddle creaking with the relaxed weight. His voice shook slightly.

"Very well, my dear. If you're bent on making an idiot of yourself, go ahead."

Paula hesitated, taking in Trace Keene's often-patched clothes, the absence of a gun at his hip, the stark reserve in his gray-green eyes. She looked faintly puzzled, as though sensing something in this man that didn't match his worn appearance. It put Trace on guard.

"Your voice," she said. "You're a Texan, aren't you?"

"Yes, ma'am."

"Did you intend to steal the buckskin?"

His laugh was a parched rasp in his throat. "I was just drifting through. This is new country to me. I've been lost in it for a week. Three weeks ago my grub ran out. My canteen's been empty for two. This morning my horse broke his leg in a pothole. I borrowed the buckskin, intending to find the owner and work out the price, if he was agreeable."

She nodded thoughtfully. "That sounds reasonable to me."

Breakenridge rapped out: "Paula, can't you see he's using a grubline tramp's gall to run a sandy on you and get a good horse into the bargain?"

"Can't you see he's half starved and nearly dead of thirst into the bargain?" she retorted. She swung back to Trace. "Get the buckskin and ride to ranch headquarters with me. We'll discuss the horse after you've had something to eat."

As Trace walked over to the buckskin, which was now grazing nearby, he heard the angry lift of her uncle's voice. "You're making a bad mistake, Paula. This will earmark Skull as a soft touch for every flea-bitten drifter in the country. Mark my words, you'll regret it."

II

It was an hour's ride to Skull headquarters, which was a hodge-podge of randomly sprawled adobe buildings set in a deep vale between grassy hogback ridges. The men dispersed to the bunk-house while the two Breakenridges, with Trace and Paula, rode on to the main house and dismounted at a hitch rack running the length of the broad front gallery.

The house, with its yard-thick adobe walls and heavy wooden doors and window shutters, had almost the appearance of a fort. Breakenridge dismounted and walked into the house without a word or glance for his niece, but Chad lingered by his horse.

With a significant glance at Trace, he said to the girl: "Sure you'll be all right, honey?"

"Perfectly, Chad," she said coolly. "I'd rather talk to Mister Keene alone, if you don't mind."

"Just as you say." Chad lifted his shoulders in a shrug and then ambled away.

Paula Harper led Trace through the comfortably furnished rooms to the kitchen. Trace drank three dipperfuls of water. Paula indicated an oilcloth-covered table. "Sit down, Mister Keene." She unpinned her hat and removed it, calling: "Sarita! Sarita! Where *is* that girl?"

A young Mexican woman entered the kitchen from a side door, smoothing an apron over her hips. She gave Trace a bold gliding glance out of dark, long-lashed eyes and said softly: "¿Señorita?"

"You may start preparing supper."

The girl busied herself at the stove. Trace Keene realized he hadn't removed his hat. He did so now, self-consciously, and set it on the floor. Paula gasped.

"Your head! There's a deep gash, and blood!"

"Yes'm. Your foreman did it . . . if Trask Ermine is your foreman."

She flushed. "He is, but Uncle Dock hired him, not I. Sarita, get clean cloths and hot water."

She came close to Trace and examined the gash in his scalp. He was conscious of her clean-scented nearness, the gentleness of her slim fingers. It made him uncomfortable.

He sat stoically, his arms folded on the table, as the girl washed his wound and dressed it with sweet oil and bluestone. She made a rough bandage from a piece of wash-faded material.

The food was ready by then, and Trace ate in silence, not speaking till he'd washed down the last mouthful with his second cup of coffee. He thanked the girl politely, reached for his shirt pocket, then let his hand fall.

"Smoke if you like," she said. She was sitting opposite him, her elbows on the table and her chin resting on her hands. "Now, about the horse. He's yours, for a month's work on my crew. And after that, if you care to stay on, you have a permanent job with pay."

Trace glanced up in surprise from his tobacco and papers. "That's pretty sudden, Miss Harper, considering that your uncle and cousin might be right about me."

Her gaze was level and searching. "Perhaps. Haven't you ever had the feeling, on meeting a person, that here was someone you could trust?"

Trace deftly shaped his smoke and avoided her eyes. He said dryly: "Can't say that I have."

"Well, I did, when I saw you. And I need a man on my crew I can trust." At the question in his face, she shook her head, smiling. "I don't mean that there's a conspiracy formed against me, if it sounded that way. But Uncle Dock does all the hiring

223

and firing, all the buying and selling for Skull, without referring to my opinion.

"Of course, Dad's will left Uncle in complete charge of the ranch till I'm twenty-one. But I want the feeling that I'm *part* of things. Instead, I'm being shut out at every turn. Uncle brushes aside my protests with 'you're too young, you're a woman.' I know he's a hard man, and he has only my interests at heart. The responsibility of running Skull is no job for a weak person."

She smiled fully at Trace Keene. "But I'm going to run one bluff on him, anyway. I'm going to hire a new hand on my own, one who will keep me informed on ranch activities. What do you say?"

Trace lounged to his feet, holding a match to his cigarette. He blew smoke at the window. "I'm a loner, Miss Harper. I like it that way."

"You have a month to think about it, won't you?"

Trace hesitated, then shrugged. It had been a long time since anyone had been decent to him. He owed her that much.

"I'll think about it." He clamped on his hat and headed for the door, but paused there and turned back. "Mister Breakenridge . . . ?"

"Will see things my way, once I've talked to him. And I'll have him talk to Trask."

He admired the flat decisiveness of her tone. There was steel in this girl. "I think he will," Trace said soberly. He touched his hat, said: "I'll turn the horses into the corral," and left.

Leaving the corral, he went directly to the bunkhouse, carrying his gear. Trask Ermine didn't seem in the least put out by the news that Trace Keene was to be on his crew. In fact there was an obscure pleasure in his manner that puzzled Trace.

"Stash your duffel under that empty bunk," he said, grinning with some secret amusement.

The cook's triangle rang then, and the crew left for the cook shack and supper.

Back in the bunkroom afterward, they lounged about, playing cards or leafing through magazines, and ignoring Trace, who lay in his bunk, smoking. Their attitude toward him was cool. He'd expected no less, for a suspected horse thief was no welcome addition to any cow outfit.

But, idly surveying them through half-lidded eyes, he wondered now if that were the whole reason. They were a tough, even shifty-looking lot, most of them, to be workaday cowhands. It added to the strange, charged atmosphere he'd felt about Skull ranch and its people from the first.

There were crosscurrents here that he did not understand — a crew of hardcases, with a Texas gunhawk for a foreman; a hard-eyed, irascible ranch manager who wanted to run Skull with a tyrant's hand. He had learned that the mistress of Skull, a seemingly sensible young woman of quiet depth, had willingly engaged herself to her cousin, Chad Breckenridge, a helter-skelter hellion.

She professed faith in her uncle's ability to run Skull, yet had evidently clashed with him repeatedly on ranch policy. Then, there was the willing eagerness of the Skull men to hang Trace on a nebulous horse-stealing charge.

Suspecting him, as a stranger, of involvement in recent rustling activities had been natural enough — but Trask Ermine had mentioned it almost as an afterthought, and Chad Breakenridge had seemed strangely amused by the foreman's remark. Finally, since Trask knew Trace Keene, why had he carefully avoided even a hint of recognition?

Trace's head ached more from unanswered questions than from Trask's blow. He snuffed out his cigarette, swung from his bunk, and walked outside, breathing deeply in the cool dusk. It cleared his brain a little, but he decided to avoid speculations that only landed against blank walls. He wondered why he gave a damn, anyway. He had only to do his job and mind his own business.

Footsteps crunched behind him. He wheeled, tense and half crouching. Trask Ermine's laugh drifted on the still evening air.

"Guilty conscience, Trace?"

Trace relaxed, straightening, facing the foreman in the waning light. "Look to your own, Trask."

Trask's white smile was blandly contemptuous. "I have no conscience to trouble me, Trace. That's an advantage you never enjoyed, if I recall correctly."

Trace's lips tightened. He said nothing.

"I *thought* something was riding you," Trask said, nodding slowly. "It had to be something big, to turn Trace Keene into a down-at-the-heels drifter. You don't even pack a gun any more. Would that have something to do with it?"

"You have all the questions," Trace said flatly. "Find yourself the answers."

"Hell, I don't really give a damn *what* happened to you, if it makes you happy. But I'm sort of disappointed . . . about the gun, I mean."

Trace saw the feverish light in Trask's hungry eyes, and now he understood. It was the old, savage pride of the professional gunny. Once, a long time ago, Trask had pulled a gun on Trace Keene and almost hadn't lived to regret it.

As though echoing Trace's thought, Trask said now, softly: "I'm still carrying that chunk of lead in my brisket, Trace. But that was six years ago. I've gotten faster since then, boy . . . a lot faster."

"If that's why you're happy I'm staying on at Skull . . . so you'll get a chance to even the score . . . forget it," Trace said coldly. "My gun's hung up on a peg back in Texas. It's staying there."

He turned his back before Trask could reply, and strode away into the darkness. He stopped beneath the shadow of a giant cottonwood, his breathing hard and shallow with the angry riptide of his thoughts. Eventually Trask would try to crowd him to a showdown. He must not let that happen. He must not permit Trask to bring back a past he'd desperately sought to submerge beyond memory.

The sound of voices drifted into his consciousness. Only then did he realize that he'd stopped close to the house. He edged his gaze around the tree trunk and saw Paula Harper, Dock Breakenridge, and his son sitting in chairs drawn up on the flagstone-floored open patio at the rear of the house. Lamplight from a window spilled over them.

There was an angry lift to their voices that now carried their words to him clearly.

"I tell you, Paula," Dock Breakenridge was saying, fury plainly clawing at him, "that Darrow *must* be in league with the rustlers. His place is located by the mouth of Cray Cañon. That's the back door to the east hills, and you know we've found enough sign there to prove that our stolen beef was driven off that way. A cow thief masquerading as an honest man can bleed a range dry . . . and there's no stopping him unless a vigilante posse runs him off. We should have done it long ago."

"No, Uncle Dock," was Paula's flat retort. "You can't condemn a man on such a flimsy premise. As far as we know, Fred Darrow is no more than he seems . . . a hard-working man with a large family to provide for, and with only a small spread and a few stringy head of beef to do it."

Chad was slouched in his chair, listening with a lazy grin. "Maybe, cousin," he offered, "Darrow got tired of working a lot for so little and decided to try an easier way."

"The damned squatter!" fumed Dock Breakenridge. "His kind, with their slatternly wives and brats and their filthy hovels,

227

are a blight on any range!"

"That's what really gets under your skin, isn't it, Uncle?" Paula said evenly. "Your ambitions for Skull are bigger than your humanity. Well, understand this. I'll endorse no action to remove Fred Darrow by force, without proof of his guilt. I'll go to the sheriff to stop his removal, if necessary."

Dock Breakenridge came jerkily to his feet. "There is no point in discussing the matter further until you come to your senses and realize that you can't maintain a spread of Skull's size and authority by coddling squatters, rustlers, and horse thieves!" He spun on his heel and walked into the house, his back ramrod stiff with anger.

Paula sat unmoving in her chair, picking absently at a fold of her skirt, her face pale and withdrawn. She was more angry than chastened, Trace guessed.

Chad watched her for a moment, then rose leisurely and walked to the back of her chair. He placed his hand on her shoulder and bent his face to her neck.

She jerked irritably away, and stood up. "No, Chad. Would you go inside, please?"

Chad's dark face settled into a scowl. "What's the matter with you lately? You're touchier than a skunk-bit hill steer. Maybe you want to call it off."

"I promised to marry you, didn't I?" she said stiffly. "I don't break my given word."

Chad's expression was sullen with an angry determination as he skirted the chair. "Then quit holding out. I want a dividend on that promise, right now. Come here!"

"No, Chad!"

Her words broke in a muffled cry as he caught her arm and dragged her close. Trace left the tree in a dozen running steps. His fingers dug into Chad's shoulder. The kid gave one scared yelp before a hard-knuckled fist smashed his mouth and dumped him full-length, unconscious, on the flagstones.

Trace rubbed his knuckles and lifted hard eyes to the girl's. "I didn't mean to listen, but I stopped by the trees yonder and happened to overhear you."

She stared at him, one tanned hand at her throat. She'd changed from riding clothes to a print dress that outlined the swell of her young breasts and hugged her slender waist.

"I think," she began huskily, "that I'd better be glad you. . . . "

Dock Breakenridge stalked from the house, his mustaches bristling. "What's going on?"

He stopped at sight of the inert figure of his son. Chad stirred and groaned. Breakenridge's frosty gaze struck at Trace.

"Get out," he breathed.

"I hired him, Uncle Dock," Paula said sharply, "and I'll keep him. Chad deserved that."

Breakenridge plainly guessed what had happened, but his temper didn't diminish. "Just get him out of my sight!" He knelt beside his son and helped him to a sitting position.

Paula took Trace's arm and drew him hurriedly away toward the shadows of the cottonwood grove beyond the patio. As they stopped, he felt her hand trembling.

"Did it scare you?"

She swung to face him, her face dimly patterned by leaf-filtered moonlight. "Uncle Dock didn't. What frightened me was the expression in your eyes when he ordered you out. You looked ready to kill. That's why I got you away."

Trace passed a hand across his eyes as though brushing something away. "There was a time when I took orders from no man. That's hard to forget."

"I don't understand you," she said softly. "I never saw a man who looked so . . . driven. When I first saw you, I thought you were just another saddle tramp, full of his own bitterness.

229

But you had something else, too . . . pride and decency and principle. I guess that's what made me hire you. Tonight you justified that estimate." She shook her head in a frustrated way. "But I still don't understand you, and somehow it scares me."

Trace was silent for a tightly withdrawn moment, then he let out his breath harshly. "You took a chance on me. Maybe you deserve to know the story. It isn't a nice one."

III

He'd been a trail-town marshal back in Texas, getting the position and holding it by virtue of a quick, accurate gun hand. Because there was no other way, he'd enforced the law by violence, until violence had become a way of life for him, and a gun the answer to everything.

He'd made enemies, more than one of whom had hired professional killers — like Trask Ermine — to make attempts on his life. All of these had failed. He'd almost come to think he was invincible. When the axe finally did fall, from an unexpected direction, it was a blow from which he'd never recovered.

In those days Trace Keene had come to be hated and avoided even by the citizenry of his own town. He was "gun poison," a man to whom they gave a wide berth. He'd one friend, however, in Chick Lawton, who owned the livery stable. Chick was his counselor, his father-confessor, his friend in need. He was a venerable man who'd seen too much of life to condemn on appearances alone.

It chanced that a jayhawker gang had raided a trail herd just beyond town, had killed the trail boss, and driven off their small remuda. The next day in town one of the trail crew saw several horses from that remuda in Chick Lawton's stable. The cowboy

230

had accused Chick of buying the stolen animals from the jay-hawkers.

Chick had protested, saying he'd bought those horses from Reimboldt, the trail boss, three days before, after Reimboldt had made him a good offer. The cowboy had jeered that Chick was safe in saying that, since Reimboldt had been killed in the raid and couldn't testify otherwise.

The cowboy had then gone to Town Marshal Keene and told him the story. Trace had gone directly to the stable and cornered old Chick Lawton. "You're in trouble, Chick," he'd told the old man flatly.

"Why hell, boy," Chick had started to say, with a look of pained surprise, and began to reach inside his coat.

Instinctively, without thinking, Trace had drawn and fired, killing the old man instantly with a slug in the heart. It had been meant as a wing shot, but there'd been no time for a careful aim at such close quarters.

Then, pulling aside Chick's coat, Trace had found not a gun but a bill of sale tucked inside the old man's vest. It was a bill of sale made out to Chick Lawton as the purchaser of three horses owned by the Long J herders and signed by Cass Reimboldt, trail boss.

Trace Keene had hung up his gun in his office, saddled up, and ridden from town within the hour. He had ridden aimlessly, not caring where so long as the trail took him away from the town and the nightmarish memory of that scene. But he'd never, even in two years, outridden the memory of the look in Chick Lawton's eyes.

A silence followed on his words. At last Paula Harper said humbly: "What can I say to that?"

"Nothing," Trace replied flatly. "Don't try. It's done with."

But it was not done with, and never would be, for him. Yet there'd been the oddly quickening relief of pouring the story out to someone at last.

Now he touched his hat, said: "Good night."

"Wait," Paula Harper said. "You won't let what Uncle Dock said affect your decision to leave or stay on at Skull?"

"That depends," Trace said slowly, "on him. I don't like a man who jumps down my throat."

She took a step toward him. She said imploringly: "I know he's a touchy and bad-tempered man to work for, but, if you know about his life, you'd understand why." She drew a deep breath. "You see, he's not really my uncle, nor is Chad my cousin. My grandfather adopted Dock when he was an orphan boy. His parents were killed by Comanche raiders. That was forty years ago.

"Grandfather raised Dock with his own son . . . Jed, my father. Dad and Dock were as close as real brothers, living in the same home, attending the same school, squiring the same girls. When they married, it was a double wedding. In turn, they raised their own children . . . Chad and me . . . together, almost as brother and sister. The deaths of our mothers drew us all even closer."

"Almost," Trace repeated dryly.

She colored faintly. "Why, it was always just taken for granted that Chad and I would marry someday."

"I see," Trace murmured. "Convenient."

Her chin lifted spiritedly. "Just what does that mean?"

"Nothing. Sorry."

She was silent for a moment. "I know what you mean. It's a natural reaction. But doesn't it stand to reason, our ties are really closer because of the way we've been thrown together?" She flushed, and he knew she was remembering the scene on the patio. "Chad is a little impulsive, even wild, but marriage will steady him."

"Sure." Trace's hand rasped his unshaven chin in an em-

232

barrassed gesture. "Your grandfather left all of Skull to your father?"

"Yes, but Dad kept Uncle Dock on as unofficial partner with an equal hand in directing ranch affairs. And Dad's will provided for Uncle Dock's management of Skull till I turn twenty-one. Sometimes I think Dock is almost resentful of what he's called the 'charitable' regard of the Harpers for him. Yet Dad had complete faith in Dock . . . and so do I."

Trace said bluntly: "How did your father die, Miss Harper?"

She looked at him strangely. "You said that almost as if you knew he'd died violently. About four months ago he and Uncle Dock were out trailing a small bunch of Skull beeves run off by rustlers, when they were ambushed. Their horses were shot from under them, and Dad was killed. Uncle Dock barely escaped."

"Hasn't the law got a lead on these rustlers?"

"No, and they've been operating from the east hills for about two years. At first it was small pickings, but since Dad's death they've gotten bolder. Our men have scoured the back country, and the sheriff has taken out a couple of posses.

"They've found several branch cañons where stolen cattle were hidden, but no one has yet caught a sign of the raiders themselves. Dad used to say that it must be an experienced, well-organized band of rustlers, like the Hashknife gang from Arizona way or the Hole-in-the-Wall outfit."

"That might be," Trace said tersely. "Sorry to take up your time this way. I just wanted to know what I was buying into. I'll say good night again."

"I didn't mind." She smiled. "Good night, Keene."

As he headed through the windless darkness toward the lights of the bunkhouse, Trace came to the bleak conclusion that Dock Breakenridge would bear watching. So would Trask

Ermine and young Chad. The kid was pure coyote.

It had sounded to Trace as though the girl were trying to rationalize her feelings for Chad to fit an expectation of her father's, a tradition of her upbringing that she'd accepted as irrevocable. For a reason he didn't attempt to analyze, this disturbed Trace.

IV

After breakfast the next morning the crew assembled down by the corrals, as was the custom, and waited for the foreman to assign the day's duties. Trask Ermine did this in a monotone as though by rote. Trace guessed that Dock Breakenridge had already given Trask the morning orders to the letter, and that Trask was reciting them from memory.

This confirmed his previous opinion that Trask was only a figurehead here so far as his ability to ramrod a ranch this size was concerned. It was plausible that Breakenridge might hire a professional gunhawk like Trask in the face of the rustler threat, but why make him foreman, a position he was in no way qualified to handle?

Trask's sly glance settled now on Trace, almost mockingly. "Keene, you ride with me today." His gaze slanted to a narrow, sallow-faced 'puncher. "You too, Alf."

The group broke up, most of them heading for a fence-repairing detail. Trace saddled up and rode out with Trask Ermine and Alf.

They rode northeast in silence across an undulating sea of grass that rose toward piney foothills and distant purple mountains. Born on a ranch in the red sand wastes of the Texas caprock, Trace Keene could not fail to appreciate the magnitude of this grazing wealth. It was a land where many men might wish to sink roots, a country too big for one man's use, for one ranch to hold.

Trask led the way, seeming to know exactly where he was going and what he had in mind. A glance at Alf's sallow mask told Trace nothing at all. Though nettled by curiosity, Trace made no comment.

The three riders reached and ascended a timbered ridge which dipped, on its opposite side, into a small valley. They halted at the crest to blow their horses. Trace saw smoke wisping up near the bottom of the slope and picked out, through the screening of the trees, the gray roof of a recently built cabin of peeled logs. He glanced sharply at Trask now, meeting the foreman's sardonic grin.

"Don't mind a little trouble, do you, drifter?" Trask asked. "You never did in the old days, as I recall."

Trace said slowly: "What is this?"

"That place down there belongs to a squatter named Fred Darrow who's suspected of rustling Skull stock. We're to give him final warning to clear off Skull range. If he gets tough, so do we."

Trace said dryly: "Breakenridge's orders?"

"Who else gives orders on Skull?" Ermine's eyes narrowed as they searched Trace's face. "What's eating you?"

"As I understand it, Miss Harper wants Darrow and his family left alone till someone gets proof that he's been rustling. She hired me. I'll observe her orders."

Trace began to rein his horse around, then stopped at sight of the pistol in Trask's hand. The foreman's frozen smile did not reach his eyes.

"No, you don't, drifter. Breakenridge doesn't want the Harper woman to know about this, and you aren't going to tell her, understand? If you tell, you'll wish you hadn't." He motioned with the gun. "I figured I'd have trouble with you, so I brought you along to show you right away where you stand. You're in this with Alf and me all the way. Move ahead of us. If there's any shooting, you'll be smack in the middle."

Trace picked his way slowly down the slope, conscious of Trask's gunsight leveled on his back. Their horses' hoofs were muffled by a carpeting of pine needles. The timber thinned out toward the base of the slope. Beyond, the trees and brush had been cleared away around the cabin.

A man and two boys, both under ten, were splitting a pine log with wedges and sledge. Close to the building a woman was making soap in a blackened iron kettle.

None of the four took notice of the riders till they had reached the edge of the clearing. Then the woman lifted her hand to push back a strand of sweaty hair from her face, and saw them. Her eyes widened, froze, and her reddened hand came up to her mouth to muffle a scream.

The man looked up and lowered the sledge. He straightened slowly, a tall, loose-jointed young farmer. His shoulders were slightly stooped with hard work, his denims tattered and dirty. But his eyes were a sharp, unflinching blue between his slouch hat and his tangled red beard.

Darrow's eyes shifted to his rifle, leaning against a stump about two yards away, gauging the distance and the risk. A shot smashed across the bright hot morning silence, and the rifle fell to the ground with a shattered stock. There were bright flecks in Trask Ermine's eyes as he cocked his pistol again.

"You shouldn't even think about things like that, Darrow," he observed. "We want you to clear out. Skull can tolerate a penny-ante squatter, but not a rustler's friend."

"I don't know about any rustling!"

"I wouldn't expect you to admit it, but the signs point that way." Trask leaned forward with a grunt, crossing his arms on the pommel. "Now, how's it going to be? Do you move

236

off, or do we move you off?"

Trask's attention was wholly off Trace Keene now. Trace knew that, if he meant to declare himself, to settle the issue for good, there could be no better time. Unexpectedly, he rowelled his horse sideways. The movement carried him into Trask's mount, almost upsetting its rider.

With an angry oath Trask turned and struck swiftly at Trace's head with the gun barrel, as though he were slapping at a mosquito. Trace ducked, and the swing carried Trask off-balance. Trace caught the foreman's gun arm and hammer-locked it behind him. Trask yelled with pain as Trace twisted.

"Drop it," Trace said between set teeth.

The gun slipped from Trask's fingers, and Trace caught it, palmed it expertly up, and had trained it on Alf before the 'puncher could finish the upward twitch of his hand to his holstered sidearm. Alf's jaw dropped at the speed of this drifter who did not wear a gun.

"Finish your draw and throw your gun down."

Alf pulled his gun and dropped it in the trampled dust of the yard, where Darrow pounced on it with a wolfish grin. "Thanks, stranger."

"Get down," Trace told Ermine, releasing the foreman's arm.

Trask rubbed it gingerly, then swung from his saddle. Trace dismounted and stepped away from the horses, feeling the familiar heft of the six-gun in his hand, and hating it. He was damned if he'd be pushed into using it, yet he had to show Trask Ermine how the cards fell. There was only one other way.

He measured the foreman thoughtfully. They were of an equal height and build, but it looked as though Trask might break him like a matchstick. Yet, he guessed that much of Trask's stalwart physique was the easy flesh of too-soft living,

237

while Trace's lean gauntness was the rawhide toughness of privation.

"Just give me a gun, drifter," Trask said softly.

"I told you once it won't be that way," Trace said tonelessly. "I meant it."

He handed Trask's pistol to Darrow, who accepted it wonderingly. Then Trace pivoted on his heel and drove straight at Trask. The force of his rush carried the foreman off his feet, carried them into Trask's horse, which snorted and shied away. They fell into the dirt, rolling over and over.

When they came to a stop, Trask was on top, with an arm around Trace's neck, while he drove long, slogging blows into Trace's ribs. Trace strained with all his strength to loosen Trask's choking hug. He wedged his palm under Trask's chin and forced Trask's head back, inch by stubborn inch, till it faced the sky at a pain-wrenched angle.

With an explosive grunt, Trask let go and rolled away, coming to his feet like a cat. His eyes swung wildly, then stopped on the rifle ruined by his bullet. He ran to it, gripped it in both hands, and bore in on Trace as the drifter came off his haunches.

Trace ducked under the first swing, catching it on his shoulder, where the splintered stock bounded off at an angle. Then he was inside Trask's guard and fighting for the rifle. For a minute the only sound was the strained panting of the two men.

Then Trask suddenly let go his grip on the rifle and threw a punch which caught Trace high on the forehead. He landed hard in the dust, now holding the rifle so he could swing it like a club as Trask dove at him. The barrel slammed Trask across the neck and knocked him sidelong into the dirt.

Trace stood up and threw the rifle aside as Trask scrambled to his feet, half stunned. He tried to retreat, but Trace crowded him relentlessly, forcing him to slug it out, toe-to-toe. Trace's arms seemed weighted with lead; his battered ribs ached with gusty breathing; his face felt like raw beefsteak. Yet, he felt Trask's blows weakening, losing timing, and he knew he had the fight won.

He watched his chance and drove a left hook to the point of Trask's jaw that snapped the foreman's head back. Then Trask's knees simply folded. He plunged face down, and didn't move.

Trace stood erect, breathing heavily, his feet planted wide. His hot glance lifted to Alf. "Get down," he said. "Help me get him into his saddle."

Alf obeyed without a word. Trask came to and fought them weakly as they lifted him between them and loaded him onto his horse. Then he subsided, his head bowed on his chest, his hands gripping the horn.

"Get out, the two of you," Trace said shortly.

He watched as Alf, leading Trask's horse, rode up the slope and vanished into the pines. Then Trace swung to face the open-mouthed Darrow, who still held the two six-guns. He now proffered them to Trace.

Trace shook his head. "Keep them. I want to talk to you."

Darrow nodded, his fierce blue eyes puzzled as he surveyed this tall, lean, ragged man with cut and swollen features. "Sure, mister. We owe you a vote of thanks. Better come inside. My wife'll look to your hurts."

V

Trace sat at the rough board table in the shack while Darrow's wife washed the blood and dirt from his face. A horde of round-eyed urchins clung to their mother's skirt and looked on.

"Your hands are in bad shape, too," the woman said.

"They'll be all right, ma'am," Trace said. "Thank you kindly."

The woman sniffed and carried the pan of dirty water outside, muttering, "Men, always battling like mad dogs."

"Hush up, Amelia," Fred Darrow said flatly. "We're in debt to this man."

He sat across the table, watching Trace in silence as the drifter, refusing help, rolled a cigarette with stiff, swollen fingers and lighted it.

Darrow said then: "You're not one of the Skull hands, are you, mister?"

"I hired on yesterday."

Darrow's eyes hardened with suspicion. "Then why'd you stop the other two?"

"The owner of Skull is Miss Harper. She doesn't want you folks troubled. I take her orders. But Dock Breakenridge is manager, and he wants you run off. Trask Ermine takes Breakenridge's orders." Trace blew smoke and surveyed the squatter through its haze. He said bluntly: "Breakenridge thinks you're in cahoots with a local rustling combine. What about that?"

Darrow bristled. "It's a damned lie! I run my own stock, poor as it is, and nobody else's."

"Where is Cray Cañon?"

Darrow glowered for a moment. "So that's it. Cray Cañon

240

is the only pass to the east hills, and it comes out on the other side of the ridge yonder, close to my place. Back in those hills would make an ideal place for hiding stolen cattle."

"Breakenridge claims Skull beef was driven off through the cañon."

"I won't deny that," Darrow snapped. "I've found plenty of cattle sign back there myself and wondered about it. But any large-scale rustling has to be done at night. I'd have spotted the thieves long ago in broad daylight."

Unless Breakenridge was right about you was Trace's unvoiced reply. But, giving the squatter his silent regard, Trace was strongly inclined to believe Fred Darrow's protestation of innocence. Darrow's fierce eyes met a man's in a way that conveyed basic honesty.

He did have a belligerent way about him that you seldom found in the usual run of spiritless drudging rawhider, but this impressed Trace favorably rather than otherwise. Darrow had guts. Maybe the squatter was the man to help Trace solve some of the unanswered questions that plagued him.

Trace ground out his cigarette and leaned across the table, lowering his voice. "Darrow, you'd like to clear yourself in the law's eyes, wouldn't you?"

"Sure." Fred Darrow spat through the open door. "But I'm damned if I care what Breakenridge or his heel-flies think!"

"All right. I want to see Paula Harper get a decent shake. Let's put our heads together."

Much later, Trace mounted up and rode away, taking with him the squatter's assurance of cooperation. He knew now that he had a trustworthy ally in Darrow.

Trace arrived at Skull headquarters by late afternoon and turned his horse into the corral. After careful weighing of pros and cons, he still hadn't decided whether to confide his and Darrow's plan to Paula Harper. To do so would be to run the risk of the girl's displeasure and resentment, because of her blind trust in Uncle Dock.

Yet she must be courting some unvoiced doubt of Breakenridge that she would not consciously admit to herself. Otherwise she would not have gone over Dock's head to hire Trace to inform her on Skull activities of which her manager kept her in ignorance. In that case, it would ease her mind to know she had two allies. And she'd certainly be interested in Dock's orders to Trask Ermine to drive out the Darrows against her express wishes.

Still undecided, Trace turned away from the corral and headed for the house. He rounded a corner of the adobe structure, then came to a stop. Voices drifted clearly from an open window of the living room.

It was Chad Breakenridge and Sarita, Paula's Mexican housekeeper. Trace flattened against the wall, hating this eavesdropping but sensing that it would be worse if Chad were to find him here.

Chad's tone was bold and cajoling, and faintly amused. "Don't be like that, honey. Come here. What're you afraid of?"

"The *señor* should know," the girl said archly. "Is he not affianced to the *señorita?*"

"The *señorita* is an iceberg. I know a real woman when I see one. You, for instance, *querida.*"

The girl gasped. "No, *señor.*"

There was a long silence, then the rustle of clothing, a sound of ragged breathing. "I'll see you later, when it's dark," Chad whispered. "Outside, in back. Promise?"

"Oh, *sí, prometo.*"

"That's more like it," Chad said.

Trace heard the girl run from the room, heard a door close behind her. Then came Chad's soft chuckle. Trace slid away from the window. When he reached the corner, he started at a fast walk away from the house. So Chad Breakenridge was cheating on Paula, and by his own admission did not find their marriage an attractive prospect!

Then why is he going through with it? Trace asked himself. The answer brought him to an abrupt stop. Because his father was forcing the marriage. Why? Because when Paula became twenty-one, Breakenridge's managership would end, and his hold on Skull ranch would be broken.

Paula's marriage to Chad would help Breakenridge retain control. Trace hesitated now, wondering whether to tell Paula of this, wondering whether she wouldn't denounce him angrily, perhaps fire him. Could she really be this blind to what was going on under her nose?

"Keene. Oh, Keene!"

Paula had hailed him. He turned his head and saw her standing by a rear corner of the house. He walked over.

"Were you looking for me?" she asked.

She'd been digging in the little garden at the back of the house, and her hands and wash-faded blue skirt were dirt-smudged. With the fine arch of her throat golden against the white shirtwaist she wore, she made a warm, earthy picture that stirred a man. Trace thought of how she'd be hurt by what he could tell her now, and suddenly he made his decision.

If she knew of what had happened today at Darrow's, or about Chad and the Mexican girl, she might, if she didn't fire Trace in angry disbelief, carry a direct accusation to both Breakenridges. It would make them realize that Trace was working in the girl's interests against them. If he kept his mouth shut, it might throw the Breakenridges off-guard enough to make them overplay their hand.

He'd tell her nothing, Trace decided swiftly, until he could offer positive proof of the secret game Dock Breakenridge was playing behind her back. Without asking himself why, Trace knew that his reasons for helping her went beyond a casual debt owed her. She wouldn't be hurt if he could help it. Years of aimless drifting had left him without purpose; now, he had purpose, and it was a good feeling.

"No ma'am," he answered her. He saw her eyes widening on his face and felt a heightened wariness. His battered features were a betrayal.

"What happened?"

"I had a difference of opinion with Trask Ermine." He made it casual, hoping she'd accept the statement at face value. He added: "Trask and I knew each other in Texas. It's an old grudge."

"I see," she said coolly. "I presume it's settled."

"Yes'm. It won't happen again."

"I should hope not. This is a working ranch, not a prize ring." Surprisingly, a humorous gleam touched her gaze. "I saw Trask a while ago. From the look of things, you both lost."

Trace touched his hat again, murmured, "'Evening," and headed for the bunkhouse before she could say more.

The supper call rang on the cook's triangle as he was cleaning up at the wash bench. Trask Ermine was wolfing his food at the head of the table as Trace entered the cook shack. The eyes of the crew shifted furtively from Trace's battered face to that of the foreman, but the black scowl on Trask forestalled any comments. The meal was eaten in a silence thick enough to be cut with a knife.

Afterward, Trask dismissed Trace and two other hands from the cook shack with a few curt words. As the three of them walked toward the bunkhouse, Trace could hear a murmured conference begin back in the cook shack. He wondered about what might come of this. *Keep your eyes open,* he thought.

244

In the bunkhouse the two 'punchers started a game of two-handed stud and ignored Trace as though he weren't there. His manner casual, Trace sauntered to the window and stared out at the ranch yard. Presently the crew filed from the cook shack and headed in a body for the corral, where they saddled up and rode out.

Holding in his mounting excitement, Trace glanced at the two 'punchers, seemingly occupied with their game. Had they been purposely left to keep an eye on him? There was only one way to find out. He headed for the door. A 'puncher's swift, clipped command halted him.

"Where're you going?"

Trace turned to regard the scowling man. "For a walk," he said quietly. "Any objections?"

He turned, without waiting for a reply, and stalked out the doorway. Immediately he heard the two 'punchers scrape back their chairs and clump after him. They came only as far as the door, but he felt their watchful stares on his back as he walked across the yard.

He was certain now that the two had orders from Ermine to see that he didn't try to get a horse and follow the crew. *Keep away from the corrals for now*, he thought. *It'll be dark soon. Maybe you can give them the slip then.*

At an idle, off-hand pace he walked toward the open-sided blacksmith shop, then hunkered down against the building, in plain view of the watching men but at a good distance from them. He shaped a cigarette and smoked while he waited for darkness.

VI

Running over the day's events in his mind, he wondered if Trask had told Breakenridge about what happened at Darrow's. Trask had failed to carry out a direct order, and Breakenridge was not the type to condone failure.

Trask would either have to run a mighty clever bluff on the manager, or else satisfy Breakenridge as to how an unknown drifter had gained the upper hand over a professional trouble-shooter. To do that Trask would have to tell Breakenridge of Trace's turbulent past which made him more than just another drifter.

The thought made Trace shift his position uneasily against the shed. He hadn't considered till now that, if Breakenridge knew about Trace Keene, he'd realize that Trace might prove a dangerous obstacle to his own plans.

For a long time Trace sat stolidly smoking in the thickening twilight. Time and again he glanced at the two crewmen who squatted against the bunkhouse, watching him. He thought he might lead them off, throw them on a false scent, double back, and get a horse from the corrals. It was growing dark enough to make the plan worth a try.

He got to his feet, dropped his cigarette, ground it out under a heel, and swung away from the shed. As he turned, something whirred past his face like an angry hornet and crashed through the shed planking. The crack of a rifle echoed the whine of the bullet.

Trace had spun on a heel and was diving for the shelter of the shed as a second shot beat through the twilight. It was deflected off the anvil in a screaming ricochet. Trace hit the dirt floor on his hip, rolled over twice, and came to a stop,

246

face down, in the shadows.

Pressed to the ground, he listened tensely but heard nothing except the angry pounding of his own heart. He placed the source of the shots as having been off toward the nearby cottonwood grove.

Either the rifleman had merely fired as a warning, or else he still waited out there to place a fatal shot. But Trace doubted that the first shot had been a warning. Probably only the uncertain light and Trace's movement, as the man fired, had saved his life.

In the gloom his gaunt face drew to a hard, cold set. It was in the open now. A bushwhacker's bullet had called the play and almost ended the game.

His eyes roved the dark outlines of the grove. There was a movement, a crackle of brush. Trace got to his hands and knees, his leg muscles gathering and bunching beneath him. A short run would carry him out of the shed, across open space, and into the grove.

The fleeting twilight, deepening into darkness, might cover his run. Then he could grapple with the bushwhacker, at close quarters, where his rifle would not help him. Trace made his reckless decision and launched himself from the shed in a pounding run. He saw a dark shape detach itself from the thick shadows of the grove and turn to meet him. For the distance of his last straining lunge, Trace wondered fleetingly why, if the man could see him, he didn't bring the rifle into play.

Then he hit the bulk figure head on and heard the man's explosive grunt as Trace's hurtling body carried him over backward. Trace grabbed for his throat, then relaxed his hold at the man's strangled curse, for he recognized the voice.

"Darrow!"

"It's me, all right. Let me up, damn it!"

Trace rolled away, and both he and Darrow came to their feet, breathing heavily.

"Someone took a couple of shots at me . . . ," Trace began.

Darrow cut him off with a swift clamp of fingers on Trace's arm. "Someone's coming. Let's get back in the trees. I can't let 'em find me here."

They faded back into the grove and crouched together in the brush, listening. Voices came to Trace's ears — Paula's, demanding imperatively to know what had happened, and Dock Breakenridge's placating reply. Trace wondered where Breakenridge had been when the shots were fired. Presently their voices faded back toward the house.

Trace said: "It's all right to talk now. Keep it low. There were a couple of the crew watching me, and they'll be wondering where I went."

"I came here, looking for you," the squatter growled. "I hitched my horse back of the grove and started to work in on foot, hoping to get your attention without being spotted by the Skull hands. I was circling the grove when I heard two shots, so I looked to see what was up."

"You didn't see anyone?"

"Not a soul. Whoever was shooting at you didn't waste time clearing out. Unless. . . ."

When Darrow paused, Trace asked impatiently: "Unless what?"

"I guess you thought the shots came from the grove. But I was standing right here, and it sounded to me as if they came from over by the house . . . or even from inside the house."

"They might have at that." Trace's chin whiskers made a stiff rasp as he rubbed a palm across them. "What's the news?"

Darrow's grimly squinted eyes made an opaque shimmer in the moonlight. "You told me to keep a night watch on the pass and let you know if any cattle were driven off that way. So I stationed myself on the rim at sunset. Along about twilight I saw some riders push a bunch of cattle through.

"I counted an even dozen riders. It wasn't a big enough bunch of cattle to warrant that many riders . . . unless some of them were just along in case of trouble. It looks as if your hunch paid off. Breakenridge is rustling his own stock on night drives! It doesn't make sense, though."

"Not *his*, Fred. Paula Harper's. It might make more sense than you think. Get your horse and meet me in back of the corrals."

Darrow melted back through the trees. Trace waited till he was gone, then cat-footed in a wide circle to reach the corrals and the harness shed. He saw no sign of the two crewmen. They were no doubt scouring the ranch for him — in the wrong places.

He saddled a horse, stepped into leather, and waited till Darrow's dark-mounted shape came up. The two rode away from Skull headquarters, heading north across a sea of moon-washed graze toward Cray Cañon.

They ascended the timbered ridge beyond which Darrow's cabin lay. But the trail selected by the squatter did not lead to his cabin. It swung wide along the south slope of the ridge. Trace could make out nothing but a dark screening of trees and brush. But Darrow, in the lead, picked his way easily by memory along what Trace guessed must be a game trail.

Finally they broke from timber into a rock-studded open park at the first undulating rise of the east hills. Darrow pulled up here and pointed to a darkly dipping slot that notched a steep escarpment.

"Cray Cañon," he said laconically, and moved his arm. "I was hidden up there on the rim when they pushed through. That was about two hours ago."

A chilly night breeze blew down from the hills. Trace shivered and wished that he'd brought his sheepskin. "How far back does it go?"

"Two, three miles. Then it breaks up into branch gullies and cross cañons. It's easy to lose yourself back there. They could take any one of a number of trails. We'd better wait here at the mouth of the pass and get a drop on 'em when they come back, eh?"

Trace shook his head. "That wasn't what I had in mind. I just wanted you to guide me here. Now you ride to the county seat to fetch the sheriff. How far is it?"

Darrow scowled. "That's Rimfire, about fifteen miles from here. But what'll you do?"

"Overtake those night riders and trail them. They won't be pushing fast with a bunch of cattle. If they're stealing for profit, they probably have a hidden base of operations somewhere back in the hills where they're holding stolen stock. I've got to locate that place so we can catch 'em red-handed with the evidence. Apparently they have a good way of covering their trail, or the sheriff's posses would've found the hide-out long ago. The only way to find it is for one man to trail those riders."

Darrow nodded in understanding. "A posse would give themselves away. Alone, you can keep those jaspers in sight without being spotted."

"*Bueno*. I'll mark the trail with plenty of sign . . . bits of cloth, piled stones. It'll be light enough to see by the time the sheriff gets here. He'll have no trouble following it. Tell him to deputize all the men he can get. There'll be fighting, unless I miss my guess. Better get going."

Darrow nodded without wasting words. His dogged, aggressive nature responded swiftly, once he knew what had to be done. He wheeled his horse and rode back the way they'd come, presently vanishing in deep timber.

Trace rode into the slot. The moonlight had topped the

cañon rim now and filled the defile with a daylight luminosity. He made his way swiftly through shadows and silver moonlight, knowing he had to catch up with the stolen bunch before they left the main stem of Cray Cañon for one of the numerous branch-offs that Darrow had mentioned.

For a mile and a half he proceeded, listening always for any sound of animals or men from downcañon. He saw plenty of recent cattle sign, but heard nothing.

Finally his plainsman's ear picked up a stir of moving animals from a distance ahead. There was also a drift of human voices, hoarse from hazing the cattle. He quickened his pace till he was riding in a moon-silver haze of dust that hung over the floor of the gorge in the wake of the cattle and horses.

Trace slowed now to keep just rearward of the raiders. He was not worried about his own sounds of movement, because the bawling and clatter of the stolen beeves and the shouts of the men would cover these.

Presently the cañon walls became bisected by scores of cross passages. By hearing alone he made out that the raiders were chousing the cattle into one of them. When they were well into the branch cañon, Trace rode to its mouth, dismounted, and built a small arrow-shaped marker of rocks to direct the sheriff.

He mounted again and rode into the deep-walled niche. In this confined areaway the dust raised by the cattle was choking. Trace had to stop, drench his bandanna in tepid water from his canteen, and tie the cloth over his nose and mouth before continuing.

After a long time a deep roar which he could not identify rose above the mixed sounds of men and cattle. As it became nearer and louder, he realized it was caused by the rush of a cañon stream, spilling headlong from the higher country to the lowland to feed Skull's rich graze.

Soon the cross-cañon trail ended at the lip of a cutbank on

the edge of the black torrent. For a moment he was puzzled. Surely the Skull renegades hadn't driven their stolen animals into this swift, rock-laced flow. But he saw, a moment later, that they'd done just that. The distant specks of horses, men, and beeves were working upstream.

After dismounting to fashion another stone marker, Trace rode down the cutbank and kneed his horse cautiously into the sparkling water. He found the mainstream to be scarcely six inches in depth. It had merely appeared deep and treacherous from above.

He felt a reluctant admiration for the manner in which the rustlers had undertaken to conceal their trail. Water left no sign, and even an Indian tracker would be hard put to find the right one out of a hundred places where they might leave the stream. Trace spurred his horse lightly, urging him upstream, knowing he might bypass the rustlers in any brief interval where he lost sight of them.

The trail was further complicated by the fact that, in another half mile, the stream split into two upper forks. The riders took the left one. When he reached the junction, Trace tore a strip from his bandanna and impaled it on a projection of rock, midstream in the left fork. Then he rode on.

Soon he saw the men driving the cattle out of the stream into another branch cañon. But, when he reached this point, he hauled up in surprise. To all appearances there was no cañon mouth, nothing but a solid wall.

He took the risk of striking a match and holding its orange flare high. Then he blew it out as swift understanding came to him. The walls of this cañon tapered inward at its high rims, roofing out moonlight, forming a vast, vaulted cavern. No doubt created by some convulsion of the terrain which had sundered the solid rock, the narrow base of the gorge had later been broadened. The eroding action of rain and melting snow in spring had drilled out a cave-like burrow which showed only a narrow streak of sky at its highest point.

Trace left another cloth marker and began to work carefully through the pitch-black tunnel. The iron clang of his horse's hoofs was picked up and amplified by stony echoes.

Suddenly he broke into full, startling moonlight. He found himself overlooking a verdant valley of rolling meadow, set in a vast pocket, competely surrounded by barrier cliffs. The cañon ended at a place where a section of cliff had collapsed long ago, forming a slope of broken shale, extending to the floor of the valley. From the crest of the slope, where Trace stood, he saw the riders hazing the stolen herd downslope onto the meadow.

Pausing to blow his horse, he admired the panoramic view of walled grassland. It was a perfect rustler's hideaway. Here, cattle could be held without need of riders to patrol the driftlines.

Trace hesitated now, wondering whether to double back on his own trail, meet the posse, and lead them here. He decided against it. He had marked a plain trail to follow. Now he could further smooth the sheriff's way by reconnoitering the valley before the lawman arrived, sizing up the layout and mapping a strategy of offense. If they could take the raiders by surprise, so much the better.

Trace picked his way down the treacherous slide area and started across the meadow. In a clump of trees a hundred yards distant a camp fire showed a rosy pattering of rising and falling flames. Spooked cattle moved from Trace's path as he advanced toward the trees.

He dismounted well beyond the fire, tied his horse to a sapling, and tugged off his boots. He tied them to his saddle, slipped his rifle from its scabbard, and moved through the trees as noiselessly as an Indian. When he was close enough to see and hear, he stopped and melted against the shadow of a thick-trunked cottonwood.

In a small clearing the tired raiders squatted around the fire, watching a pot of coffee come to a boil. Their talk was low. Trask Ermine stalked restlessly back and forth across the clearing, his battered face sallow and malignant in the firelight. Trace wondered if he were still brooding over the beating he'd taken.

One of the riders stood and walked to the fire, cup in hand. He hunkered down to fill it from the coffee pot. As he straightened, the orange light shone squarely on his narrow features. It was Chad Breakenridge.

The sight of Chad erased any remaining doubt in Trace's mind. The Skull crew was an organized rustler band, led by Trask Ermine, but masterminded by Dock Breakenridge. The latter had no doubt appointed his son to ride with Trask to see that Dock's interests were not betrayed. That was not surprising, if you knew Trask.

Chad sipped the scalding brew and made a wry face. "Swill." He poured it out on the ground. Trask slid an ugly glance in his direction but said nothing. Chad hooked his thumbs in his belt and demanded arrogantly: "When are we riding back?"

"When I say so," Trask answered, his flat, pale gaze hitting young Breakenridge's like a striking snake.

It was a battle of wits but a brief one. Soon Chad's glance fell away. Chad might be representing his old man, but Trask was in command here and meant to leave no doubt of it.

"The men are tired," Trask said. "We've been pushing cattle through rough country half the night. We'll head back at daybreak."

Daybreak, Trace knew, should give the sheriff time to get here and catch them with enough evidence to convict the lot. He started to move back to his horse. One groping foot caught in a forked rock. He fought for balance but couldn't save himself from spilling headlong. His falling body made a distinct thud, mingled with the crackling of twigs.

"What's that?"

Trace lay flat on his belly, not daring to move, as Trask Ermine rasped the question. Through a screen of twigs and leaves he saw the foreman balancing on the balls of his feet, his gun out, straining to see into the wall of darkness beyond the rim of firelight.

"A rabbit, maybe," Chad said irritably. "Relax."

"It's too big for a rabbit." Trask cocked his pistol.

"A deer, then. Or one of the horses pushing through the brush. Take it easy."

"I haven't stayed alive this long by taking it easy, sonny," Trask told him. "I'm having a look."

Trace lay motionless, hoping the thick ground shadows would cover his prone body. Trask was beating the brush, kicking his way aimlessly but dangerously close to where Trace sprawled. Trace was waiting and wary, yet was not prepared for Trask to blunder squarely into him. That the foreman did, almost falling over him.

"What the hell!"

Trask's exclamation was choked off as Trace swung his rifle in a sweeping arc from the ground, smashing the foreman's shoulder and knocking him from his feet. Trace lunged upright and ran for his horse, ducking low and dodging among the trees.

Shouts broke out from the camp. Wildly flung shots slashed the foliage. Trace had reached his horse and was fumbling for the reins tied to a sapling when a bursting pain caught him in the head.

As he sank down, clutching at the bark of the sapling, Trace's last thought was an incongruous anger at having been hit by a stray bullet — and at the last moment.

VII

He came to by painful degrees, inching his heavy eyelids open. He flinched as bright firelight hit his aching eyes. He tried to move his cramped and aching limbs and found himself tied hand and foot. His scalp, caked with dried blood, exploded with pain when he lifted his head.

He was lying on his back near the fire, with the Skull renegades hunkered close and fixing him with unsympathetic stares. Trask Ermine was on his feet by the fire, kneading his shoulder with a palm. His lips were skinned back from his teeth as he regarded Trace.

Knife-like pain ripped Trace's ribs at every breath, and he wondered if any bones were broken. Trask had evidently vented his fury by a savage booting. Chad sat cross-legged on the ground, sipping coffee, with a sly smugness in his grin. Trace guessed the kid had gotten in his own kicks, remembering how he had knocked him unconscious in the patio.

Trask said now: "The slug just creased you, Trace. That's not the worst you're feeling, though, eh?" He laughed.

"Guess I'm lucky." Trace's lips barely formed the dry statement.

"Think so? You're alive, but not for long. I guess you haven't changed as much as I'd thought. You're still a lawman at heart." Trask lifted his hand in mild salute. "I've got to hand it to you. It was a neat job of trailing." His tone hardened. "You pushed it too far, though."

Trace sat up, holding his breath with the painful effort. "Since I'm as good as dead, you won't mind telling a dead man a few things."

"Not at all," Trask said equably. "Old Dock engineered the

set-up. A couple of years ago, when Jed Harper was alive and running Skull. Dock explored this back country and found the valley here. More than likely he was the first white man to set eyes on it. There's only one way in, which isn't easily seen, as you know.

"Dock figured it'd make a foolproof rustling set-up. He could drive off small bunches, hold 'em here till he had a sizable herd, then drive to a remote market and a cattle buyer who wouldn't ask too many questions. As manager of Skull, he could even sell them under the Skull brand.

"There are always plenty of penny-ante stock thieves living off a wealthy cattle country. Dock got in touch with a few of them on the quiet, organized a small gang, and worked it that way. It was small pickings, but it totaled up. And there was no danger of anyone finding this place."

"Till Jed Harper got too smart," Trace guessed.

Trask's pale gaze sharpened on him. "You figured out quite a bit on your own, didn't you? After I told Dock who you were . . . who you'd been . . . he said you were too dangerous to live. I guess none of us knew *how* dangerous."

"An ex-lawman never loses his suspicious mind," Trace said. "Miss Harper is prejudiced in Dock's favor, but she told me that her father had been killed while he and Dock were following up some stolen cattle. With what I had already seen of the way Breakenridge is running things, I guessed Dock's story of how Jed died was all wool and a yard wide."

Trask nodded smilingly, his eyes glinting. "Jed was getting too close that day. Dock had been throwing the sheriff's posse off by driving a few head of cattle into branch cañons or coulées, and leaving 'em there for the posses to find so they'd think it was the work of a few amateurs. They'd never look for a place like this.

"But Skull's latest range tally had showed a loss that couldn't be explained by penny-ante theft or even a heavy winter kill, and Jed was getting suspicious. The few stolen head that did turn up, and the fact that nobody had ever caught sight of the thieves, made Jed figure there was a well-organized bunch behind it. He also guessed that they had a well-hidden place where they were driving the bulk of their steal.

"That day Dock and Jed were on the range alone. Jed, once he'd figured what to look for, was turning up all sorts of sign. He followed it as far as the stream, in fact. Then he knew it was a planned operation.

"When he told Dock that, Dock knew Jed would find out the rest of it, if he kept looking. Jed was a human bloodhound, once he got the scent. Dock weighed his chances and knew there'd never be another opportunity like that, while he was alone with Jed.

"On the ride back he fell behind Jed, plugged him in the back with his rifle, shot both their horses, and came in with the story that the rustlers had ambushed them and gotten Jed. Nobody questioned it. Dock's a respected man in this county. It took a stranger like you to see through him."

Chad Breakenridge was squatted by the fire, listening with a morose scowl. "You talk too much, Trask. The old man wouldn't like it."

"Relax," Trask said easily. "Trace won't be telling anybody anything."

Trace felt cold, his limbs numb with the bite of ropes. His mind searched desperately for a way out. For more than the sake of getting information, he wanted to keep Trask talking. "It must have been a blow to Dock when Jed's will left everything to Paula."

"I suppose it was," Trask agreed, "but he didn't let it faze him for long. He was manager of the gal's ranch till she came of age. That gave him time. He could keep draining off Skull

258

stuff till he made a clean sweep.

"He gradually got rid of the old Skull crew and replaced 'em with his own tough hands. That not only made stealing ten times as easy, it let Dock break Skull without the danger of word leaking to outsiders . . . or even to Miss Harper."

Chad put in sullenly: "I never could see why the old man went to all this trouble to break Skull. Once Paula and I are married, it won't be hard to persuade her to let the old man keep running things. It'll all be in the family, then."

Trask's gaze slid to the kid. "Maybe Dock doesn't want to risk all his cards on a weak hand like you."

Chad Breakenridge went pale but held his temper. Trask swung to face the men. "Let's get to the horses," he ordered.

The men rose and straggled from the clearing. The gray light of false dawn had begun to dissipate the darkness. The night riders would return to Skull now to resume their rôles as honest cowhands. Trask lingered behind the others, giving Trace a hard stare. Trace's stomach muscles tightened. They wouldn't leave him here alive.

One of the men paused at the edge of the clearing, jerking his head toward Trace as he said to Trask: "What about him?"

"I'll take care of things," Trask said softly, not taking his gaze off Trace. "You boys go along. I'll catch up. Wait . . . Jules, give me your gun belt."

"What?"

"Hand it over, damn it!" Trask's tone had gained a sharp, uncompromising edge.

The man called Jules shrugged, unbuckled his gun belt, and tossed it to Trask. The foreman caught it, then dropped it on the ground.

"Get going," Trask snapped.

Jules followed the others. The clearing was deserted in

the gray stillness except for the two men, one lying bound near the crumbling embers of the fire, the other with his hand on his gun, a glimmer of indecision showing in his taut face.

"Get it over with," Trace said, his voice holding steady. A numb paralysis of resignation filled his cramped body.

Trask's hand fell from his gun. He pulled a clasp knife from his pocket and opened the large blade. *So it would be a knife*, Trace thought, the sickness welling high in his throat. Since a knife had never been Trask's style, this could mean only that he meant to make the man he hated die slowly.

Trask bent, and Trace felt the knife part the ropes that secured his wrists. Before he had time to wonder at this, Trask was cutting away the ropes on his feet. Then Trask stepped back, pocketing the knife and palming his gun with a swift gesture. Trace maneuvered stiffly to his feet, closing and unclosing his hands to restore circulation.

Trask put his toe under Jules's gun belt and kicked it toward Trace. "Put that on."

Trace stared at him.

"Put it on, I said!"

Under the threat of Trask's pistol, Trace slowly stooped, then straightened with the shell belt in his hands. Just as slowly he buckled it about his hips, feeling an angry revulsion at its old familiar weight — a revulsion that vanished swiftly in the urgent concern of the moment.

Trask's eyes were varnished with a fevered brightness. His voice sounded hollow. "Now," he said, as though to himself, "we'll see."

Trace understood then what was passing through the gunman's mind. He'd sensed somehow that it would be this way, but it had seemed fantastic that Ermine would really carry it through. Driven by an ancient obsession he could not control, the man was gambling his own life against Trace's life and freedom.

"So that's it."

"That's it." Trask's face was gray in the half light, the skin drawn taut across its bony planes. "I've only been beaten once. You did it, Trace. I say you can't do it again. You wouldn't meet me before. Now you have no choice."

Trace said harshly: "Do you think you can push me to it this way?"

Trask sheathed his pistol with a lightning motion, but his hand remained poised. "You've been away from it for a long time. I'm giving you the draw."

"Trask, you're raving mad!"

"Suit yourself," the gunman snarled.

Trask's hand dipped and swung up.

Trace, caught off-guard in that split second that made the difference between life and death, reacted in the only way left to him. His reflexes carried him in a swift sideways leap — a basic gunman's trick he'd learned long ago. As he moved, his hand stabbed down, then lifted, thumbing the hammer with automatic precision. He realized that there were some skills you could never forget, no matter how you tried. They stayed a part of your bones, muscles, and nerves.

Trask's bullet cut air where Trace had stood a fraction of time before, then Trace's gun was spouting once, twice, again.

Trask did not get off a second shot. His heavy frame stood loosely erect for a moment. Frustrated rage showed in his face, then vanished, and left a blank stare. He toppled like a downed tree.

Trace held his crouch, his gun pointed before him, coldly alert and waiting. But there was only silence beyond the trees, except for the receding sounds of the Skull horsemen. They'd suppose the shots were Trask, finishing him off. But they'd return when Trask failed to join them. Trace had to work fast.

He paused by Trask's body to remove the gun belt, knowing he might have to burn a lot more powder to get out of this. He saw that his three bullets had taken Trask squarely in the chest, within a two-inch circle. He shuddered faintly, but the moment passed without the retching sickness he had expected.

The cold necessity of this had abruptly broken through the block he'd thrown up in his mind after the killing long ago of Chick Lawton. The sudden sense of self-exoneration from an old guilt gave him an overpowering feeling of relief, even in this hard-pressed moment.

He found his rifle. Then, with Trask's shell belt slung from his shoulder, he pushed through the trees to where he'd left his horse. As he hastily pulled on his boots, he assayed his position.

He was one man against eleven. A running break for freedom was out of the question, for they could easily block off the one exit from the valley. His best chance was to hole up in a strategic spot, hold them off while his cartridges lasted, and pray that the posse would arrive in time.

As he caught up his reins and piled into the saddle, an outbreak of gunfire rolled across the meadow. With a quick surge of relief, he knew that the posse had made it.

He spurred his horse from the trees onto the open meadow. Sunrise was topping the eastern summit of the barrier cliffs and picking out the distant forms of mounted men. They were pouring out of the notch and spilling down the shale slope, their guns blasting at the demoralized Skull men.

Five of the quicker-witted raiders, accepting the realization that the game was finished, had wheeled their horses and were racing back toward the trees to make their stand there.

A grim smile touched Trace's lips. His nerves were steady now with the cold precision of the professional lawman he used to be. He pulled his horse up in the face of the oncoming men, jerked his rifle from its boot, and systematically emptied the magazine with carefully placed shots.

Two horses went down, spilling their riders headlong. One of them lay unmoving; the other lurched to his feet in a futile staggering run, then finally fell on his face and lay sobbing in disgust. The other three pulled up and directed a panicked fire at Trace but were too rattled at being caught between fire from two sides to place their shots with accuracy. Trace bowled over two more horses. The remaining horseman threw away his gun with an oath, and raised his arms.

Trace rode forward to collect his prisoners. He dismounted and herded the dazed men to their feet. The man who had not moved when his horse fell would never move again. His neck was broken.

Trace held his four captives at gunpoint till several of the posse men rode up. He recognized the lean-jointed form of Fred Darrow in the lead. Beside him rode a swarthy man of middle height who wore a dusky town suit. Authority showed in his seamed face and brisk movements as he swung from his saddle and approached.

"That's Trace Keene, Brodie," Darrow said. "Trace, meet Sheriff Brodie Dutcher."

The lawman's handshake was hard and vigorous, like his appearance. "It looks as if you had things well in hand without us, son."

Trace shook his head. "I'd say you got here just in time. As for these men, you got them so shaken up by the way you rode down on them, they didn't know what they were doing. I just herded them up."

The sheriff's quick gaze moved over the barrier walls encircling the valley. "This is quite a set-up. I guess they figured no one would ever find this place. We never would have, if you hadn't marked the trail. I thought Fred was crazy when he woke me up in the middle of the night and told me to organize a posse. I couldn't believe it when he told me Dock Breakenridge was behind this business. I went along against my better judgment. I'm glad now that I did."

The remainder of the posse, made up of Rimfire citizen volunteers, joined them, herding more Skull renegades at gunpoint. Trace's eye ran over the prisoners, then he swung to face Dutcher.

"Chad Breakenridge is missing. Did he break through your men?"

"Any of you boys see young Breakenridge?" the sheriff asked.

A lean rider with a bloody bandanna tied around his wrist nodded. "He rode straight between two of us. He shot Charlie's horse from under him, hit me in the arm, and got away through the notch. That kid's no slouch with a six-gun."

"We'll pick him up later," Dutcher said. "He's not worth worrying about."

"There's more than that to worry about," Trace said tersely.

"Eh?"

"Chad'll ride to warn his father. Dock must have enough money salted away to get both of them clear of the country. They'll do it, if they have a good start."

"You mean the money from the stolen Skull beef he's been selling?" Dutcher questioned. When Trace nodded, the sheriff growled an oath. He snapped orders as he headed for his horse. "Half of you take these lads to Rimfire and have my jailer lock 'em up, pending trial. The rest of you come with me. If we can't overtake Chad, we can reach Skull before Breakenridge has time to get his money and make a break."

VIII

The sun was high in the mid-morning sky by the time the tired men halted their blowing horses at the crest of the grassy dip overlooking the Skull buildings.

"It looks peaceful enough, Brodie," one of them drawled.

"That's Chad's horse, tied at the rail by the house," Trace pointed out.

A harrying worry had grown in him during the return ride. He was thinking of Dock Breakenridge's explosive fury when Chad told him what had happened. That fury might turn on Paula.

Sheriff Dutcher turned a grim stare on Trace. "Dock's warned, and he's probably primed to the teeth for us, figuring to make his stand here. You said there were a couple of Skull hands left behind on last night's raid? With Chad and Dock, that makes four men. Even four men can hold out for hours in that damn' fort. I reckon we'll just have to smoke 'em out, if that's how Dock wants it."

"That's not the worst of it," Trace said quietly. "Miss Harper's in the house, too."

The sheriff's stocky frame jerked with this realization. He swore blisteringly. "We'll have to dicker with Dock, then. We can't run the risk of her getting hurt. The old devil's holding all the cards, and he knows it." He swung from horseback, saying: "You boys stay here. Hold your fire until I give the word. Keene, you come with me."

One man said sharply: "You're not going down to the house, Brodie?"

"Breakenridge won't shoot," Dutcher said, "if he figures he can bluff us some other way. Coming, Keene?"

Trace stepped to the ground, hesitating as his eye fell on Trask Ermine's fine-tooled gun belt looped around his saddle horn. The holster was made of supple, well-oiled leather. He drew the pistol, hefting its weight and feel. It was a finely balanced gunfighter's weapon. Without hesitation now he unbuckled Jules's gun belt and strapped on Trask's.

Then he looked at the sheriff. "Let's go."

Dutcher and Trace walked down the slope, keeping to the open and holding their hands well away from their guns to make their intentions unmistakable. Between them was the tacit knowledge that Breakenridge might easily cut both of them down. But, with the ingrained fatalism of experienced lawmen, neither mentioned the risk. Nor did they speak of it now as they came within a hundred feet of the sprawling, thick-walled adobe house.

The door opened suddenly, and Dock Breakenridge moved onto the wide verandah, pushing Paula Harper ahead of him. The girl's face was white with pain, for the man had one arm twisted behind her back in a cruel hammerlock, while his other hand held a pistol against her throat.

"Close enough, gentlemen!" he called.

Trace and the sheriff halted, dead in their tracks.

"Let the girl go, Dock," Dutcher called sharply. "You can't play this dirty."

"Can't I?" Breakenridge mocked.

His eyes were wildly bright. His white hair made a tangled nimbus around a tight-drawn fanatic's face. Seeing his expression, Trace had the sickening realization that Breakenridge would kill Paula at the least excuse. Breakenridge's unstable temper had been only a token symptom of something far worse that festered inside the man. Now, with his back to the wall, that something had broken into plain and ugly sight.

"We're riding out of here, Dutcher . . . me and my men . . .

266

with her," Breakenridge said. "Keep your posse off our backs, or I'll stick this gun in her mouth and pull the trigger!"

Trace heard Dutcher's breath suck in hard. The sheriff said: "I think you really would," as though he couldn't believe it.

"Damn' right he will, lawdog."

It was Chad Breakenridge, stepping from the house to his father's side. The two remaining Skull hands followed, looking anything but sure of themselves. Chad's sneering smile was twisted in a face pasty with fright.

"Those're real fire-eaters you have siding you, Dock," Dutcher commented. "How far do you think you'll get with them?"

"As far as need be with her as a passport." Paula winced as Breakenridge's pistol nudged her neck.

Trace whispered from the corner of his mouth, "Keep him talking."

Dutcher gave him a swift sidelong glance and then shuttled his hard gaze back to Breakenridge. "Why did you kill Jed Harper, Dock?"

Paula gave a broken cry. "Uncle Dock!"

Breakenridge laughed harshly. "You never did suspect, did you, my dear? Not even when I began to replace your old crew with my gunnies. You had too much faith in your old Uncle Dock." Again there was the jarring laugh.

Trace's muscles tensed. His eyes narrowed to watchful slits. Breakenridge's gun was still against Paula's throat, and he couldn't take the chance.

Trace said: "Why did you steal Miss Harper blind when you could've named your terms legally through Chad after they were married?"

Breakenridge shook his head, sweat glistening on his face. "I had too good a thing started to cut it off after I killed Jud. It was sure money. Anyway, I couldn't take a chance on Chadwick, the way he plays around. There was always some woman. That's one thing I never could control in him. Nothing worked. When he started fooling with the Mexican filly right in Paula's household, I knew it was only a question of time before she found out and broke with him."

Chad gave a sickly laugh that didn't come off. Breakenridge went on without a glance at his son. "Besides, I figured I could bleed Skull dry, then make Paula an offer" — he chuckled — "out of the proceeds from her stolen cattle to take the losing proposition off her hands. In another year, the way things were going, she'd have sold at any price."

"What about Darrow?" Trace pressed. "Why were you so eager to move him off?"

"Partly because I didn't want any squatters on Skull when I took it over. Both Paula and Jed were always too lax about that. But mostly because Darrow's place was too close to Cray Cañon where we were driving off the cattle. There was the danger that he might start prying and catch Skull hands rustling their own stock. But I saw a worse danger in you, when Trask told me who you were. I'd heard of *that* Trace Keene."

Dock's pistol moved slightly off Paula and toward Trace.

Sweat broke out on Trace's forehead and ran into his eyes in a stinging wash. He blinked it away. *Keep talking*, he thought. *You're getting his whole attention.*

"Is that why you shot at me last night? Darrow heard the shots and thought they came from the house."

"They did," Breakenridge admitted. "I fired from my office window." His voice took on a menacing edge. "So Darrow was with you. You two were working together against me."

"The end you really had in sight was owning Skull, wasn't it? Even when you were rustling its stock, your only reason was to force Paula to sell out." Trace played his trump card then

— the only one remaining. "You must have hated the Harpers like poison!"

Breakenridge seemed to swell with the bristling rage touched off by Trace's words. "The high-and-mighty Harpers! I was always the poor orphan brat they took in, and they never let me forget it. Owning the biggest ranch in the territory, they could afford to throw pearls to swine. Jed's old man willed the whole show to Jed, and Jed left it to Paula.

"I was the hired hand, nothing more. Long before Chad was born, I'd made up my mind I'd own every blade of grass that Skull ever claimed. I'd be a bigger man than the Harpers ever dreamed of being!"

The last words tore from him in a shout. Forty years of pent-up hate and twisted reprisal were boiling from the man. But Trace's watchful eyes were concerned only with the fact that Breakenridge's angry movements had partly exposed his body to view from behind Paula. Now Breakenridge's gun steadied on Trace.

"You wrecked it all, damn you!"

Trace made his draw, a blurred motion that sent his shot crashing off with Breakenridge's. He felt Dock's slug furrow hotly along his forearm. Then his bullet knocked Breakenridge over, pulling the girl down with him.

Chad was fast, surprisingly fast. He had his gun out before Trace broke his arm with a second bullet. Chad yelled and went down on his knees, holding his wrist. Trace was covering the two Skull hands before they could even complete their motions of drawing. They stopped, paralyzed with slack-jawed astonishment.

Dutcher's gun was only half drawn when it was over. He breathed: "I never saw anything like it! You got Dock cold and still had time to cripple Chad with a wing shot, instead of dropping him dead center. I've seen handy gun play in my time but nothing like that."

Trace said softly: "You'd better get their guns."

He walked to the verandah and helped the dazed girl to her feet. Wracked with sobs, she buried her face in his chest. Trace, like a sensible man, held her close.

"It's over now," he kept telling her. "All over."

IX

The Skull ranch yard lay silently in the long shadows of ending day. Trace Keene and Paula Harper sat on the verandah, neither saying much. Trace was thinking of the contrast of this quiet scene, now that the posse and the prisoners were gone, to the seething tensions and erupting violence of a few short hours ago. It was like a bad dream whose memory was already fading. Skull ranch seemed as deserted as a graveyard.

The girl spoke for the first time in many minutes. "He was crazy. He must have been crazy."

"Breakenridge?" Trace thought that over. "Maybe he was, toward the last. But he let it build in him over the years. He knew what he was doing when he set out to wreck you. Don't waste sympathy on him."

She said slowly, as though absorbing a relief gained by his words: "I guess I was hanging onto childhood memories of Uncle Dock and Chad. I should have seen what was happening, yet I never really would have believed it . . . because I didn't want to. But a person has to grow up, don't they? I mean, things don't stay the same . . . even from minute to minute. You can't live in the past."

"I guess you can't." Trace thought of the past with which he'd ridden for two years.

Paula guessed his thoughts. She said haltingly: "You had to

use a gun today. I'm sorry, Trace."

He stood up, leaned against a porch column, and stared across the plain. Then he cuffed his hat back and looked down at her with reflective eyes.

"First I had to use it on Trask Ermine, because he pushed me to do it. Then I realized there was nothing else I could've done. Finally I had to down Dock, figuring it was the only way to save your life. The way he hated the Harpers. I doubt if he'd have let you go alive. I figured . . . in a way . . . that sort of squares things for Chick. He'd've been satisfied."

"One thing is certain," she said gently. "He wouldn't have wanted you to go on torturing yourself as you had been."

Trace nodded gravely. "That part of my life is finished . . . the drifting part."

"I'll need somebody," she said. "Somebody to hire a new crew and to put this ranch back on an operating basis. Will you stay, Trace?"

Trace sensed the bewildered, frightened sense of loss behind her words. Paula Harper's whole world had collapsed in a minute of violence. She seemed desperately to need to believe in something, in someone. It was a start for them, anyway.

"I'll stay as long as you want me."

There was more he wanted to say, but it was too soon. Too much had happened. There would be time enough to tell her the rest when Paula was sure in her own mind. There would be all the time in the world for both of them.